BU

UNIV

Mina Bancheva

A Secret Life

 europe books

ISBN 9791220134149
First edition: March 2023

A Secret Life

To Siân and Sophie with all my love

First and foremost, my gratitude and thanks go to Tricia Wastvedt without whose encouragement, help and support this novel would have never been written.
My thanks also go to Kylie Fitzpatrick whose careful and thoughtful last edit gave me the confidence to submit my work for publication.

Big thank you also to my writing partner, Susan Beale who kept me going at times of doubt and to the members of my writing group: Jane, Mary, Christine, Wilma, Ali and Fiona who have all been an inspiration on my writing journey.

Last but not least, thank you to the team at Europe Books and in particular to Ginevra, who commissioned the novel and to Rachele for her help with editing it.

Thank you also to Eddie for his support and useful suggestions.

Mina Bancheva
October 3, 2022

Part One

Chapter One

June 1974, Sofia

The passport official behind the glass screen takes her passport and she gives him her sweetest smile. He doesn't smile back. He is young, about her age, with soft blue eyes under dark eyebrows.

He leafs through the pages; back and forth and back again and glances past her at the queue forming behind. He looks weary as if he's had as little sleep as she's had. Sweat trickles down her spine.

'Get on with it,' the woman behind her says under her breath.

The man picks up the phone. *Keep your nerve*, Yana says to herself, *don't run or break down or it would be the end of everything.* A tiny muscle twitches in the temple by her right eye. She must look calm, casual, a phone call is not unusual at passport control at Sofia airport.

Two soldiers with rifles walk towards the queue. Her blood pounds in her ears. This is it; she thinks. I am done for.

But now the man is tapping her passport on the glass, tetchily as if it were she who was keeping him waiting. He hands it back with a brief, hard look into her eyes.

The soldiers walk on. The barrier clicks open. Yana exhales and realises she has been holding her breath.

In the departure lounge, she finds a seat and puts her bag on her knees. Suddenly all courage vanishes and she wants Mammy and Katya and home but it is too late. She tries to quieten her lurching heart. They're letting me go, her mind is saying over and over. He let me through.

Maybe he didn't want the paperwork, the hassle, the late coffee break that questioning her would have meant. She had the correct documents, but he wasn't stupid. His training would have sharpened the instinct they all possessed; he must have known she had paid for this somehow. What he did not know was how and who he'd anger if he stopped her.

So, in the end this is how freedom comes; because a young man decided she wasn't worth the trouble.

She takes out her book and holds it tightly, staring at the pages. The words are strings of letters and in her head, she hears Comrade Ivanov's voice: *People have been taken off planes minutes before take-off.* Ivanov knew these things. He was an insider who, like her, wanted out. He didn't say it in so many words, but she knew he envied her and that made her feel that in the power stakes, they were equal.

When it came to it, Comrade Ivanov had been a gentle lover and she was surprised at how easy it was. Afterward, she didn't hate herself, or him or feel ashamed. It had been a fair exchange: two nights in his bed for a visa.

Mammy never asked how she got it. Perhaps she guessed. All she said was, 'If you want to go, *dushko*, then you must'.

As for her friends, if they had known about Comrade Ivanov, they would have thought her a traitor. But that was the hardest thing, not telling them she was leaving. Right to the end she was making arrangements with Rossi

His kindness makes her blush. She wonders what he might want in return. But he just smiles, hardly looking at her, then walks away and she wonders if all Englishmen are like him, kind and chivalrous, willing to help without expecting anything back.

She writes to Mammy: *Here I am in France, just for an hour.* She can't *think* of anything else to say. *Thinking of you. Love Yana.* To Katya she writes: *The lipstick is fab. Thank you. Love, Sis xxx*

Back on the plane, the trolley comes along the aisle again and she has another of the small bottles of wine. The man folds his newspaper and asks, 'Your first visit to Britain?' He must have known she isn't a seasoned traveler because of the postcards.

'I will be studying,' Yana says.

'Ah yes,' he says mildly. 'Excellent.' He takes off his horn-rimmed glasses and wipes them with a piece of cloth.

She tells him she is going to Cardiff. She has always wanted to live in London, but she has a friend in the capital of Wales, and she is going to live with this friend, Mary, while attending university.

She is glad she has her facts right about the countries and the capitals of Great Britain. It is complicated. When she first met Mary, she thought that London was the capital of the whole country, but Mary explained that Wales had its own capital, and England had London.

'I'll be studying Psychology,' Yana tells the man. She sips her wine, feeling sophisticated. 'Actually, it interests me very much because it's all about how we see the world, why we believe different things and even how we fall in love and who we choose. It all depends on how we are brought up and how our culture conditions us.' She'd read this somewhere and liked the idea but doesn't know if it's true.

'So, one studies love at university these days,' the man says with no irony in his voice at all. He is too polite to tease her. 'I regret reading Classics. It's done me no good at all. A first-class degree in love would have been much more useful.'

She blushes profusely, she feels a fraud.

'Your English is very good,' he says.

'My father was educated in Britain,' Yana continues, grateful to him for changing the subject. 'He taught me. And I studied English at Sofia University.'

She doesn't know why she is telling this man so much about herself. She knows she is smiling too much. Perhaps she is a little drunk.

'Your friend is meeting you at Heathrow?' the man enquires gently.

'Yes, and I hope I can see a bit of London before we travel to Wales.'

London. The city of her dreams. Tatti studied journalism there before the war and he told her stories of buses like scarlet houses on wheels, with an upstairs and a downstairs. The buildings were grey, or red or yellow brick and the policemen rode bicycles. The banks of the River Thames were lit with skeins of lights that shimmered in the water on summer evenings, and in the winter, street sellers roasted chestnuts over barrels of hot coals.

But every country carries darkness in its heart, Tatti told her. The Tower of London had dungeons and terrible machines to torture people, although that was a long time ago.

And every country carries hope, he said. There was a diamond in the Tower so precious and beautiful, its worth was beyond a figure anyone could calculate.

Like life, Tatti said. Like freedom. She tries not to think of what she had do to get here, the land of freedom.

The plane judders to a stop and the man helps her get her bag from the overhead locker. 'Good luck,' he says as he moves down the aisle to the door. She makes her way down a long corridor and follows the signs for arrivals. At the barrier she looks around and sees Mary and all tension drains away. She feels light and dizzy.

'Welcome, my lovely Yana,' Mary says as she hugs her. They hold each other close and Yana inhales Mary's perfume, which is warm and spicy. Her body softens.

It is two years since they met in Sofia, but Mary hasn't changed. Yana knows she is in her forties, but she looks not a year older than thirty. She is wearing a flowery summer dress, the wide skirt skimming her knees and showing off her shapely legs. Her hair has grown a bit longer and it falls to her shoulders in a cascade of burnished gold. Yana is conscious of how drab the blue suit Mammy made for her looks in comparison.

Mary works for a prestigious gallery in Wales and had been invited by the Ministry of Culture in Sofia to organize an exhibition of works by a British painter. Yana had been hired to interpret for her and they became friends, Mary's warmth and grace quickly winning Yana's affection.

'I'll take you for a drive along the Thames,' Mary says, 'before we get on the motorway to Cardiff. Would you like that?'

Evening is settling over London, and it veils the city in a violet-grey light. It makes the buildings look like a

19

stage set. The twinkling lights are there, just as Tatti had said and as they drive along the embankment, people are strolling, some eating ice cream. There are no steaming barrels with hot chestnuts, it is the wrong time of the year, but the red double-decker buses are here and so are the brick houses, solid and reassuring in their uniformity.

A mixture of emotions takes hold of Yana as they drive through the city and onto Wales. As they pass through streets, bustling with life and colour, she feels as if she is in an enchanted land, strange and exciting. But anxiety worms itself into her heart. Will she find her way in this unknown country? And what would happen when her six months visa expires? Will she have to go back, and will it all have been for nothing? The thought compresses her chest, heavy like a stone inside her.

It is dark by the time they get to the outskirts of Cardiff.

Mary's house is large and stands on its own. The road has big leafy trees, which make the area look elegant. In Sofia the shabby blocks of flats give the city a tired look, like its inhabitants; grey and worn-out, scurrying around with their shopping bags, hoping to find something in the shops, which are often empty.

Inside, Mary's house has a bohemian grandeur. It is on two floors, three very large rooms downstairs and five bedrooms on the first floor. Mary's children, Jason and Lily have long gone; Lily to London to pursue a career in fashion and Jason, travelling in India. Their father left Mary for a woman twenty years younger. Mary never talks about him.

Yana has the second largest bedroom, at the other end of the corridor from Mary's. A double bed covered by a brocade bedspread in mulberry and orange stands at one end of the room. The window opens on to a narrow balcony and has heavy velvet curtains the colour of red wine.

Yana puts down her suitcase and sits on the bed. So different from the room at home that she shares with Katya; their two beds at an angle, the desk by the window, the mountain rising in the distance, blue on a clear day.

A sharp, cutting pain in her chest; what has she done? The nights she spent in Ivanov's bed burn her cheeks. Will she ever see Mammy and Katya again? There is no going back. She'd wanted this. She'd prayed that she would be allowed to travel, she must not now give in to shame or regret.

In the morning she walks around Mary's garden, which is filled with herbs and flowers. She finds a couple of secret places; one behind the rosemary bush, the other, tucked away at the far end, where a Japanese rose trails on the brick wall, its delicate sugar-pink petals scattered on the grass like confetti.

It is a sunny day and Mary has gone to work. Yana takes her mug of coffee and a rug and spreads it behind the rosemary bush. She picks a few of the sharp green needles and inhales their rich, lemony aroma. She floats a couple in her coffee and when she takes a sip, she finds that they have softened its bitterness and made it taste like summer. At long last, she feels safe.

Two weeks later, there is a letter from Mammy on the mat by the front door and Yana takes it to read outside on the wooden bench by the Japanese rose.

My dearest Yana,

I hope you are settling in Cardiff OK and that life with Mary is good. What a kind woman she is to take you in

21

and look after you, I will never be able to express enough gratitude to her. Would you please tell her that?

Katya and I are well. I am so proud of her, she has a place on the course for Illustrators at the Academy and she is full of it, can't talk about anything else. And the course hasn't even started.

Baba and Diado are keeping healthy despite their advancing years. I visited them yesterday and Baba cooked a lovely lunch, I wish I could cook like her! They miss you as much as I do.

I lost my job at the theatre. They said there was someone better qualified, but it turns out she is the sister-in-law of the manager, surprise, surprise! I should have known it was too good to last.

Look after yourself, dushko and don't worry about us. Will try to find you some lukanka, I know how much you love it, and if I do, I'll send it straight away.

Much love for now,
Mammy xx

Guilt and longing cloud the brightness of the morning. The letter brings back her old life, which from a distance, doesn't seem so bad. She longs to be back, living it with Mammy and Katya and all the others. She longs to feel the breeze that comes from the mountain and heralds spring. Hard as it was, it was the life she was born into. It got even harder after Tatti died and there was no money and Mammy had to take odd jobs and knit sweaters for a state-owned textile company, but they were all together in it. She has to remind herself why she left. She has to remind herself of Tatti. She must think of the sacrifice he made in the hope that one day, she might know what freedom means.

She mustn't show regret to Mammy, she mustn't let her know how desperately homesick her letter has made her and how every time someone asks how she's settling here, she wants to cry. She's made her decision, and she must stick with it. So, she writes Mammy a jolly letter, describing Mary's house and the garden and telling her she's got a job waitressing in an Italian restaurant and is hoping to hear soon that her application to study at Cardiff University has been accepted. Mary is kind to her and all is well.

In the afternoon, she is getting ready to go out to post her letter when she hears the doorbell and finds herself face to face with a tall, dark - haired man, with an aquiline nose and a slightly protruding chin. 'I am a friend of Mary's' he says and asks if she is in. 'Tell her Daniel called,' he says when Yana tells him Mary is out. 'Tell her I'll call her tomorrow.' He walks down the path to the gate, then turns around and smiles at her. 'You smell of violets,' he says.

After he's gone, Yana wonders who this mysterious person is and senses anxiety creeping in again. It's probably nothing, perhaps he is Mary's boyfriend, then wonders why Mary hasn't mentioned him.

Chapter Two

Katya watches her sister as she walks across the tarmac, waiting for her to turn around and wave good-bye. But Yana keeps walking, she doesn't look back. She climbs the airstairs and vanishes from sight.

Katya looks at Mammy, her eyes have clouded over. The brave smile she had for Yana before she left has gone and Katya knows she is hurting. She puts her arm around her shoulder. 'Let's go,' she says gently.

In the taxi, she holds Mammy's hand. They don't speak, each wrapped in their own thoughts, each trying to come to terms with Yana gone.

For weeks, Katya watched her sister getting ready for the trip and tried her best to appear cheerful. She was pleased that her sister had finally managed to get her visa, of course she was. She knew how much Yana wanted to go. After Tatti's funeral, she told her she was not going to live in a country where people get murdered for their views. 'No way,' she'd said, 'no way am I going to be part of a system that stifles people's freedom to speak or travel.'

Katya said she understood but her eleven-year-old self couldn't for a minute contemplate not living at home with Mammy. Despite the sorrow and the poverty after Tatti died, she liked how her life was. She liked school where she was encouraged to draw and paint, a talent she was told she had and she liked her friends and playing with them and on warm summer evenings, chatting outside, until the sky would darken, and Mammy would call her home for supper.

It is difficult to believe that Yana has gone. The finality of it doesn't sink in until they get back to the flat. Mammy busies herself getting supper, while Katya goes into the bedroom, which she shared with Yana until only last night. Yana's bed is carefully made, the pillows plumped, the duvet smoothed. She opens Yana's wardrobe, which is empty apart from her old dressing gown hanging forlorn on a metal hanger. And then she notices that Yana's left her slippers behind and the sight of them, neatly arranged under the bed, cuts her open and the tears she's been holdings since the airport finally, mercifully flood her vision. She lies on Yana's bed, face down on her sister's pillow and sobs.

After a few minutes, there is a light tap on the door and Mammy comes in. She sits on the bed beside her and strokes her back.

'Don't cry, *dushko*,' she says. 'Your sister has done what she always wanted to do, and we should be happy for her. Get up, wash your face, supper will be ready in a couple of minutes.'

But Mammy's eyes are puffy, and Katya knows that she too has been crying.

'She didn't look back, Mammy, not one last time to wave good-bye. How could she just leave with not a single glance back, how could she?'

Tears flood her eyes again but this time they are angry tears.

'Perhaps it was easier for her that way, *dushko*.'

'Easier for her? And what about us?'

'Let it go, Katya, you have things to do. Start getting ready for your course in September. Go out with your friends, go to the cinema with Vlado. Live your life and let Yana live hers.'

26

Katya knows that Mammy is right, she will have to get used to life without her big sister. But knowing that doesn't take away the heavy feeling in her chest.

Chapter Three

The restaurant is busy today and Yana's legs are beginning to ache. She is on her ten- minute break and grabs a cup of coffee then sits down and puts her feet up on the little stool in the kitchen. Joe, one of the other waiters pulls a chair and sits next to her.

'How are you doing, gorgeous Yana?'

She pushes a strand of hair away from her face, which is damp with sweat. Gorgeous is not how she feels.

'I feel as if I am on my last legs,' she says.

'Gosh, isn't your English good? Where did you learn such an expression?'

'Reading mostly. I did study the language at the university in Sofia.'

'My my, a university graduate. What are you doing working in a dump like this?'

'Waiting to study again at Cardiff University. Psychology.'

'Psychology? Does it mean you will be learning how to read people's minds?'

Yana laughs. 'I don't think so. But maybe I will learn how to understand myself better.'

'Deep, aren't you?'

Before Yana has the chance to reply, they are joined by Ben, the manager.

'Could you please pop into my office after you've finished your shift, Yana?'

'Sounds ominous,' Joe says after Ben has left.

'Sit down,' Ben says later in his office. 'How are you settling here, Yana? Are you managing all right?'

'I think so,' she says. 'Why? Have there been any complaints?'

'As a matter of fact, yes. I am afraid so. Apparently, you gave the wrong change to the couple at table 7 earlier on. You need to be more careful, Yana. And please do ask if there is anything you don't understand.'

In the toilet she washes away her tears with cold water. Her dream to leave Bulgaria has come true but the reality of living it is something she had not contemplated. She had set her heart on leaving so fervently, she hadn't considered what the consequences might be. The loneliness, the homesickness, the feeling out of place, of not always understanding. All the anxiety, the uncertainty, was it worth it? Maybe freedom is just an illusion she thinks, perhaps we are never truly free. Perhaps we always remain prisoners of our own fears.

Later she sits at one of the tables at the open- air café in the Hayes and orders her regular cup of coffee. Her eyes must be still red from all the crying at the restaurant earlier because the man who usually serves her says: "Jui Jui what's the matter, caeriadd?'

Which makes her cry again; she doesn't understand the language, but she understands the kindness.

'Nothing is worth it, I tell you,' he says and brings her a Welsh cake with the coffee. 'On the house,' he says. She is touched to the core and her eyes well up again.

'Thank you,' she says, 'so kind of you.'

He waves her gratitude away. 'No need,' he says as he starts to clear the table next to hers. 'It must be hard being so far away from your home.'

If only he knew, she thinks.

Chapter Four

It's been raining for three days, a fine misty rain that has permeated the air with the soft smell of summer. Yana folds the big black umbrella she's borrowed from Mary and places it in the oriental looking jar by the door. The gallery is brightly lit and crowded with people and the din of voices assaults her as she stands by the door. For a moment she contemplates walking out, but she knows Mary would be hurt. And she has spent most of her first wages from the waitressing on clothes and make-up to wear to the private view. The week before, Mary took her to Biba; a cave- like place, dimly lit, with large black and gold- framed mirrors, potted palms in dark corners and Art Decco lamps scattered on polished surfaces. She bought a maxi black and white striped dress and a pair of white PVC knee-high boots, just like the ones the girl on the plane had on. She is wearing her new outfit now. It makes her feel fashionable and sophisticated. She's never in her life had such lovely clothes. Mammy did her best to make her and Katya pretty dresses, skirts and blouses, sometimes re-fashioning some of her own clothes but compared to what people here are wearing, her outfits back home seem dowdy and old-fashioned.

Before leaving Mary's house, she'd made herself up carefully, applying a thick coat of metallic blue eye-shadow on her lids and as she appraised herself in the full- length mirror, she thought she looked glamorous, mysterious and seductive; her long red hair shiny, the fringe just touching the eyebrows, her green eyes made brighter by the eye-shadow.

A table in the corner is laid with glasses and bottles of wine. Mary is standing behind it, handing out drinks She looks beautiful tonight. Her low-cut red dress hugs her tiny waist and shows off the curve of her breasts and hips. She is talking with a tall man; Yana recognises him as Daniel who called at the house a few days earlier.

'Come here, honey, have you got yourself all wet?' Mary waves her over. 'Have some pink bubbles, nothing better to lift the spirits, what a soggy few day it's been.'

Daniel's eyes narrow as he appraises her. 'Hello, we meet again,' he says with a smile but there is something in his dark eyes that doesn't match the smile. Something broody that makes her feel uneasy. Yana smiles back a polite hello, unsure of what to say next. Mary comes to her rescue.

'Daniel's been to Sofia, honey, he knows the place quite well.'

'I've been a couple of times,' Daniel says, 'as part of an Arts Council exchange with the Ministry of Culture there. They put my work up in the *Rodopi Gallery*. Do you know it? The one in the narrow street by the statue of the Russian Tsar. Not far from the cathedral.'

Yana nods as a surge of homesickness threatens to choke her. She takes a sip of pink champagne and looks away. When she looks back at him, his face is serious. 'You must miss Sofia,' he says. It's too much, she doesn't want to hear the words, she doesn't want him to know.

'I am going to look around the exhibition,' she says and starts to push through the crowd; past a fat man in a pinstriped suit who is talking to a pretty blonde woman in a colourful kaftan and past two long- haired men in embroidered shirts with coloured beads strung down to their waists. She feels hemmed in by all these people, light-headed and hot, still trying to hold back tears. She orders herself to calm down and stops in front of a canvas of a woman, leaning on her elbow on a sofa. Her naked body is voluptuous, the contours painted with precision and her eyes are smiling. Yana moves closer and reads *Daniel Greenberg, 'Nude' 1966.* As she stands back to get a full view, she feels a gentle touch on her shoulder.

'Do you like it?' Daniel asks.

'She is beautiful.'

He turns his face away for just a second, then takes her by the elbow and leads her away from the painting to a group of people, chatting and laughing.

'George, this is Yana, a friend of Mary's from Sofia.'

George is thin and so is the smile he offers her. 'How are you settling down in this rainy country of ours?' he asks, and she thinks no, not settling, longing to be home and fed up with this question. Can't people think of anything else to say?

'I like it here,' she says. 'People are kind.' Her standard response to this kind of question.

George smiles absently and his eyes dismiss her. Daniel introduces her to a few more people. A woman with long braided hair, beaded bracelets on both arms tells Yana she'd heard that Bulgaria is beautiful, she'd like to visit and what time of the year would be best to go?

The champagne has gone to Yana's head. She rather likes the feeling. It makes everything cloudy. It takes off the edge and helps the loneliness subside. It makes it easier to talk to people, to answer questions. She follows Daniel back to the table where Mary is talking to some people, all laughing loudly. He fills her glass and then his and she can feel Mary's eyes on them. They join the group. People are talking about the work of someone called Rauschenberg and about a pile of bricks someone has apparently assembled at a gallery called the Tate and they all seem to have different opinions about something called 'Happenings.' She is struck by the ease with which they express themselves, without fear of criticism or repercussions. So unlike home. Just listening to them makes her tense and uneasy. She knows she is being paranoid but what if someone here is listening in order to report? She knows nothing about Art, and she can't join in but just being present at such a discussion could mean being arrested and sent away. It is her fear speaking, she knows that and tries to shut off the voice in her head. The feeling of being separate, of not belonging overwhelms her again.

She tries hard to follow the conversation but none of the names mean anything to her. When Daniel joins in the discussion, she slips away, takes her umbrella out of the ornate holder and goes out into the wet and windy street. A gust of fresh air fills her lungs, and she breathes in its moisture. She is glad to be out of the gallery. Anonymous in the dark street, she can be herself again.

Waiting for the bus to take her home she notices a short stocky man standing at the corner of the street, looking at her. Her heart starts pounding. No, not here, not possible. Stop imagining, she orders herself. All is well, she's left the country legally, why would anybody be following her? But all the way home she can't stop thinking about the man. Will she ever be free of the fear?

Later, she dreams of home; the fountain in the square by the National Theatre, millions of jewels rising and falling in the sun. Old men are playing chess under the chestnut trees while a gypsy band makes music by the fountain. In the dream, she kicks her shoes off and joins the band. She sings and dances with the players and others join in, and they make a circle round the fountain.

Waking up, she wills herself to go back to the sweetness of the dream, but it pales away as dawn lights the sky outside her window.

'Why did you disappear last night?' Mary asks at breakfast in the kitchen, which overlooks the garden. Light seeps through the glass patio door and throws shadowy patches on the polished floor.

'I didn't know what people were talking about, Mary, I don't know anything about art. I felt ignorant and stupid. And I don't know how to talk to people I've never talked to before. How do you do it, Mary?'

'You just do it,' Mary said, 'you go up to someone and say *hello* and ask them questions. Everybody likes being asked questions.'

The dream comes back and longing clamps her chest again. She can't tell Mary that, lovely as being with her is, she wants to be back in Sofia with Mammy and Katya and her friends who know her and love her.

Mary puts her arms around her. They stay like this for a while and gradually, the pain eases. Her body relaxes and she remembers Daniel and the quizzical look her gave her last night. She wonders who the mysterious woman in his painting is.

'Who is Daniel?' Yana asks Mary.

'A successful painter,' Mary tells her, 'Mostly portraits. He trained at the Slade, one of the most prestigious Art Schools in this country. I was in Sofia to set up his first exhibition there when you and I first met, remember? His wife died in a car accident soon after.'

'Was that her in the picture in the gallery?'

'Yes, Jane. He painted her all the time, but we managed to get one of the best for the exhibition, they are showing all over the country.'

'She was beautiful.'

35

'Yes, she was and such a lovely person, we were all bereft when it happened. They were our 'golden couple.' I think I was in love with them both.'

Yana feels a stab of jealousy and wonders why. Is she jealous of Mary's love? Like she was jealous of Mammy's love for Katya when they were growing up? She wonders if that makes her a bad person.

Washing up while Mary gets ready to go to work, Yana feels deflated, out of place, restless in her skin; the memory of being told off at the restaurant still weighing heavily on her. She wonders yet again if her application to study at the University has been accepted; it's a month since she applied and she hasn't heard anything. And she is still waiting for uncle Nicolay in Munich to wire her the promised first instalment of the fees. Nicolay married a German nurse during the war and left Sofia before she was born but he and Mammy had been close, and Mammy assured her that he would do anything to help her in Wales.

He'd better hurry up or I am done for, she thinks.

Later, she is getting ready to go to work when she hears to doorbell and runs downstairs.

'A letter for Miss Yoakimova. It needs to be signed for.'

'It's me, I am Yana Yoakimova.' Her heart is thumping so hard she fears he might hear it.

'Sign here,' the postman says, and he offers her his pen. She signs her name slowly, trying to steady her hand.

And then the letter is in her hands. She tears the envelope open; the paper is headed *CARDIFF UNIVERSITY*, with the Welsh writing underneath: **PRIFSSGOL CAERDYDD** and informs her that she, Yana Christova

Yaokimova has been offered a place to study on the Psychology Course starting this October.

She feels lightheaded and breathless, she is afraid her legs might give away. She sits on the bottom step to calm herself.

This is it, she thinks, my new life is starting now. I have to learn how to live in this country where people are unafraid, where the walls don't have 'ears,' where people go about minding their own business and where no one seems to mind who you are or what you believe.

The freedom that Tatti wanted so much that he was prepared to give up his life for it.

Chapter Five

August soaked and soggy is drawing to a close. Yana has never seen so much rain, day after day, week after week, steady and relentless. The grass in Mary's garden is glassy green and she walks there in the mornings, breathing in the soft air cleansed through and through by the water. She must get used to it; she has to learn not to mind it. She has to learn not to miss the sun. And she must think of her course starting in October. She must get ready for that.

Then one Sunday morning they wake up to a perfect sky and a sun that is shining hot and bright, as if making up for lost time. 'We must have a barbeque', Mary says, 'it will cheer us up after all this rain.' She rings around her friends with invitations, they drive to the supermarket and load the car with sausages and rolls and chops and salad. Yana offers to make some *koftas* and a tray of *banitza*.

By lunchtime, the sun is scorching. They get out the parasol and the wicker chairs from the garden shed and lay the marble- topped garden table with glasses, plates and napkins. The guests start arriving: a couple with a young girl who flies into Mary's arms, her plats swinging in the air, four women in colourful summer dresses and two young men, who Mary later tells her are friends of Jason's. The garden fills with noisy chatter.

Daniel is one of the last to arrive and when she sees him, Yana realises she's been waiting for him. He is wearing a blue linen shirt that shows off his olive complexion. She thinks he looks distinguished and handsome.

'Hello again,' he says and kisses her cheek, and she can smell the traces of soap on his freshly laundered shirt.

People are drinking and laughing, and the sun beats down. Most of the guests stay in the shadow of the large parasol or under the trees but Yana can't get enough of the heat, her body is starved of it. She finds a hair band in the pocket of her sundress, scoops up her hair and piles it up on top to let the slight breeze cool her neck. She passes round platefuls of salad and bread and people complement her on her *koftas* and a woman wants her recipe for the *banitza*. When she starts to feel her back burning, she joins Mary and Daniel under the cherry tree.

'Are you having a good time, Yana?' Mary asks. 'Look, the sun has come out specially for you. I know how much you like it.'

'Are summers always hot in Sofia?' Daniel asks. 'It certainly was very hot when I was there.'

'Oh, yes,' Yana replies, 'sometimes it is so hot that we have to stay indoors to keep away from the sun.'

'The rain here must get you down.'

'I like a bit of rain, it keeps everything here so fresh and green but no, I don't like it when it rains for what seems like forever.'

'Look at us,' Mary laughs, 'talking about the weather. So English.' And with that she stands up, saying she must get people more drinks.

Daniel moves closer to her, and she feels her pulse quicken. She sits very still, her insides vibrating. She likes the feel of him being close to her, his body is solid and warm, and she would like him to put his arms around her.

'Tell me about you,' he says.

'What would you like to know?'

'What was it like growing up in Sofia?'

Where to start? Snowfalls and knee-high drifts, feet frozen to the bone, starlit nights, kissing boys on the corner of her street. The sound of Mammy's knitting needles clicking and her pale face leaning over in the morning light. Misty November mornings, dew-sprinkled cobwebs hanging from the rose bushes in the park across the road. People whispering, afraid. Or people like Tatti speaking their minds. Eating jam with a spoon. The sunlight so sweet and golden, it tastes like honey on your tongue. The pain of being sent to live with Tatti to the other end of the country when he and Mammy divorced. The feeling of being unwanted, so unbearable she had to shut down. Policemen at Tatti's funeral. Next doors neighbour Mad Magda whispering on the stairs. Mad Magda who knew everything because people thought she didn't understand and talked freely in front of her. What was it like growing up in Sofia? How can she ever explain that she had to leave her beautiful homeland because she felt imprisoned there.

'A big question.' she says.

They sit in silence for a while watching the light fade, leaving a lilac sky striped with orange and gold. 'Why did you leave?' he asks.

'It's a long story'

'Tell me sometime, maybe over coffee or dinner one night?'

'Perhaps.' She knows she should avert this awkwardness. 'Tell me about you,' she says.

'I grew up in East London. My father's parents came from Hungary and my mother was born in Latvia. She managed to get away after her parents were killed in the Holocaust.'

Yana had already guessed that he isn't of British origin because of his complexion and had wondered if he was perhaps Spanish. She didn't know any Jewish people but of course, she knew about the horrors of the Holocaust. She wishes she hadn't asked the question.

'I am so sorry,' she says and is relieved when Mary joins them, bearing a tray laid with a pot of coffee, cups, biscuits and chocolates. 'They've all left,' she says, 'time for a cuppa.'

They drink their coffee in silence and watch the sky. Evening advances and it turns dark violet. A few stars come out hanging like tiny lanterns twinkling far away. More stars appear as the night unfolds around them, velvet on Yana's skin and she feels the ache for Mammy and Katya ease. Perhaps this place could be home after all. She hears children's voices in the garden next door, clear like bells ringing in the darkness and the smell of fading roses fills the garden, sweet and intense like church incense that lingers long after the flame had turned to ash.

Taking his leave, Daniel exchanges kisses with Mary then kisses her on the cheek too. She feels herself blush and hopes the darkness will hide her burning cheeks.

'Come to my studio,' he says on his way out, 'I'll show you more of my pictures and we can talk about Art. Mary here tells me your grandfather was an artist too.'

'I think he likes you,' Mary says back in the kitchen as they are washing up.

'Maybe.' Then not wanting to sound ungrateful, she adds, 'I do appreciate everything you are doing for me, Mary, I really do.'

And she means it with all her heart and puts her arms around Mary who strokes her hair.

'You are most welcome, sweetheart and always will be.'

'It must be nice to meet somebody in Cardiff who knows about your country,' Mary says after a while.

'Good and bad,' Yana replies. 'Daniel talking about Sofia the other evening at the gallery made me very sad. It made me long to be home.'

'Have you heard from Mammy and Katya recently?'

'Not yet, waiting for a reply to my last letter.'

She busies herself drying the coffee cups to hide the pangs of homesickness but something else too. Daniel's good-bye kiss has stirred her body and the thought of him floods her with warmth, her fingers tingle and her heart flutters. Don't be silly, she tells herself, it was just a friendly kiss, it didn't mean anything.

Chapter Six

Daniel drives them out of town and along narrow country lanes, past fields dotted with bales of hay and dusty hedges stretching out in the heat. It is two weeks into September and summer, late in arriving is hanging on.

His studio is a barn at the end of a gravel driveway and as Yana enters the white -washed space, the sharp smell of turpentine and linseed hits her senses. It takes her back to another studio, at the top of her grandparents' house in Dondukov Street. Diado, short and slightly bent, stands in front of the portrait of her grandmother he's been painting for as long as she could remember. Baba has long auburn hair and when the sun comes in through the dirty windows, it looks as if it is on fire. Her handsome face is unsmiling but there is love in her eyes. Next to her, on a different easel is a painting of another woman, blue eyed with black hair. 'Someone we used to know when we lived in New York,' Diado said when she asked about her.

Baba's love was a constant in Yana's life. When Mammy was distraught with grief, she went to Baba for comfort. Not one for many words, Baba cooked instead and when Yana tasted one of her sugar-crusted dough-nuts, pleasure took over the pain and for a few moments all that mattered was her and Baba sitting in the small kitchen, eating doughnuts, not talking, just being to-gether.

She hasn't thought of Diado and Baba for a very long time.

While Daniel is making coffee in the kitchen, Yana sits in an armchair draped with a blue paint- splashed cloth. She looks around at the stacked canvases in one corner, the pots of paint, the rags and the brushes piled in another and the clay torso of a woman waiting to be finished. She breathes in the smells, familiar but different, sharper and cleaner.

Daniel brings in a pot and two blue mugs and pours the coffee. She watches his hands, large and strong, the hands of a maker. She imagines them touching her skin and feels her spine tingle.

He sits on a stool beside her.

'I grew up watching my grandfather paint,' she tells him. 'I loved being with him in his studio, sitting on the little stool he had made specially for me. They were happy times. I still remember the smell of his studio, a bit like yours but mixed with the smell of his cooking.'

'He cooked in his studio?' Daniel looks surprised.

'Oh, yes. He was quite eccentric. By the time I knew him, he had moved out of the apartment he shared with my grandmother, and was living in his studio, at the top of the building, painting and cooking, mainly boiled carrots, lentils and rice.'

'Vegetarian before his time?'

'I guess. Are you?'

'Yep. What did he paint?'

'Portraits at first. Then he was sent to the front as a war artist when the Great War broke out. I remember he used to tell me off for wearing eye shadow and mascara. Take that muck off, your face,' he used to say, 'it spoils your beautiful eyes.'

'You do have beautiful eyes.'

She is blushing and hopes he hasn't noticed.

'What about your grandparents, did you know them?' she asks to break the awkwardness she feels. Awkwardness tinged with excitement.

'I didn't know my grandparents, but my parents told me a lot about them.' Daniel tells her. 'My Grandma, my mother's mother played the guitar, it must have been unusual for a woman in Latvia in those days.'

Yana wants to know more, but something in his eyes tells her she shouldn't ask. She gets up and looks at the canvas on the easel, a woman, her outline blurred, walking away through a yellow field.

'What are you working on now?'

'Playing around with some images.' His voice tells her he isn't going to say anymore. She sits in the chair and sips her coffee, and the room fills with heavy silence. Minutes pass, Daniel gets up and starts to wash his brushes. She watches his back, his shoulders slightly stooping, his head bent over the sink, his body totally focussed, consumed by the task.

The afternoon gathers around them.

'You lost your father when you were young, Mary told me.' Daniel says after he's put his brushes away.

It takes Yana by surprise; she hadn't realised he knew. He must have seen the shock in her face. 'I am sorry for intruding,' he says. 'It was clumsy of me.'

The afternoon takes on a different hue as if darkened by shadows. Silence stretches wall–to- wall, taking up all the space where words might come. She hadn't wanted thoughts of Tatti to intrude on her day with Daniel but unbidden they come, and the image of his battered body emerges as if on a screen.

'I need to go home,' she says and gets up.

He comes close and puts his arms around her. 'I am sorry,' he says again. He holds her for a moment, just

47

close enough for her to feel the warmth of his body. It feels good, she wants to relax into his arms, longs to lose herself, to forget. But it is as if her body is on guard, it holds itself, silently resisting, the pain too intense to allow in the possibility of joy. She gently pulls away.

She goes to bed thinking of him. The feel of his arms around her has awakened her body and she twist and turns, unable to switch off desire. She drifts into sleep imagining him lying next to hers, then the weight of him on her and at last she drops off into a dark and dreamless night.

The alarm brings morning light flooding through the half-closed curtains, and she can hear Mary moving downstairs in the kitchen. The smell of coffee and toast wafts up and Yana is seized by hunger sharp and sudden. And with it comes the memory of yesterday and it makes her smile.

She hears Mary leaving the house and goes downstairs to eat toast, bacon, eggs then more toast thickly spread with strawberry jam. Then she lets herself out into the sunny street. It is warm and she feels light. A small girl is skipping on the pavement, and she catches herself wanting to join in.

For now, she can put the past behind her and live this new life and see where it might take her.

At the bus stop, someone taps her on the shoulder, and she jumps, startled.

'Have you the time, love?' It's the stocky man she saw at bus stop on her way back from the private view at the gallery. Her heart starts its crazy beat again. But he is obviously local, the accent she now recognises as Welsh, maybe a neighbour. 'Diolh,' he says and smiles at her sweetly when she tells him the time.

You have to stop this, she tells herself firmly, nobody is after you. Nobody cares, you are not important enough. But her body is refusing to believe her thoughts and her stomach clenches in fear. For a few seconds her feet refuse to take her towards the bus approaching from around the corner but when it arrives at her stop, she wills herself to move.

Chapter Seven

The University is in a grand Victorian building in the centre of the city. Yana makes her way up a wide staircase, past groups of students noisily coming down. She finds the lecture room, which is already full and chooses a seat at the end of the fourth row. The noise subsides and all eyes turn to Professor Hepple, a slight man who has quietly slipped into the room.

It's strange being a student again and being at least ten years older than most of the first-year students. And having to work and study at the same time which certainly wasn't the case when she started her English Language and Literature course at Sofia University at 18. Strange and exciting. It makes her feel confident, in charge of her life. She thinks of Daniel and hopes he thinks of her from time to time too.

They have met a few times now and a friendship is growing between them, but she wants more. He took her to the cinema to see Murder on the Orient Express and she loved it and thought that Lauren Bacall and Albert Finley were wonderful in it. She'd read the book while at University and got hooked on Agatha Christie, proceeding to read every book she'd ever written. Last time they met, Daniel took her out to dinner to a very grand hotel called the Angel just across the road from the ancient castle. She was amazed when she noticed that no one was smoking. So not like home, she thought, where most people smoked while eating, fork in one hand, a cigarette in the other. She'd ordered gammon steak with chips, food she'd never eaten before. He laughed when she carefully arranged the apricots that garnished it in a small heap on the side of the plate.

'We never mix sweet and savoury food back home,' she'd told him. 'I'll eat the apricots for dessert.'

She loves spending time with him, her body tingles all over when they are together. She would like to kiss him and be kissed by him. She would like to make love with him. She knows he likes her too, she can see it in his eyes, but he is holding back, friendly pecks on the cheek when they part company, once or twice a hug. She thinks he is still grieving for Jane. Maybe when he is with her, Yana, Jane comes to him and claims him, and he grows distant with longing for her. Maybe it is the ghost of Jane that stands between them.

An eruption of laughter brings her back to the lecture hall. She realises that the professor has made a joke and she has missed it. The old familiar feeling of being outside, looking in as if through a glass pane, makes her want to get up and leave. Just as she had wanted to run away when Mammy sent her to the other side of the country to live with Tatti and his new wife.

Professor Hepple has come to the end of his lecture on child development and Yana gathers up her books. Some of the students are chatting in the corridor. She feels awkward standing by herself. Mary's advice seems useless, she doesn't know how to speak to people she doesn't know. She must find out how it's done, she needs to observe and learn.

Outside, the sky is heavy with rain. She runs to a café round the corner, finds a little table by the window and orders an espresso. The café seemed a popular haunt for students; its brown walls are covered with postcards of the Beatles and posters advertising gigs and mike nights and pub crawls. The jukebox in the corner is blaring

Abba's Dancing Queen and grey wreaths of cigarette smoke hang in the air. The café in Sofia where she and her friends met after lectures was always smoky too but there were no pictures of pop stars on the walls, just portraits of Lenin and Stalin and posters of the October Revolution.

Within minutes rain starts to pelt the pavement and the wind picks up clumps of leaves and swirls them in a wild dance and into the gutter. She sits alone, shutting out the noise of chatter and music and remembers Daniel's arms around her when he last hugged her. She welcomes autumn and his arrival in her life and for a while, her mind is free of longing for home.

The waiter brings her coffee and at the same time a tall blonde girl stops by the table. 'I saw you at Hepple's lecture,' she says. 'What did you think?'

And before Yana has the chance to respond, she continues: 'I noticed you, we're both older than the others. It feels strange, don't you think?'

Yana smiles. Could this be a new friend?

'Do you mind if I sit with you?' the girl asks.

'Yes, of course.'

'I am from Manchester,' the girl whose name is Jenny says. Yana tells her she comes from Bulgaria.

'I didn't think you were English, but I wondered if you might be Irish, with that hair of yours.'

Yana has never been taken for Irish before and she likes it, it seems romantic.

'Bulgaria,' Jenny says, 'I'm ashamed to say I don't know much about your country. You are the first Bulgarian I've met. What is it like?'

'It's beautiful. Lots of sun in the summer, lots of snow in the winter. Mountains that go down to the sea. Sandy beaches that go on for miles.'

'Sounds wonderful.'

Yana's heart contracts. How is it possible to explain that the most beautiful place in the world becomes a prison when you can't speak your mind and you can't leave? When fear is a shadow that follows you wherever you go.

They finish their coffees and promise to look out for each other at Hepple's lecture the following week.

Out in the street it is still raining, and Yana makes a dash for the bus. She hears footsteps behind her. She wants to turn around and confront whoever is following her but keeps walking. Stop it right now, she says to herself, stop always imagining that people are following you. Once and for all stop it! I am here legally, why would anybody want to follow me? Ivanov. It could be a trap. Perhaps he let her have the visa only to trap her. But what would he want from her here? She'd thought that sleeping with him had been the price for the visa but maybe there is another, higher price to pay?

Just before she gets to bus stop, she turns around. It's a young man who is running for the bus like she is. You have to stop being paranoid, she admonishes herself again.

She watches the rain trickle down the steamed-up window. Meeting Jenny had been a nice surprise. She hadn't thought she might make a friend on her first day at university.

Mary meets her in the hall holding an envelope. 'A letter from home, sweetheart, hope all is well there.'

The writing is Katya's. Katya rarely writes to her; Yana gets all the news from Mammy. She feels weak in the knees and her stomach hardens.

Monday, October 2nd

My dear Yana,
Please don't worry too much when you read this. We didn't tell you earlier because we didn't want to make it difficult for you to settle down to your studies and your new life in Wales. A few weeks after you left, the doctors found a tumour on Mammy's left ovary. It was malignant and they took it out last Friday.

But please, please don't worry, the op was successful, and she is recovering well, she'll be out of hospital at the end of the week. She'll have to have a course of chemo after that but hopefully, that will be the end of it.

I wrote to tell Uncle Nicolay in Munich too and he phoned straight away to see how she was and he asked after you too. He wondered if you might be coming back to be with Mammy and worried that you may not be able to leave again if you did. But honestly, you don't need to come. You've just started your new course; I understand how important this is for you.

Otherwise, no other news from here. I am trying to get on with my Art and Design course, I am loving it, it's so interesting and I am learning such an awful lot. How is your course? Are you enjoying it? Are you making new friends? Does it really rain all the time in Wales?
I do miss you big Sis, it's lonely without you here,
Write soon,
Love and kisses,
Katya xxx

The ground is shifting under her feet again.

A week passes. She goes to her classes, works in the restaurant, writes her assignments, meets up with Jenny for coffee and drinks and tries to put Katya's letter to the back of her mind. When she thinks about it, it seems unreal, like a story in a book. Mammy can't be ill, or if she is, she'll recover, of course she will. Nothing needs to be done. She writes back asking for more news of Mammy's recovery and sends her a card and a pretty scarf patterned in dark blue and violet, the colours Mammy likes.

She doesn't tell Mary what is in Katya's letter. She can't explain to herself why, maybe speaking about it would make it more real. Most of the time, she manages to turn her mind away. She longs to see Daniel again. She longs to talk to him, to touch him, just to feel his presence.

One morning she wakes up early, before dawn and listens to the rain beating softly against the window. And suddenly she knows. Katya's letter is urgent, she didn't mean it when she said not to come back.

She gets up and opens the heavy velvet curtains. It is still dark, but she knows she won't be able to go back to sleep. The thought of Mammy's illness, the possibility that she might not survive it makes her heart so tight, she can hardly breathe. She must go home and be with Mammy, she mustn't leave Katya on her own. But a voice in her head whispers *if you go back, your hopes of a free life would be dashed forever*. It is highly unlikely they would let her out again, even if she slept with Ivanov; they must know that it is her intention to stay here. And it would mean that she would lose Daniel, just as she has found him. The thought makes her chest ache.

Chapter Eight

Dawn is breaking and the birds outside are noisy. She goes downstairs as quietly as she can, not wanting to wake up Mary. The kitchen is stuffy, the stale smell of last night's cigarettes mingling with the heavy odour of coal from the fire that had died down during the night. She opens the back door and breathes in the damp, cool morning, then walks down to the end of the garden and sits on the wooden seat under the trellis of Japanese roses. Their heads, white and pink in their second bloom are delicately bowed under the weight of the rain, their smell intensely sweet in the first light of the day.

Daniel comes into her thoughts. First his eyes, gentle and thoughtful. Then his lips. She wants to speak to him. Best to go out now and get a coffee somewhere near college. She can ring him after the first lecture.

Jenny is already in the lecture hall and has kept a seat for her.

'You look pale,' she says, and Yana tells her about the letter. It seems easier to tell someone she doesn't know well than tell Mary who she knows loves her and would feel her pain.

'It sounds urgent, Yana. Let's have coffee after the lecture is over.' she suggests.

They go to the cafe on the corner where they first met and order their coffees, double espresso with hot water, half and half for Yana and a frothy cappuccino for Jenny.

'Have you got money for the ticket?' Jenny asks.

'Not enough, the tips haven't been all that generous.'

'What will you do? What can I do to help?'

Yana feels a wave of gratitude for having met Jenny. They are so different and yet she feels close to her. She loves her for her kindness and her feistiness, the way she seems to look at the world straight in the eye. She wonders if one day perhaps she could tell her about Tatti.

After parting with Jenny, she phones Daniel from the box by the café.

'Do you need money?' he asks, 'Let me buy your ticket.'

'Thank you, Daniel, I do appreciate the offer. I have an uncle, Mammy's brother who lives in Munich, I am sure he'll wire me the money if I ask.'

'Let me at least take you to the airport.'

'I'd like that very much.' She feels a flicker of disappointment. He didn't sound sad, just matter of fact.

Yana has never met Mammy's elder brother Nicolay or his German wife, Gertrude, a nurse he'd married during the war. Mammy had told her they left Bulgaria as the war was ending. Rumours had spread that the Soviets were advancing across Eastern Europe; terrifying tales of Russian soldiers raping women and looting and even killing children. Uncle Nicolay had urged Mammy and Tatti to leave too but Mammy was pregnant with Yana. But the pictures Yana grew up with were of joyful crowds throwing flowers and cheering the tanks as they rolled into the streets, women in summer dresses, children running beside the marching soldiers and the tanks, clamouring for a handshake or a kiss.

Uncle Nicolay and his German wife never returned, too scared of the communists, too scared that he would not be allowed to leave again. Yana understands the fear, she has lived with it all her life. Her heart tells her she must return, it gives her no choice but her body resists, it tenses itself around the thought and cold sweat runs down her forehead.

In the afternoon, after lectures are over, Daniel takes her to a bar and orders a couple of brandies with their coffees. The brandy loosens her limbs and the tension eases, giving way to tears. He takes her hand across the table. 'Come back home with me,' he says.

In bed, he holds her, their passion for each other spent. She wants this moment to last forever; the solid feel of his body as she lays her head on his chest, the beat of his heart, the feel of his skin on hers.

'I'll find you,' Daniel says. 'What is between us can't stop. You have brought me back to life.'

She doesn't need to say she feels the same because he knows.

Chapter Nine

Katya, late October 1974, Sofia

The sound of the radio next door wakes her up. At first her mind is blank, as if refusing to face up to the day ahead. Slowly she wakes up as the image of Mammy's bald head rises to the surface. She throws off her bed-clothes and stands at the window. The mountain rises in the distance, silent and brooding.

'Breakfast, Mammy,' she says as she enters Mammy's bedroom. 'What do you fancy?'

Mammy is sitting in bed, propped against a pile of pillows, reading the paper. She has already wrapped the dark blue and purple scarf Yana sent her round her head; she doesn't like anybody seeing her hairless. 'Good morning *dushko'* she says and smiles, a happy welcoming smile. The sight of her, so vulnerable and so brave pierces Katya's heart. She wants to climb into bed with her and hold her and never let her go but she knows she mustn't show Mammy her fear and her sadness. She must be brave; Mammy doesn't want sympathy.

'How about if we went to Misho's *sladkarnitza* round the corner,' Mammy says, 'and treat ourselves to cake and coffee and maybe some *boza?'*

'Yes, that would be lovely, Mammy, if you feel up to it.'

'Of course, I am up to it, *dusko,* I wouldn't have suggested it otherwise, would I now?' The irritation in her voice has become familiar to Katya since Mammy became ill.

'I need to get some milk and bread first, the queue yesterday was so long that by the time my turn came, there was none left.'

'The story of our lives now,' Mammy says. 'It didn't use to be like this before Yana and you were born. Not in the old days.'

Katya loves to hear stories of Mammy when she was a little girl. The large house on *Oborishte* street where she grew up with her father until after the war when the new government took it away from them and made it into the Argentinian Embassy. Every time Katya goes past it now, she thinks of Mammy and her grandfather, the judge living there with the housemaid Louise and Emily, the French nanny. Mammy playing in the large garden at the back with *Lucky*, her little dog, not a care in the world. 'Did you not miss having a Mammy?' Katya had asked listening to Mammy's stories. 'I was only six months old when she died so I had no memory of her. I was happy with my life, I felt loved by the people in my life.' Mammy had replied.

Katya lets herself out and takes in the moist October air. A flock of birds passes overhead flying south. Two girls chase each other around the pavement, and it makes her think of Yana. She misses her badly, especially now that Mammy is so ill. Her big sister who always took care of her is not here. There is a missing feeling in her chest but there is something else in her body too, a tensing in her stomach and in her shoulders.

Her sister's letters are cheerful and full of interesting observations. Apparently, it is allowed to sit on the grass in the parks there, it doesn't carry a stiff fine and a loud telling off. And there are fabulous clothes shops in Cardiff and most women wear very short skirts. Yana told her that Mary shortened all her skirts when she got to Cardiff, so now she feels more 'with it.' And apparently, she counted more than fifty kinds of biscuits in the super-market there.

Katya is not envious; she has never wanted to live abroad despite all the limitations here. She likes her hometown with *Vitosha* rising above it and she likes the routine of her life, living with Mammy and spending time with Vlado on weekends. She is enjoying her course and loves spending time with her friends, she can't imagine life without them and often wonders how Yana managed to leave all of this behind.

But Yana was always different. Restless, dissatisfied and disaffected, always looking ahead, wishing for a dif-ferent life. More like their father. Katya is glad that Yana has found a new life for herself in Wales and that she is happy there. She felt awful having to write to her about Mammy. But she knew Yana would never forgive her if she didn't and she is glad her sister is coming. She is longing for her, can't wait to see her.

By the time she gets to the shops, the milk has gone but she manages to get a loaf from the bakery and walk-ing home, she can't resist tearing off the still warm crusty bits and savouring the slightly acetic taste of the sour-dough. Yana and she used to do that when they were young and sent on shopping errands. Her heart is soft and tender for her sister when she remembers.

Later Katya takes Mammy to the *sladkarnitsa*. Mammy has dug out her father's walking stick from the ancient trunk where she keeps old photographs and letters and is propping herself on it, its gilded lion's head catch-ing the late afternoon sun and shining as if newly pol-ished. Katya remembers her grandfather using it in his later years and how once, when they were at the circus

63

and a large woman had obstructed their view, he used it to tap her on the shoulder and ask her to move so she and Yana could have a better view. Katya still remembers the embarrassment she felt when the woman turned around angrily, saying 'Who do think you are??' But she did move, and Yana and Katya had a good view of the acrobats on horses and the magic lady who got cut in half.

At the *sladkarnitza* they order *baklava*, coffee and *boza*. Nikolova, from next door is at a table near them. She turns around to face Mammy.

'How are you doing, Leni?'

'Doing well, comrade, doing well,' Mammy replies.

'And Yana, is she coming back? You must miss having her with you at such a difficult time. I always wondered how you felt about her living abroad, so far away. I wouldn't like it; I wouldn't like it at all if mine decided to leave.'

'Yana is coming back shortly,' Katya says, then turns away from Nokolova indicating that the conversation is closed.

'I wish people would mind their own business,' Mammy says when they get back to the flat.

'It must have touched a nerve, Mammy,' Katya says. 'You've never talked about it, how you felt when Yana left.'

Mammy sighs, then straightens her back, lifts her head and looks Katya in the eyes.

'I always want what is best for my children,' she says firmly. 'Now I must lie down and have a nap.'

If only she would talk, Katya thinks, share a bit instead of keeping all her pain inside. This is how it was when Tatti left, this is how it was when he was killed.

Which made it so much more difficult, the unspoken grief hanging over them like a dense black cloud, permanent and unsolvable.

And all of it because of Tatti.

Chapter Ten

Early November, Yana

In the departure lounge, Yana gets herself a coffee and finds a seat near the checking-in desk. She can tell, by what they are wearing that most of the passengers waiting there are either from Bulgaria or from another one of the Eastern Bloc republics: badly made suits of coarse material, the colour mostly grey, the shoes a particular give away, roughly cut, the leather hard. So different from the colourful clothes in the shops and on the streets of Cardiff. She looks around at her fellow passengers' faces, which are sullen and closed and reminds herself of what a different reality she is about to go back to.

The plane shudders as the wheels touch the runaway, coming to a stop smoothly. A round of loud clapping follows and the woman sitting next to her says, 'Ours are the best pilots, don't you think? They can teach the British a thing or two.'

Yana has been talking to Vera on and off during the three-hour flight and they established they were born a few streets away from each other. Vera is a big-busted woman, her hair dyed orange, with black roots on the top. She is a schoolteacher and a know-all who espouses the virtues of socialism. Yana is reminded of Comrade Stoyanova, her primary school teacher. She once brought the ruler down on Yana's fingers when Yana told the class that she prayed to God with Mammy and Katya every night before she went to sleep. 'God doesn't exist,'

Comrade Stoyanova had hissed through clenched teeth. 'God', she'd raged, 'has never existed. God is an insidious invention of the corrupt capitalist system of the West which has caused the unhappiness of millions and millions of poor working-class people all over the world.'

Yana continued to pray even though she couldn't find any proof for God's existence. Her heart felt soft and quiet when she prayed with Mammy and Katya. But she never told anyone about it again.

Listening to Vera reminds Yana why she left; communism and its slogans, its constant presence and the fear to speak one's own mind because 'the walls have ears.' But when she thinks of Mammy and Katya, her stomach tightens. She has deserted them, wanting a better life for herself. Just like she did when she agreed to live with Tatti.

A deep yearning for home rises inside her and her body relaxes. She shuts her eyes and allows herself to sink into the feeling.

When she opens her eyes again, the passengers are scrambling up, looking for their hand luggage in the lockers overhead. She takes down her bag, her hands shaking so badly she thinks she might drop it. She struggles to contain the energy that is rushing through her, hot one moment then freezing, joy and fear jostling for primacy. She follows the man in front who has started to move forward, trying hard not to push past him to the exit.

Waiting to get her passport stamped seems like eternity. Her stomach is churning. Her body remembers the fear.

The man behind the screen is older than the one who let her go through six months ago. He takes her passport and spends a long time leafing through the pages. Finally, he stamps it and gives it back to her.

'Make sure you submit it to the Department for Internal Affairs within a week, comrade. Failure to do so will result in a prison sentence.'

Yana knows about the procedure and yet she is surprised by the violent jolt of anxiety. Here we go, she thinks.

Katya is waiting at the barrier holding a bunch of white carnations. Seeing her, tears burn behind Yana's eyelids. Katya looks thinner and when they hug, Yana can feel her ribs under her blue jumper. Her hair, jet black as ever is longer, with a fringe, which makes her look both older and more vulnerable at the same time. It's been nearly six months and holding her now, Yana feels sorrow for the passing of time. Then love surges and she presses Katya close to her chest.

November sunshine, pale but still warm makes her blink as they step out of the airport and into the waiting taxi.

'Try not to look shocked when you see Mammy,' Katya says, 'she's lost her hair.'

Yana knew Mammy was going to lose her hair because of the chemo, that's why she'd sent her the scarf. But hearing Katya say it is like a punch in the stomach.

'How is she though? In herself?'

'It doesn't look good Yana; they think the cancer may have spread to the lymph nodes.'

Yana remembers the nightmare she'd had two days before she left Cardiff. Mammy wearing her wedding dress, happy that she is marrying Tatti again. She is veiled in a red flag, old and tattered with the sickle and hammer and the five pointed- star in one corner. When Yana woke up, she knew that that the news at home wouldn't be good.

The taxi speeds down the boulevard to the centre of the city. Past the Institute of Science and Technology, a tall ugly building where Yana once had a part-time job teaching English to engineering students. Then past the supermarket, it's grimy walls peeling. She used to go for her lunchtime sandwiches there. When they come to the Orlov bridge, its two large cast iron eagles standing erect on each side, she sees the mountain in the distance, intensely blue against the pale autumn sky and she knows she is home.

In the lift she inhales the familiar smells wafting from neighbours' apartments; red peppers roasting on hot plates and herby garlic beans stewing for supper. It is as if she's never been away.

The lift comes to a stop and Mammy is already at the door. Her head is covered with the blue and violet patterned scarf that Yana had sent her; her cheeks are sunken which makes her brown eyes look even bigger. She smiles a broad happy smile that floods her face with light. It is if a little lamp inside her has been switched on and for a moment, Yana feels as though time has stood still and everything is as it always was. But when she holds Mammy she knows this is not so; her smell is different, pungent, unfamiliar.

The flat is the same though, and Mammy has kept Yana's bedroom just as she left it. She puts her bag on the carefully made bed. She feels like a stranger intruding on her own life.

In the dining room, the table is laden with her favourite food; roasted red peppers and *banitza* and a whole plate of *lukanka*. For some reason, this makes her feel even more of a stranger, a guest in her own home.

'Eat,' says Katya, 'we got the *lukanka* specially for you. Nikolova next door has a new boyfriend, he's the manager of the grocery shop on Oborishte Street. We told her you were coming and how much you love *lukanka* and she got him to put a couple of pieces behind the counter, you know how quickly it goes.'

There is a lump in Yana's throat, and she finds it difficult to swallow. She takes a sip of red wine, and it slides down, velvety and smooth but the lump is still there. Mammy reaches across the table and holds her hand. 'Cry if you want to, *dusko*, don't hold it in. It's not going to upset me, bawl your eyes out if you need to. It will do you good.'

Katya is looking at her plate, arranging and re-arranging the slices of *lukanka* in a line. The lump in Yana's throat would not dissolve into tears. The evening spreads around them, silent and unobtrusive and then it's dark. Mammy puts on a light and kisses them both good night. Katya and Yana sit quietly for a while, together but alone in their grief.

The surgeon's office is large and brightly lit. The surgeon, probably in his sixties is sitting behind a mahogany desk, with a cluster of family photographs at one end and a telephone at the other. The room smells faintly of disinfectant. He confirms what Yana already suspected; that the cancer has taken over Mammy's body.

'I hate to be the bearer of bad new,' he says, 'but there is nothing more we can do for your mother now. The chemotherapy worked for a while but sadly the cancer has spread and is inoperable.'

A wave of sadness floods her chest, and she knows she has been hoping against hope. Her stomach sinks, becomes a hollow space inside her body. She looks across at Katya who is crying and puts her arm around her. They sit in silence for a while as the surgeon looks through his notes, then he closes the file and Yana knows that the consultation is over.

Afterwards they go to the coffee shop on Stamboliiski street. It hasn't changed much. The wood-panelled walls are still lined with books and Yana remembers sitting, reading and drinking endless cups of coffee with Rossi and Leni and sometimes Katya on the days before exams. She looks around remembering that she once belonged here. She would like to sit with her friends here again but so much has happened since she last saw them that it now feels like another life. Now, she is adrift between two realities; her life in Wales and freedom and here, her childhood home, with roots of love and fear so deeply entangled they threaten to strangle her.

The waitress comes to take their order and Yana is surprised at how hungry she is. It is as if her grief about Mammy has carved a hole in her stomach and she needs to fill it in, pack it with food so there would be no space to feel. She orders a slice of chocolate cake and wolfs it down, then orders a slice of *baklava* to follow. Katya orders just coffee.

'Are you not hungry?' Yana asks, 'you've had no breakfast. I am worried about you, Katya, you've lost a lot of weight.'

Katya sips her coffee and looks away. When she looks back at Yana, there are angry tears in her eyes.

'Yes,' she says,' I know. I haven't been able to eat much since Mammy got ill. All the worry and no one to share it with. I am not having a dig at you, Sis but that's the truth. I have felt so alone with it all.'

'You wrote to me, Katya, telling me not to come, that she would be OK. You never said how you felt.'

'And was it that difficult to guess? Or was it that you didn't want to?'

'That's not fair. I would have been here like a shot, had I known the reality of it. You hid it from me, you wanted to protect me. Now you blame me for not coming earlier. It's not fair.'

No more words now, just silence. Guilt mixed with anger churn in Yana's belly. She should have come straight away, of course she should have. Would she ever forgive herself for choosing to delay because of Daniel? She doesn't know how she will face what must surely come. Losing Mammy frightens her to the core. But she can't tell Katya this. She is the older one, she has to look after her, she must not leave her alone again. She will write to Daniel to tell him she won't be going back. The thought cuts through her like a knife.

Chapter Eleven

Katya

It's strange having Yana in the flat again. She missed her terribly after she left back in the summer but then she settled into her life without her. Until Mammy got ill, her course and Vlado took up most of her time and she'd felt contented. Then everything changed. She is glad Yana is back, but she has to get used to having her around again.

She goes to the kitchen to make coffee for them both. Since Mammy was taken to hospital two weeks ago, Katya and Yana had not been as careful to keep the flat as tidy as when she was there, and Katya has to stack a pile of dirty dishes to one side to make room for the coffee grinder. But the coffee grinder is not in its usual place, and she can feel her jaw tightening, the angry devil sitting on her shoulder. *Why is she always moving things around? As if she knows better*. That's how it always was, her older sister knowing more, knowing better, always being in the right.

'I can't find the coffee grinder, Yana. I wish you wouldn't move things around. It gets on my nerves, it really does.'

Yana looks at her surprised. 'I put it where we used to keep it. What's all this fuss about?'

'Well, we changed things after you left, you can't expect us to keep everything in the same place just in case you ever came back.' Now her stomach is rock hard.

Yana's face reddens and Katya can hear her breath coming out. 'Sorry,' Yana says.

The familiar whirl of the machine is comforting and so is the rich aroma of the ground coffee that infuses the room with a caramelly smell.

Katya pours the coffee into two large mugs, places them on the wicker tray puts a couple of chocolate biscuits on a plate and takes them to the sitting room.

'I'll be going to the hospital in about an hour, are you coming with me?'

'Yes, of course.' Then after a pause: 'I didn't tell you, but I had a letter from Daniel the other day, he is arriving in Sofia on Saturday.'

'A bit unexpected, isn't it?'

Katya knows that Daniel hasn't been in touch with Yana since she got here a month ago. She knows that her sister is hurting, and she is angry on her behalf.

'So, what brings him here so suddenly?'

'Friends of his are having an exhibition at the Arts Centre. They invited him to the opening night.'

'And he is fitting you in while here?'

'Don't be horrid,' Yana says and bursts into tears. The truth hurts, Katya thinks but it hurts her too to see her sister upset. She thinks of Valdo and their solid commitment for each other, the way he is always there for her, ready to listen and hold her and her heart goes out to her sister.

Later, at the hospital, they sit on each side of Mammy's bed. Mammy looks brighter today and a tiny sliver of hope sneaks into Katya's heart. Maybe the doctors are wrong, maybe there are still miracles in this world, maybe Mammy will survive. But deep down she knows that Mammy will die, and the truth sinks deep into her body.

She takes hold of Mammy's hand which is thin and dry, and Mammy gives her such a sweet smile that it takes all the strength that Katya could muster not to cry.

Chapter Twelve

Yana

She spots him in the line of passengers heading for the exit and her heart starts drumming. She makes herself take a few deep breaths to stop herself from running towards him as he comes to the exit.

'Daniel,' she says, 'good to see you again.'

He puts his bag on the floor and hugs her. 'You still smell of violets,' he says and her resolve to keep him at an arm's length melts away.

In the taxi, sitting close to him, she forgets the distance and the tears and lets him hold her hand. 'I've missed you,' he says.

It has just started to snow, large wet flakes that melt as soon as they touch the windscreen. A tram packed with people, sitting or standing, holding on to the leather loops hanging from the ceiling and swaying with the movement, catches up with the taxi. As the taxi driver opens his window to throw away the stub of his half-smoked cigarette, a gust of cold damp air enters the cab, and she shivers.

Daniel's friends, Elka and Vancho live on the outskirts, in one of the large blocks of flats the government built in the fifties when a lot of people from the countryside came to Sofia in search of work. They climb the stairs. The walls are peeling, and dust is curling in the corners. But when Vancho opens their door, they step into a world suffused with colour. There are brightly coloured paintings everywhere, hanging on the walls, the small apartment struggling to contain the outpouring of its occupants.

Elka comes out of the kitchen, taking off her flowery apron as she walks. She is a small middle-aged woman, with a compact body, and a striking-looking, dark- complexioned face with high cheek bones, a prominent nose and large brown eyes. As if sensing her shyness, she embraces Yana as if she were a long -lost daughter. 'Welcome, welcome,' she says. 'Come and sit down.'

The table is laden with salads and freshly baked bread and Yana can smell lamb cooking in the kitchen. A bottle of *rakia* stands on the table and as she and Daniel sit down, Elka brings out more dishes: plates with stuffed vine leaves, their dark skins glistening and plumb roast peppers with scraps of charred skin still on them, garlicky beans, grilled *kofta*, and bowls of apples, grapes and walnuts and cheese.

Vancho is a tall man, with a slight paunch and a face remarkably unlined, rosy-skinned and smooth like a baby's. He pours the *rakia* into small crystal glasses.

'Here's to Art and friendship,' he says as he raises his glass.

'To Art and friendship,' Daniel repeats. He catches Yana's eye and gives her a re-assuring smile. She is grateful to him for trying to include her, he must sense how awkward and out of place she feels.

The conversation turns to Elka's exhibition, which is opening with a private view in a couple of days.

'It took ages to find the right strings to pull to get the permission,'Elka says, 'and then it was given only on the condition that at least two thirds of the paintings would be in the approved style.'

'Well, that's something,' Daniel says, 'things must be loosening up, I guess that wouldn't have happened a few years ago.'

'It's getting easier to bribe people,' Vancho says, 'everyone is doing it. It's getting looser in this sense. You can do more or less anything if you know the right people.'

'I envy your freedom to paint what you want,' Elka says to Daniel, 'I am fed up with having to jump through hoops to be able to show anything that even vaguely resembles contemporary Western style. They rejected one of the paintings I put forward because it gave 'no clear message to the people.'

'I don't always paint what I want either,' Daniel says. 'I may not have to paint for socialism but sometimes I paint what I know the galleries want because it sells.'

'But you do have a choice,' Vancho says.

'You have a choice too. You could stick to social realism and paint factory workers and life on collective farms and pretty sunsets, but you have chosen to paint outside the system. I admire your work, some of Elka's paintings remind me of the lyrical abstraction of Hyland but I have often wondered why you have chosen to go in that direction.'

'I'll tell you why,' Vancho says. 'I believe that Art is political, as I think that Lenin said.' 'And when an artist works in an environment in which there is no freedom of expression, it is the artist's duty to turn his work into a negation of oppression. I see it as my duty to show what lies beyond the boundaries of totalitarianism. Then people have a choice too. They may not like what I paint but if they are not allowed to see that there are alternatives, they are like the proverbial horse with blinkers, as we say here. They have to toe the line because they can't see the bigger picture.'

'Well, I think you are both brave to do what you are doing.' Daniel says and turns to her. 'Don't you think so, Yana?'

Her heart drops to the pit of her stomach. He doesn't know, he doesn't realise what he is asking her to do; asking her to take part in a discussion, which is so subversive that if the walls do indeed have ears, they can all go to prison or be sent to the camps. But he doesn't know that, he has not a clue, he is ignorant of her reality. He doesn't know what it means to never feel safe.

'I don't know much about Art,' she mutters.' I need to go soon, or it would be too late to visit Mammy in the hospital.'

The following day, Sunday, she takes him to the Park of Freedom. It's a bright day and the sunshine is warm. They walk past the statue of the Russian soldiers and come to the lake where the water lilies are still open. Beneath the floating leaves, fish move, their golden skins translucent in the sunshine. There are people everywhere, young mothers pushing prams, old people sitting on benches taking in the sun and children everywhere, running, jumping, laughing, fresh faced, with none of their parents' greyness upon them.

They walk further, to the woods that flank the southern side of the park. There the trees throw patches of dark shade woven with bands of golden light. They sit on a bench under a spreading chestnut tree and Daniel takes out his sketch book.

'Do you mind? I want to paint this place when I get home. It will remind me of you.'

'Of course not,' Yana says, and she watches the trees around them grow on the page, charcoal back against the white paper.

Chapter Thirteen

Katya

Vlado's apartment is small and crammed with books. He is in the kitchen cooking moussaka. Katya joins him and starts cutting up the tomatoes, the cucumber and the cheese for the *shopska* salad. She piles it all up in the large glass bowl, mixes it with olive oil and a little vinegar and takes it to the table in the sitting room. In a few minutes Valdo joins her and pours them their pre-dinner *rakia*. They toast each other and help themselves to the salad.

'How was Mammy today?' Vlado asks

'Not good. She didn't open her eyes the whole time. But I think she knew I was there.'

'Tough for you, my love.'

Katya's mouth is dry. She takes a sip of the *rakia* and swallows it with some water.

'I am worried about Yana, Vlado.'

'How come?'

'Daniel arrived yesterday, and she doesn't seem to be able to think about anything else. Wants to spend every minute with him. I am afraid she is going to get hurt; I don't think he is as keen on her as she is on him.'

'Well, darling, don't forget he is English. From what I've heard, English people don't wear their hearts on their sleeves.'

'Perhaps. But he hadn't been in touch for over a month. She would rush to the door every time the post came, and I could sense how disappointed she was. I really felt for her.'

'She is a grown up, Katya, she can fend for herself.'

'Even so, she is my sister.'

As always when he can't offer a valid solution, Vlado changes the subject.

'Shall I come to the hospital with you tomorrow?'

'Please. It's lonely on my own and I am sure Yana will be spending the day with Daniel, I think it's his last day here.'

'Sure, sweetheart, I'll be there.' And as always, Vlado's solid presence calms her down. She wants to tell him that being with him helps her face the worst, but she knows his shyness, she knows he gets embarrassed when she tells him how much he means to her, so she just squeezes his hand as a way of showing her gratitude.

The smell of disinfectant assaults Katya's senses as they enter the hospital. A doctor in a white coat comes out of Mammy's room as they approach. He stops them from going in.

'She hasn't got long, Katya,' he says, 'It could be tonight, it could be tomorrow, it's difficult to be precise.'

Katya's legs give away from under her and Vlado props her. He takes her to the nearest bench by the wall and sits her down. She can feel all blood draining from her body. She knew it wasn't going to be long before Mammy died but to be told this in no uncertain terms takes her breath way. She gasps for air like a woman drowning,

Yana is already in the room, sitting on the side of Mammy's bed, holding her hand. Daniel is also there, standing at the foot of the bed.

Katya feels her skin flushing. She clenches her hands. The shock of seeing Daniel, a stranger by Mammy's bed grips her chest and blood starts pounding in her ears. *How dare she bring him here, why does she always feel she is entitled to do exactly what she wants? With no consideration for anyone else? How dare she!!*

Mammy is unconscious. Tubes are attached to her mouth and arms; her head is inclined to one side of the pillow. Rasping breaths come from her open mouth. Tight-lipped, Katya sits on the other side of the bed and takes Mammy's other hand.

Chapter Fourteen

Sofia, 1975

The shabby furniture and carpet are suffused with the warm glow of sunlight streaming from the open window. Yana watches the dust motes shimmer like a swarm of gilded insects as a gentle breeze from the window whirls them round and round. The mountain is glowing with light too and she whispers 'Hello' to its quiet immovable presence. Today, this only makes the ache of Mammy's absence sharper. A month since she's gone and the empty apartment gapes like an open wound.

Katya moved out to live with her boyfriend Vlado two weeks after Mammy died. She was tearful and apologetic but said she couldn't bear to be in the apartment and Mammy not being there and Yana said she understood.

Mammy had been conscious for most of the week before she died but Yana could sense her detaching from life as if whatever little energy she had left was now directed towards the journey ahead. And then, the morning before she died, Yana found her sitting up in bed, alert and smiling, her eyes full of light. She patted the bed for Yana to sit and held her hand.

'I am so very sorry I sent you away when you were little, *dushko*,' she said, 'I have never forgiven myself.'

Yana wanted to ask why, why did you do it, why did you let me go, did you know what it did to me. 'I have come home,' she said instead. 'I am here now,' and something in her chest shifted and she felt lighter.

They held hands for a long time, until the evening slowly dimmed the window and night advanced, painting deep shadows across the floor. Yana straightened Mammy's pillows and watched her drift to sleep.

Sometime later, when the room was nearly dark, Mammy let out a few rasping sounds. Yana tried to catch the words, but Mammy slipped back into the current that was taking her and Yana knew she was losing her. 'I love you Mammy,' she whispered and listened to her breaths getting weaker and weaker until there was silence. She put her face next to Mammy's and felt the coolness of death gradually seeping through her skin.

After a while, Yana called the nurse who told her Katya was on her way. She was still sitting with Mammy when Katya came in.

'Vlado is outside,' Katya said, and Yana joined him, not wanting to intrude on Katya's time with Mammy.

When they returned to the flat and Vlado went to the kitchen to make coffee, Katya shut herself in Mammy's bedroom. After a while Yana knocked on the door and went in. Katya was holding Mammy's pillow to her chest and staring into space, dry-eyed. Yana sat next to her and tried to hold her, but Katya pushed her away. There was rage in her eyes.

'Leave me alone, where were you when she needed you?' she said. 'You can't make it up just as easy as that, turning up at the end to make your peace. She missed you, you know; she needed you, she called for you when you weren't there.'

Why didn't you call me earlier, Yana wanted to say, I wanted to be with her too. Her throat was tight with guilt. She had left and not looked back.

They'd got through the funeral somehow, Katya keeping Vlado close to her side, Yana feeling utterly alone.

She watched Mammy's friends and neighbours filing past the open coffin to pay their last respects. When her turn came, she stroked Mammy's icy face and kissed her forehead. She didn't let herself cry.

During the wake she and Katya got drunk on whisky and hugged and cried and made incoherent promises never to leave each other ever again. But Katya left the flat soon after, seeking refuge with Vlado. The rift between Yana and her sister was as wide as the Danube.

Chapter Fifteen

May the First, International Workers' Day. The parade that every able-bodied person must join will be starting in a couple of hours. They will be led to the boulevard and past the Mausoleum of Georgy Dimitrov, the Father of Socialist Bulgaria. There on the balcony will be the government dignitaries watching over the waving crowds below, their hands raised in a regal salute.

When Yana was in primary school, they were taken on a class outing to visit the Mausoleum and pay tribute to Comrade Dimitrov. Their teacher, Comrade Stoyanova told them that they must be quiet in the Mausoleum and think respectful thoughts about Comrade Dimitrov, thanking him for all he had done to make their lives happy and free. This confused Yana because she had heard her parents describe Georgi Dimitrov as an evil man who had ruined their lives and made their country hell to live in.

She lined up with other children, some of whom had travelled from far away. They waited a long time. Her legs ached and it was hard to keep quiet and still. Then at last they came to a metal-studded door and into a cold vaulted hall. The attendant told them to walk in a single file and not stop or hold hands. They mustn't talk, not even whisper, he said.

The hall was dark and silent, and the heels of their shoes made a soft clicking noise on the hard floor. In the centre was a marble dais and on it was a coffin, with a glass lid. In it lay a small dark-haired man, his face waxy yellow, his black moustache glistening in the dim light. As Yana passed by the coffin, she thought she saw him bare his teeth in a snarl. She panicked and tried to push her way out and her teacher rushed forward and pulled her outside, her face full of anger. The following day, Mammy was called in to see the Headmistress and was admonished for not instilling in Yana the appropriate reverence for the Memory of The Father of the Glorious Revolution. 'I am sorry you got so frightened *dushko*, it's insane to make small children look at a dead man,' Mammy said to her later at home.

She is a child of the Glorious Revolution, born at the dawn of 'freedom' but she has never felt free in the country of her birth. Today she must parade under the watchful eyes of the Party and tomorrow, she will queue with all the other freedom-seekers outside room 44 to collect her passport, hopefully bearing the stamp that would allow her to find it in a foreign land. When they parted, Daniel had looked sad and said he'd write soon but he hasn't been in touch and Yana wonders if she has imagined love where there was only friendship. Mary, on the other hand has written many times to say she is waiting for Yana to return.

The street is heaving with people. The women are wearing colourful summer dresses, some have ribbons in their hair. Even Mad Magda, who lives in the apartment above Mammy's is there, accompanied by Comrade Angelov. She grins at Yana and waves her over. 'Take no notice,' she whispers in Yana's ear. 'They are all mad, why else go around murdering people?' She squeezes her hand and Yana sees that Comrade Angelov is straining to hear. She nods at him and moves on.

She joins a group of old school friends who squeal and appraise her, her hair, her clothes, her shoes. They walk together to the main street, which is teeming with people carrying banners and flowers, crowding the pavements and spilling onto the road.

Someone taps her shoulder. A tall gangly young man is smiling at her. 'Yana? Do you remember me?'

And as clear, as if it was yesterday, she sees them walking hand –in –hand along the banks of the Danube all those years ago.

When she was eight, Tatti came to visit in the summer holidays and Yana was so excited about seeing him that she decided to put on her best dress and black patent shoes, even though the dress was scratchy, and the shoes were tight and hot.

She was ready to run to him for a hug, but a woman was standing next to him, so she stopped in her tracks. It was Tatti's new wife, Danna. Why was she here? Why had Mammy let her come when she'd told Yana and Katya that this woman had taken Tatti away?

Katya had been sent to play with a friend while the four of them, Mammy, Tatti, Danna and Yana sat around the small table in the sitting room sipping their drinks, tea for the adults and lemonade for her. Nobody was saying anything. Yana listened to the voices of the children play-ing outside and wondered why she was here with the grown-ups who looked thoughtful and serious. She wanted to be outside with her friends.

'Mammy and I have been thinking,' Tatti started. He stopped for a while then continued, 'It would be nice for you to come and live with me and Danna in Svishtov. In September when the new school year starts.'

Yana looked at Mammy who smiled at her reassur-ingly. 'Yes darling,' she said, 'Tatti hasn't got a little girl to look after and I have two, so we thought it would be a good idea to share. And I am going to study in the autumn, so I'll have less time to look after you and Katya.'

Yana thought she might be sick.

She looked at Danna who smiled at her. They were all looking at Yana intently, all smiling.

'What do you think?' Mammy said.

'Will I get new schoolbooks?' Yana asked. 'Not passed down from the year above, all marked and scribbled upon?'

'Oh yes,' Tatti said, 'brand new, never touched before.'

'And new shoes? Red ones?' She knew Katya would be jealous.

A month later, Yana and her grandfather Dadan took the train to the town on the Danube River where Tatti and Danna lived. They travelled many hours. The train stopped at a few stations and Dadan bought her drinks and sweets and *kifli*. She thought of Mammy and Katya back in Sofia and of Kircho, her best friend and her heart squeezed but she thought it best not to cry. She didn't want to upset Dadan.

But she also felt excited. She had liked Danna with her dimples and kind blue eyes. The promise of new books and pens and pencils, not to mention the red shoes had helped her make up her mind, although a small voice inside her said it wasn't right to accept such an offer and leave Mammy and Katya behind. But she was fed up with all the hand-me-downs and Mammy saying 'we don't have money' whenever she asked for anything new.

Tatti and Danna lived in a big white house with a turret on the roof. Her bedroom was airy, with white walls and daisy-patterned curtains. It was in the turret and when she stood on the little stool by the window, she could just about make out the banks of the Danube. She liked her room and not having to share with Katya but sometimes at night she missed Katya so much she thought her heart would break.

The first few days in the new school were hard. The other children stood back from her to view her from a safe distance. She knew they thought her strange, a girl from the city who spoke oddly. It was nearly a week before some of the braver ones were curious to find out why she was there and what it was like living in the big white house that stood by itself in the hills above the river.

She liked living in her new house, which had many rooms with soft carpets, and a garden full of fruit trees and fresh herbs. Tatti was always out working but Danna cooked nice food and made delicious cakes, especially for Yana and she had pocket money to buy snacks and sweets at the school kiosk. She'd never had pocket money before and she felt rich. If it wasn't for missing Mammy and Katya at night, she would have been happy. The missing sometimes came in the day too, in the playground. She tried her best to join in the games and be friendly, but she never felt at ease like she did with Katya and her own friends back home.

One day when the teacher asked to see their homework, Yana didn't have anything to show him because she hadn't done it. It was arithmetic, a subject she hated because she couldn't solve the problems. She told him she'd left her book at home, and he sent her back to fetch it.

She didn't go home; she went down to the river instead. It was a hot September day, and she took off her school blazer and her shoes and socks. She sat on a grassy bank and watched the lazy waters drift along, swollen with autumnal rains, brown with mud and sticks and dried leaves. It was quiet, just the gentle buzz of insects and a bird calling. She wondered what to do. She had lied and didn't know how to get out of the lie.

After a while the heat made her sleepy and she spread her blazer on the grass and lay on it. She shut her eyes and listened to the buzz of the insects and a bird calling desperately as if it had lost a friend.

She must have fallen asleep because she didn't hear the footsteps. She felt someone touch her shoulder and sat up startled. A boy, about her age was kneeling beside her. She had seen him in town and knew he was taught at home and that his name was Mitko. She scrambled to her feet and smoothed her skirt down, feeling drowsy and confused.

'Let's go looking for worms, my Tatti needs them for the fish,' he said.

'Have you ever eaten snails?' she asked him.

'Ugh, no. Have you?'

'At home, they catch them in the garden and eat them. But I don't.'

'Why not?' he asked.

'I play with them. I like it when they hide in their little houses on their backs. Sometimes I wish I had a little house on my back too, then I can hide in it when I am scared.' She felt brave telling her secret to a boy she didn't know.

Mitko nodded then took her hand. They walked by the river for a long time, stopping here and there to look for worms under the stones. Mitko placed the worms carefully in a tin box he carried in his pocket while she threw stones into the river and watched the ripples dance.

The willow trees on the banks swayed gently in the breeze and some of their leaves dropped in the water and she watched them swirl around, then drift slowly downstream. It was very quiet, except for birds rustling in the leaves and the distant croaking of a frog. She could feel the sun burning her neck.

When they turned back it was dark. They held hands all the way to her house. The windows were lit up, the front door was open, and neighbours were coming in and out. There was a police car and inside, Mitko's mother was crying. When she saw them, she gasped then rushed to Mitko wrapping her arms round him. Her sobs echoed in Yana's ears, 'Where have you been, where have you been, you naughty, bad child?' Yana started to cry too. Tatti had gone to help the police searching for them but Danna who had been comforting Mitko's mother, scooped her up and held her close. 'It's Ok, it's OK, don't cry, you are safe.' she tried to soothe her.

After Mitko and his mother had gone home, and Tatti had returned, he sat with her in her bedroom for a long time. He asked her what had happened, but she couldn't explain why she had run away. He must have understood anyway because soon afterwards she was assigned a special tutor to help her with her arithmetic. And each night Tatti would come up to her room to ask about her day and to read her a bedtime story. In time, the pain of leaving Mammy and Katya lessened and she started to feel almost at home in the big white house with the turret that overlooked the river. After a while she was allowed to play with Mitko again and they spent many weekends by the river collecting snails and skimming stones and listening to the birds rustling in the trees.

When Dadan came to take her back to Sofia because he said Mammy wanted her back, she felt bad about leaving Tatti and Danna. She felt as if she was betraying them, just as she had felt she had betrayed Mammy and Katya the year before.

'You don't remember me, do you?' Mitko is saying.

'Mitko! What are you doing in Sofia?'

'Studying Physics at the University. Took me a while, but I got there in the end.' He grins and his teeth are slightly crooked. 'Shall we go looking for worms after this is over?' Yana laughs. 'A coffee maybe.'

They find a table at the students' café. 'How have you been?' Mitko raises his voice above the din of people talking and the clatter of china.

'Lots has happened since we last met. Too much to tell you all at once. Anyway, how about you? Do you still go fishing with your father?'

'The Danube is dirty now, not many fish in it, it makes the old man bad-tempered. Do you remember how good it was back then when we were kids? Endless sunny days, the water cool, racing each other? You wouldn't want to dip your toe in the water now.'

How simple it all seemed then Yana thinks, and how much has changed since. Just as well we can't see into the future.

'Shall we meet again?' Mitko asks. 'Go to the cinema or something?'

They exchange numbers before they part and walking back home, the streets emptying of people, Yana feels soothed by her unexpected encounter and the memories of childhood Mitko has brought back to her. It is refreshing to be with someone who speaks the same language, shares in her experiences and is light and funny. No serious talk of art and politics!

That night she dreams she is in a cellar. Inside a plastic bag there is meat cut up as if ready to cook. She knows it is human flesh and tries to call out, but Comrade Angelov appears and puts his hand over her mouth.

She opens her eyes. The apartment is silent and knowing.

There are dark shadows in the corners of the room.

She must see Katya. She feels utterly alone and can't
bear it anymore.

Chapter Sixteen

Katya

The flat is empty when she gets back from her course at the Institute. It's six o'clock, Vado should be home by now. The worms of worry start wriggling in her gut again. She hates it, the way it happens every time he is late. She starts getting their meal ready, trying to distract herself but the thoughts keep coming, *where is he? What is keeping him late? What if something has happened to him?*

It happens every time since Tatti died, this worry about losing the people she loves. In her mind she knows it's irrational but her body refuses to believe reason and every time someone she is close to is late without an explanation or a warning, fear clamps her body with a vise-like grip and her heart starts pounding. She feels caged by it, with no way out. It happens with friends too; like two weeks ago when Julie was thirty minutes late for their date at the local café. Katya was on the verge of tears when she finally turned up.

The relief she feels when Valdo gets back comes out in tears.

'What's the matter, sweetheart? Why the tears?'

'You should know by now, Vlado. You should know by now how I panic when you are late.'

'That's how much you love me, I know,' he says making light of it. He doesn't like to see her cry.

Later, they are in bed when the phone rings. It's Yana and she sounds tearful.

'I miss you Sis, the flat is empty without you and Mammy.'

'I can imagine it, Yana.' The angry devil is sitting on her shoulder again. 'Talking about leaving, you have no idea what it was like for me when you left. And what it was like when Mammy got ill, and you weren't here. And the way she went on about you, saying how much she missed you, sometimes it was as if she didn't see me!'

'That's not fair, Katya, you told me not to come.' Yana's voice is tight now, there are no tears.

'And you could not read between the lines? You couldn't for a moment imagine what it was like for me?'

Yana comes back quick as a flash.

'And you have no idea what it was like for me when Mammy sent *me* away and kept *you.*'

'Listen Sis, I was four. What did I know about it? And you can't go on and on about it either, using it as an excuse for the things you do. You took off with no thought of us, you knew what you wanted, and you were going to get it even if it meant walking away from us with not a second glance. I remember you at the airport, Yana, you didn't turn back to wave one last good-bye. I hated you then. Then I missed you so much I couldn't bear it.'

'It was the most difficult thing I've ever done.' Yana says and her voice is tearful again. Katya feels a pang of sadness softening the anger.

'I miss you too, Yana.'

In the silence that follows, she can hear Vlado stirring in the room next door. The grandfather clock strikes one, they have been on the phone for nearly an hour. She needs to see her sister; she needs a hug badly.

'I'll come over tomorrow,' she says, 'we can talk more then if you want to.'

Back in the bedroom, Vado is sitting up, propped on two pillows.

'What is it with you two?' He asks.

'It's difficult for you to understand, you have no siblings.'

'Maybe, but I don't like to see you upset, Katya.'

'I can't help it, Vlado. She does upset me. First going away with no thought for anybody else but herself, then coming back and rearranging the flat as if she owns it, as if she is the one who always knows best. Well, she doesn't. We managed perfectly well without her. Who does she think she is?'

'Come back to bed,' Vlado says, and she does and slides down next to him. She feels the buzzing energy in her body seeping out and shuts her eyes. She is tired of it all, the accusations and the fights. She thinks of Yana holding her after they found out about Tatti, how she took care of her and of Mammy too and warmth spreads in her body. She loves her sister much more than she hates her.

But the anger returns the following morning when she remembers Mammy's grief –stricken face at the airport when Yana left.

Chapter Seventeen

Yana

Room 44 is on the second floor of the Ministry of Internal Affairs, a monolithic building in the centre of the city. Its spire is adorned by the five-pointed star and inside the building, the granite walls and marble floors keep the heat out even on the hottest summer day. Heavy oak doors line the wide corridors and flags on the walls commemorate Bulgaria's friendship with the other republics in the Socialist bloc.

There are two benches outside room 44 and a middle-aged woman and two young men are sitting, waiting. Yana sits next to the woman who glances at her then goes back to the handkerchief she's been twisting. Her face is lined and there are bags under her eyes. The men stare into space, alone and contained in the silence of waiting. A door opens and closes somewhere along the corridor.

Minutes trickle away then the door to room 44 opens and a young fair-haired girl comes out. She is crying and her sobs echo as she runs along the corridor to the stairs. The woman stares after the girl, still twisting her handkerchief, her face like a carving on a stone wall.

Fear grips. She wonders what happened behind the closed door and what will happen when her turn comes. What's the worst she thinks, they won't let me out again and I will never see Daniel and Mary again. But he hasn't called or written since they parted eight weeks ago, perhaps she had imagined there was love between them.

With Mammy gone and Katya now living with Vlado who has she got? I need to get out and build a new life for myself, she tells herself firmly. A short man wearing round steel -rimmed glasses comes out of the room. He inspects the little group for a second or two. Looking for fear she thinks. They are like dogs; they can smell it from miles away.

He calls her name, and she feels a film of sweat on her forehead. Her mouth is so dry she can't swallow. The man looks at her intently as if she might be a rare specimen in a glass box. He shows her into the room and leaves.

At the desk, by the window a man with grey hair and heavy jowls stubs out a cigarette in an overflowing ashtray. The room is large and bare, save for the desk and a chair and a couple of pictures. It stinks of stale tobacco. She sits down. Lenin and Stalin, side by side on the wall behind the desk look down on her.

'So, Comrade Yoakimova, you want to leave again? Don't you like your country? Are we not good enough for you?'

'I love my country, but I am enrolled at University in Wales and would like to complete my studies.' Yana's voice does not tremble but is a little too loud.

'Or is it that you have fallen in love? With an Englishman? Because you don't think our men are good enough for you?'

In a flash, Yana knows that they have read the letters. Rage takes over the fear. It pounds in her ears and heats up her blood. She clenches her teeth so hard her jaw starts to hurt.

'Tell you what,' the man behind the desk says. He pauses, picks up a gold pen and twists it between his fingers. He glances at her then he puts down the pen as if he's made a decision. 'We'll let you leave but first you must prove you love your country.'

Now her mind is blank.

'These friends of your English boyfriend,' the man continues, 'Elka and Vancho Danchevi, we have reasons to believe they may be engaged in anti-government activities. The British Council is organising an exhibition of their work in London, and they will be there for the opening. We want you to keep an eye on them, see who they talk to, where they go. That's all. Then report to our contact at the Embassy.'

'Mr Greenberg is not my boyfriend,' Yana says, 'and I have only met Elka and Vancho once. I may not be invited to the exhibition.'

'See what you can do,' the man says with a rubbery smile that makes Yana's flesh creep. 'We'll be in touch when your passport is ready. All we'll need then is your signature.'

Outside it's hot but Yana shivers. She wonders if she will ever feel warm again. The fury that took hold of her in the room returns. It runs through her veins like electricity and makes her cheeks burn. How dare they.

She wonders what to do. Daniel is now an unknown entity. Still, could she betray him by betraying his friends? Tatti would be dismayed if he were alive, a daughter of his selling out to the enemy, he who spent his life using his pen to fight against the killers of freedom.

But he is not alive, and she needs the visa, she wants to get out again. He wanted that for her. Danna told her this some years after he died. 'You must be free,' she'd said. 'You must go to London. Your father loved London. It's too late for me, I'll never leave this country now, too many memories, but you are young, go. He'd have wanted that for you.'

And they are not asking much, are they. Just to watch, listen and report. Her signature in return for the stamp in her passport. There is nothing for her here now. In Wales she can make a new life for herself, she can put the past behind and start again. And perhaps she can win Daniel back and he needn't know how she got the visa.

Chapter Eighteen

Dear Yana,

I am so sorry it's taken me so long to write back and I was so very sorry to hear about Mammy. I am glad you were with her when she died. Are things with you and Katya better now?

I have been busy preparing for my new show in London and work seems to be going well. Mary and I met for a drink the other night and talked about you, she sends you her love.

I don't know when I might be able to come over again, Yana. Life is busy but I have to be honest with you, it's more than that. We are so different, Yana, our lives are so different. Not that in itself that is bad, but we are too far apart to get to know each other properly, to learn how to be with each other day to day. I couldn't live in Sofia, and you might not get out again.

This is difficult for me to write because a part of me still wants you so much.

You are lovely, Yana and you should be loved unreservedly. It is me who is at fault for not being able to do so.

Please don't think badly of me and please let's keep in touch.

Daniel.

Dear Yana,

I hope you are OK my darling, things sound quite grim for you right now. Have you and Katya made it up? It must be so difficult living by yourself. Sharing grief with those close to us lightens the load and I do think of you so often.

I spoke with the Dean of your faculty last Thursday and the good news is, they have agreed to keep your place on the course for a year so I do hope that you can get your visa soon and come back.

I saw Daniel the other night, we had a drink at the Angel and talked about you. I think he misses you too, but he seems pre-occupied with his new show in London. It will be big! He told me he hasn't been in touch with you much because he's been busy.

He is a difficult man to pin down, Yana, I guess most artists are. I have known him for years and still don't know what goes on inside him. A difficult nut to crack, as we say in English.

The garden has come into its own this spring and the Japanese rose you so love is coming into bloom. Your little room is ready and waiting for you my darling and I do hope to see you very soon!

Will write again in a couple of weeks,
With all my love, Mary.

The two letters came on the same day and confirmed what Yana already knew. She read them once and put them away. She'd write back to Mary later but there was nothing she could say to Daniel. She tried to reason with herself, just because we spent a night together, he doesn't owe me anything.

She would see Daniel when she returned to Wales. She would get herself invited to Elka and Vancho's exhibition so she could complete her assignment. She would pretend it was OK to just be friends. His letter has made it easier to do what she has to do.

It's late May and summer has arrived. Sitting on a bench in the park across the road from the flat, she thinks of Mammy gone. Katya and Daniel have left her too. Her visa has still not arrived.

The trees in the park are tall now. She remembers when the council planted them. One Sunday, Mammy took her and Katya for a walk there and they saw men planting saplings in tidy rows, a few pale leaves on fragile branches. Now the trees are dense and cool, throwing patches like inkblots on the sun-bleached path.

It is Sunday and the park is crowded with babies and small children, some in their prams, others tottering on their chubby legs, their mothers keeping a watchful eye on their first stumbling steps. A little girl offers Yana her toy, a grey rabbit, one ear chewed to tatters, the other flopping over a blue glassy eye. 'Kiss him,' the child says, and Yana does. The girl's mother laughs and gently scolds her daughter. The little girl giggles and skips away and her mother waves Yana good-bye. Yana likes children, she loves their pure, undiluted energy but long ago she decides that she won't have any of her own. She likes her independence too much.

A bird, she can't make out what it is, flies overhead and last night's dream comes back to her. She is walking up a grassy hill and an eagle, black against a brilliant sapphire sky is hovering overhead. She feels awed by its strength and majesty and in her dream, she calls to Daniel who is climbing behind her. 'Look,' she says, 'isn't it amazing?' But he is gone.

She takes his letter out of her bag and reads it again, the dream still with her. She wonders if their love had been a dream too. Reading Mary's letter again, she feels a pang. Jealousy? Surely not.

Mary and Daniel are old friends and Mary is so much older than Daniel.

She remembers the eagle in her dream. I am that bird, she thinks, I am young, and my life is in front of me. I will find a way through the loneliness.

Chapter Nineteen

The phone is ringing when she gets back to the flat.

'Fancy coming to a party?' Mitko sounds excited.

'Whose party? Where?'

'One of the guys on my course, his parents are away for a week, he's got the apartment to himself. Pick you up at seven?'

Why not, Yana thinks, I am here for now, so I might as well make some new friends.

But longing for Daniel makes her tired. She would rather sleep. She had wanted a life with him but now this seems impossible.

At seven Mitko is at the door with flowers. 'For you,' he says as he thrusts the pink roses wrapped in newspaper into her hands.

Yana is taken aback and blushes, then quickly composes a thank you.

Mitko smiles sheepishly. 'From my landlady's garden, she said she didn't mind. I like your dress,' he says.

Coming from him, this makes Yana laugh and he laughs too, standing at the door, tall and gawky, shiny blond hair to his shoulders, his blue jeans immaculately pressed. They run for the bus holding hands, as they did all those years ago on the banks of the Danube.

The party has started, and they push their way to the drinks table through clusters of people chatting and smoking. Cigarette smoke hangs in the air like a grey curtain and Yana's eyes are stinging. Mitko lights up too. He offers her a cigarette, but she declines. She started smoking when she was sixteen because all her friends did, but her time in Wales has cured her of the habit. Apart from Mary, few people she knew smoked there.

Everybody here smokes and she feels like an alien among the natives. She slips out onto the balcony while Mitko is chatting to a pretty girl, her dark hair cut very short. Yana looks out onto the city, the first lights of the evening twinkling here and there. If she stayed here long enough, evening would settle in velvet darkness and thousands of lights would outshine the pale stars above.

How strange it feels being here. On the one hand, it is as though she's never been away but on the other, she feels as if the six months she was away have so changed her that she can hardly recognise the young girl who left for Wales nearly a year ago. She has grown up and does not fit her old life anymore and yet, she can't discard it either. It is as if she were two separate selves, unknown to each other.

Mitko hands her a glass of beer. It tastes bitter but it is refreshing, and Yana savours its cold touch on her tongue. She is glad he's stopped talking to the pretty girl.

'Let's dance,' Mitko says.

In the sitting room the music is so loud, Yana thinks it might burst her eardrums. She dances with Mitko to the sound of the Stones, and she can feel the beat of the music in her pulse. Her feet stamp the floor as the Stones bellow *'I can't get no satisfaction; I can't get no satisfaction.'* Everybody is singing along now, a collective chant of dissatisfaction. Then Elvis croons *It's Now or Never, Please Hold me Tight and* as if following instructions, Mitko puts his arms around her and clamps her body in an awkward embrace. 'Hello,' she whispers in his ear, as a way of easing his tension but he fastens his mouth onto hers and she has to push him away to get some air. They look at each other and laugh with embarrassment. 'Better luck next time,' Mitko says, and she feels a stab of anxiety that she might hurt him. She mustn't let him think that there can be anything more than friendship between them.

Many beers later, a tall girl, her hair in a ponytail comes up to her. 'You are Katya's sister, aren't you? Katya and I were at school together, I remember you from parent-teacher meetings. You used to come instead of your mother. I often wondered why.'

Because Mammy didn't know about the meetings. Katya and she used to hide the notices because if she attended, Mammy would find out about all the skipped classes and the homework that never got done and the boys that got kissed. So, Yana would go in Mammy's place and tell the teachers their mother was ill or held up in work. Until the Headmistress came to the house one day and it all came out. Mammy was furious and she and Katya were banned from going out for a month.

It is a sweet memory of a time when things seemed so much simpler.

The girl is smiling.

'You've been in England, haven't you? What is it like there? Did you like it?' She asks.

Yana doesn't want this conversation. How can she answer such questions when she herself is not sure of the answers?

'I was in Wales,' she says. 'It's different from here.' Her voice tells the girl the subject is closed. Fortunately, the music starts again, and the girl joins the others on the dance floor.

Mitko comes up to her. 'Shall we?' he says and leads her to the music.

Chapter Twenty

Weeks pass but the call she has been expecting from The Ministry of Internal Affairs does not come. The little money that Mammy had left Yana is beginning to run out, so she puts an advert in the local paper offering English lessons. A few pupils from the school round the corner sign up. It isn't much but it helps with the bills and keeps her occupied.

Early one Sunday, she joins Mitko and four of his friends for a picnic. They catch the tram to the foot of Vitosha mountain, rucksacks heavy with food and wine on their backs.

The tram rattles through the streets until the last ramshackle houses on the outskirts of the city disappear behind the forest. The early morning sun comes through the trees and makes patches of light on the ground. A fresh breeze carries the sound of birds celebrating the morning.

When the tram reaches the small station at the end of the line, it is only eight o'clock, but the sun is already hot on Yana's face. The path is narrow, and they walk in a single file, Yana behind Mitko, followed by Rosa, the girl Yana met at the party and another girl and two men whose names Yana can't remember. All around are hay meadows filled with flowers, yellow lizard orchids and foxgloves, red-veined and ochre –coloured, they fill with air with the smell of summer. Higher up they find wild strawberries and fill the plastic containers they had brought with them and when Yana savours one, it tastes warm like sunshine. They stop to look at the view of Sofia below, hazy in the distance. The sight of her city and the warmth of the sun and the smell of the wildflowers make Wales feel far, far away, almost like a dream. This is where she belongs, this land of hers, this is where her roots are, in the soil beneath these rocks and in these meadows. She offers her face to the sun and the warmth spreads through her body and makes it soft and light.

By midday, the sun is getting hotter, and they look for a shady place to have their picnic. They follow the sound of water to a clearing where a stream runs over stones and boulders. They spread rugs, unpack rucksacks and start tasting each other's offerings. Yana has made some *banitza* to Mammy's recipe, which the others find delicious. Rosa has brought pomegranates; when Yana scoops out the pearly seeds and puts them in her mouth, they burst with flavour that make her taste buds come alive with the sharpness and blood-red juice dribbles down her chin.

'You didn't tell me much about England when we last spoke,' Rosa says, 'I want to go there more than anywhere else in the world.'

'I lived in Wales, in Cardiff,' Yana says, 'it's different from England, they have their own language, although few people speak it nowadays.'

'What are the English like?' a young man, called Georgi asks. 'I've heard they are polite but cold.'

Yana thinks of Mary and Daniel and Jenny and smiles. 'I don't know many English people,' she says, 'but the ones I've met are very kind.'

'But they seem arrogant, from what I've heard,' Georgi says, 'and so proud of their country and their traditions.'

'Well, they were nice to me.'

'The trouble with us, Bulgarians is that we don't value our country and our traditions enough,' Mitko says. 'And we have so much to be proud of.'

'Like what?' A man whose name Yana doesn't know chips in.

'Like the fact that we didn't allow a single Jew to be sent to the camps in Germany during the Holocaust,' Mitko retorts. 'Like the fact that the Nazi trains left our country empty.'

'Perhaps, perhaps not. That's what they'd like us to believe.'

'It's all in the Jewish Chronicles if you want to check your facts.'

'Well, maybe so,' the man says, 'but this wasn't to do with us, the people, it was the king, he was German as everybody knows.'

'So that makes it even more remarkable, doesn't it?' Mitko says. 'He went against Hitler, even though we were on the side of the Germans. OK, there may have been a few Jew-haters amongst us and there were camps here too, but nobody was sent to the gas chambers. On the whole, I think we are a pretty tolerant nation.'

'So, you think it was OK to have camps here? How come we had them if we are so tolerant?'

'Every country in Eastern Europe had the camps and most of them sent thousands of Jews to Germany. We didn't.'

'And what about Macedonia? Our troops were there with the Germans and thousands of Jews were sent to Germany from there.'

'Maybe so, but no Jew left Bulgarian soil for the gas chambers in Germany.'

Mitko's voice is steady, but his face is tight, and his eyes are narrow. A vein on his forehead is pulsating angrily. It makes her feel uneasy, it is a side of him she hasn't seen before. The Mitko she knows is placid and sunny. She starts to feel irritated too, she hadn't come here today to talk about politics.

'Of course, another way to look at it,' Rosa says, 'is that we are and always have been too scared to stand up for ourselves. Remember that old proverb from the time of the Turks? ''Keep you head down, and you'll be spared the sword?'' That's what we do, we keep our heads down, too scared to speak, too scared to breathe.'

These people must trust each other to allow themselves to speak like this. Yana's chest tightens around her heart. What if there is an informer amongst us, what if one of them is making mental notes and will report every word of what is being said? All of it going into our dossiers and making it even more difficult for her to leave again? Speaking is dangerous. Look what happened to Tatti.

Mitko isn't an informer for sure; his parents had been interned for their political beliefs. But she doesn't know anything about the others. And even keeping quiet wouldn't protect her if someone here were an informer; being present at the conversation would be enough to get punished. She would never get a visa now even if she has agreed to sign the papers. Two of her classmates, Spas and Hristo tried to defect to the West by hiding in the undercarriage of a train heading for Yugoslavia. They were caught at the border and all their friends were punished even though nobody knew anything about their plan. Yana was stripped of the honour of being a Young Pioneer and the disgrace was compounded by having her red kerchief taken away. They were expelled and dispersed to different schools round the city. To this day Yana wonders who informed on Spas and Hristo.

How awful living like this is, always in fear of speaking, always scared of who may hear you and what they may do. She remembers all over again why she wanted out of it, this constant fear to speak out, to live freely. But when she looks at the mountain against the blue expanse of the sky, Cherni Vruh shrouded in cloudy mist, and when she listens to the silence, her soul is divided and love for her country makes a bid against fear. Could she stay and make a life for herself here? And have the mountains and the lakes and the rivers and go to the Valley of the Roses and breathe in the heady scent? And in the summer, stand among the tall green stems in the sunflower fields and see their faces turned to the sun?

If she stayed, she would have all of this and much more. She could spend time with Katya and live in Mammy's flat and cherish the memories of her. She could walk in the park and maybe start to draw; she's always wanted to draw. Perhaps she would marry Mitko, he'd been in love with her since they were children and walked hand-in-hand on the banks of the Danube. They would have a couple of kids and build a life for themselves with friends and family around. They would take picnics to the mountain, like today, go skiing in the winter and in the summer, they would sunbathe by the Black Sea where the golden sands stretch from one end of the coast to the other. It could be a good life, even a happy one.

But another voice speaks in her head. She hears mad Magda on the stairs telling her how Tatti died. Mammy had told her and Katya that it had been an accident but one morning, on her way to school, she met Mad Magda. 'They cracked his skull open, with a hammer,' Magda said. 'Blood everywhere, his skull cracked open, and his shoulders smashed to smithereens. But he wouldn't die, they said, not for a long time. His heart was strong, it wouldn't stop beating so they shot him in the end. Buried

121

him deep somewhere in the mountain for the wild dogs to find him.'

How did she know? Mad Magda knew everything. She sneaked around, eavesdropping and people didn't mind what they said when she was there because they thought her mind had gone. But she listened and remembered.

Only the mad are not afraid to speak the truth. There must be so much hatred in those who rule us to kill a man like that, to smash his skull with a hammer. Mammy never recovering, Yana growing up fast to take care of her and Katya. She couldn't take it anymore, she wanted out, out of her life in a country ruled by people full of hatred. A country of killers. The only way for her spirit to be free was to leave.

She wants Daniel and she must be with him, she can't go against her love for him even if they would only ever be friends. She is tired of the fear. She would do what they asked of her so she could be free to be near him. Perhaps in time she could persuade him to love her.

He almost did, she saw it in his eyes.

But is love enough and how can she love him, knowing that she is betraying his friends? And she and Daniel are so different. Would she ever feel she belonged in his world as she does here today, with Mitko and his friends, speaking the same language and sharing their country's history? Daniel's friends are kind, but they are cultured and serious and talk about things she knows nothing about.

And yet, when she remembers him, it is as if all the parts of her join together and she is whole again.

Chapter Twenty-One

Still no call to sign the papers for her visa. She wonders why. Perhaps they had changed their minds. Perhaps they have found out about the picnic on the mountain. Found out she had been spending time with people with 'undesirable ideas.'

Comrade Ivanov might know something about this. She tracks down his phone number, he sounds surprised to hear her voice. He suggests they meet at the Russian Club and when she gets there, she finds him in the garden. He is drinking ra*k*ia and a plate of *shopska salad* is on the table. She remembers the feel of his bulky but strong body. 'The same?' he asks and his blue eyes twinkle under a set of dark thick lashes. She signals her agreement.

It is early evening, but the restaurant is already full. It is not a cheap place and Yana wonders how so many people could afford to eat here when everyone is complaining of hardship all the time.

Around her, people are smoking, chatting, eating and as the day starts to fade, the waiters come to light the candles. Darkness thickens and the little lanterns that festoon the trees are lit up, making the place look like a magical cave.

It has been over a year since she last saw Ivanov and he seems the same.

'You haven't changed,' she tells him.

'Maybe not to look at but a lot has happened since we last met. I got 'released' from the Ministry.'

'Really? How come?'

'I wasn't fervent enough,' he says. 'I let people out too easily.' He winks at her and the memory of the two nights in his bed comes back; the feel of his body on hers and the sharp smell of his aftershave that stayed on her for days. Unexpectedly, desire stirs up in her belly.

He orders another double *rakia* and she wonders if it was the alcohol that stood between him and his career.

'There is a child, since I last saw you,' he says, 'I am not with his mother anymore, she left soon after he was born. My mother is looking after him.'

'Does he look like you?' she asks on an impulse. But he must have read something else in her question because he takes her hand and says:

'They won't let you out this time, Yana. The only way I see you getting out is marrying that Mr Greenberg of yours.'

Yana is startled. 'He hasn't asked me,' she replies sharply.

'You could explain to him that it's just a formality, to get the visa. Then once you are out, he can divorce you and you'll be free.' He adds, 'You won't be the first or the last to get out that way.'

Yana feels queasy. She gets up and heads for the Ladies and is sick in the washbasin. Too much rakia. She steadies herself and looks at her white face in the mirror. She could never make such a suggestion to Daniel; how could Ivanov even think about it? Of course, he doesn't know about her feelings for Daniel, he just assumes that like many others, she could strike a marriage of convenience just to get out. She feels indignant at the thought only to reminds herself quickly that she is planning to do something far worse. She is planning to damage people's lives by spying on them.

She knows now there is no way out unless she signs the papers. If they still want her to. It is clear that Ivanov is in no position to help. If they don't call her to sign, there really will be no escape this time.

When she gets back to the table, Ivanov has ordered another two double *rakias*, one each, and more salads. Her stomach revolts at the sight of the alcohol but she makes herself drink it and accepts the cigarette he offers her, even though she had promised herself that she would never smoke again. She inhales the bitter, acrid smell and nearly chokes. 'Out of practice,' she says, 'I haven't smoked for nearly a year.'

'Do you want to meet my boy?' Ivanov asks. She sees the pride and love in his eyes. 'Yes,' she says, she can't disappoint him. 'But not now.'

He looks at her pensively. 'You really are in love with him?' More of a statement than a question.

'It's complicated.'

'Of course, it would be. With an Englishman.'

'He is a painter,' Yana volunteers, wondering why she is telling him this.

'Mixed up then,' he says and orders more drink.

People are leaving the garden, it is late. She should go home but the thought of the empty apartment makes her want to stay.

'Come back and lie with me,' Ivanov says. 'We won't do anything, I am too drunk anyway, but I think we both need company tonight.'

She wants to, the sexual energy between them is palpable. And it would blunt the loneliness and make her forget the fear.

'Let me at least walk you home,' he says and calls for the bill.

It's a warm night as they walk through the Doctors' Park. Lovers are sitting on almost every bench, huddled in passionate embraces and when the moon comes out from behind the clouds, it lights them up, so they become like actors on a stage, cast in a play about love.

Walking down *Oborishte* street Ivanov takes her hand in his big bear paw, and she knows she will sleep with him again. Not because she needs to but because she wants to. She wants to lose herself in his big arms and fall asleep there.

'Are you coming up?' she asks him as they approach the building. I've run out of coffee, but I can offer you some more *rakia.*'

'It's not *rakia* I want,' he says. 'It's you.'

But the *rakia* he drank at the Club, multiple doubles of it, has taken its toll and they end up just holding each other which feels nice.

Chapter Twenty-Two

Katya, August 1975

'Something is afoot with Yana,' she says to Vlado. It's Sunday morning and they are in bed. Sunlight streams through the half-opened curtains and brings the August heat into the room.

'What is it now?' he says, and she can hear the impatience in his voice. He puts his arms around her and pulls her closer.

'Not sure but I know her well, Vlado. She is holding something back. And listen to this, she rang me last night to tell me that Daniel is arriving here on Saturday and that's she is meeting him at the airport. Would you believe it?! She hasn't heard from him in weeks and here she is, ready to be at his beck and call. What on earth is the matter with her?'

'Calm down, my love, she is a grown-up, she must know what she is doing.'

No point talking to Vlado about it, Katya thinks, he is always so neutral, always pointing out the other side of things. She wriggles out from his embrace, gets out of bed and puts on her dressing gown, frowning with the effort to contain her annoyance. He means well, she knows that.

'I am going to go over later on,' she tells him, 'I need to pick up a few things from the flat any way.'

It's the perfect summer's morning outside. The sky is spotless and the birds on the tree outside Vlado's apartment are loud. She wishes her heart wasn't so tight. She

127

knows her sister is unhappy, and she doesn't know how to help her.

It's a twenty minutes' walk to the flat. The lift is not working so she has to climb the stairs to the third floor. The plant on the windowsill is dry again, nobody thinks of watering it since I left, she thinks.

Yana is in the kitchen, making coffee. 'Oh, hello Sis,' she says, 'I wasn't expecting you. Do you want coffee?'

They take their cups to the sitting room. The windows are wide open, and the room is flooded with light. But something isn't quite right, Katya thinks, the room is unusually quiet. She looks around and notices that the old grandfather clock has stopped, it needs winding.

'Have you got the key?' she asks Yana.

'I can't find it. I can't remember where I put it last time.'

'Typical of you! You know how much the clock meant to Mammy, but you don't care, do you? Just like Tatti. He didn't care what his actions meant for us, the consequences we had to suffer. The poverty, the fear. All he cared about were his ideals. You are just like him!'

'And I am proud to be like him because I am proud of what he stood for and was willing to die for.'

No point going further with this, Katya thinks.

'Have you heard from the Home Office about your visa application? 'She asks instead.

'Yes, they asked me to go there.'

'And?'

Yana looks into her cup as if she can find the answer there. After a while she looks at Katya.

'You wouldn't believe this Sis, they told me they would give me the visa on the condition that I agree to spy on Daniel's friends, Elka and Vancho.'

Katya gasps. 'What?'

'Yes, no kidding.'

'Surely you didn't agree?'

'Of course not. But I need to find a way to get out again, Katya. Mammy's gone and you are with Vlado, what is here for me? And I want to finish my course. It's important to me.'

Katya's lungs deflate, sadness takes over from the shock and the indignation. She is going to lose her sister again, this time probably forever. What about me, what about your friends here, don't you care? She wants to plead but there is a glint of steel in Yana's eyes, and she knows it's pointless.

Chapter Twenty-Three

Yana

He reaches for her hand and at that moment a small bird flies through the open window and lands on the floor by the bed, stunned.

'Shhh,' Daniel whispers. He gently scoops up the tiny creature and releases it and he can feel its heart beating wildly against the palm of his hand. He goes to the window, releases it and watches it fly off to the roof opposite. In the distance, the mountain is covered in white mist.

Making love to him after all this time felt strange. It was as if it was the first time and yet when their bodies met, they knew each other. Hungry and eager, they tore at each other's clothes, mute with desire and desperate as if in slowing down, they might see the doubt in each other's eyes. Afterwards, they still didn't speak. Yana lay in his arms, her limbs loose, her hair spread on the pillow.

He gets back into bed, and she smiles at him. He takes her in his arms again and she feels her body softening. His skin smells faintly of paint and linseed oil and she breathes in the smell. It makes her feel warm. Her mind is quiet, she knows all she needs to know for now. Tomorrow or the day after or the one after that she will have to think about the visa and what she will have to do to get it but for now there is only the beat of their hearts and the warmth of his skin against hers.

Later they go to the park near the apartment, and she tells him about the trees, how she 'd watched them grow, and about the child that had come to her last time she was here. She tells him about Tatti and how it was as if a part of her had died with him. 'But life is stronger, isn't it?' Daniel says, because he too has felt such mortal grief. 'Meeting you has brought me back to life.' They walk in the sunshine amidst the prams and the tricycles, and the laughter of children being chased and chasing, and it feels as if this is how it should always be.

This is how she wants it to be. She silences the voice inside that tells her she is planning to betray his friends. But what if he asked her to marry him? Then she would have everything she wants and there would be no need to become a traitor.

They visit Vancho and Elka and Daniel talks with them about the show he is trying to organize for them. Before he leaves, he tells her the last few days have been some of the best he can remember, perfect days he will always cherish. He will write and they will speak, and they will meet again. Then he leaves her with one last wave at the departure gate and she has to let him go because for now, she has no other choice.

She goes to Katya's flat straight from the airport.

'Come here,' Katya says and opens her arms to her. Yana buries her head in her chest. The tears are there but they won't come.

'So, did you tell him? About the 'proposal.' Katya asks.

'No, of course not, how could I?'

'So, you missed the perfect moment? If you had told him, he would have understood how impossible it is for you to get out. He might have realised that the only way for you to be together would be for him to marry you.'

'They *were* perfect moments, and I didn't want to spoil them.'

Katya asks quietly, 'You are not going to do it, are you? Become an informer? Betray his friends? You can't. You would be betraying Tatti, not just Daniel. Tatti would be turning in his grave if he knew.'

'I know. He chose death because of his principles, and I want to live. I want to live the life I choose for myself.' There is no way she could tell Katya that she is considering it precisely because she wants to live the life she chooses for herself.

Silence settles between them. Could Katya really understand? That she loves Daniel and the only way to have him would be to betray him. And risk losing him. She wants him but she wants to be free too, however high the cost of that freedom might be.

Chapter Twenty -Four

Weeks go by with no news from Daniel. She meets with Ivanov again; he buys her supper at the Club but there must be something wrong with her because the smell of food and alcohol make her want to retch and she has to breathe deeply to stop the nausea rising up her throat.

'You seem peaky,' Ivanov comments. 'I wonder if you are sickening for something?'

'Time of the month', she re-assures him and is glad of the excuse. She knows he wants to sleep with her, but her mind is on Daniel. She wonders what's happened to him, why he doesn't write. It's eight weeks since he left, telling her their time together had been the best ever and then disappearing as if swallowed in a void, vanished without a trace. She feels angry with him but then blames herself. Maybe I just read too much into it, she thinks. And maybe he did feel these things at the time, but the memory didn't last, his life in Wales and his painting taking over and blotting out their time together.

'Never mind,' Ivonov says, 'we can go to the pictures instead, would you like that?'

'I think I need to go home,' she tells him, 'This time of the months can be quite painful. I think I need to go home and lie down.'

And so he walks her home, the perfect gentleman, and kisses her on the lips before they part.

October and the evenings are drawing in. Autumn chill has crept into the air. Most mornings, the mountain is screened by a ragged curtain of clouds, which today are grey, turning black at the edges. Yana opens the window, and the sharp moist air fills her lungs and clears away the last traces of sleep from her eyes.

She thinks of making herself a coffee but the thought of it makes her want to be sick again. She has been vomiting most days this week and is beginning to think that there must be something seriously wrong with her.

'When was your last period?' the doctor, an old friend of the family asks her after examining her.

She has to think, it must be well over a months ago. Then realises that she hasn't bled since Daniel's visit.

'I am pretty sure you are pregnant,' the doctor says, 'but let's test you to be absolutely certain.' He sends her off to the bathroom with a little plastic tube to pee in. The bathroom smells strongly of disinfectant and she wants to throw up again.

'Wait outside for twenty minutes,' he tells her when she hands him the tube, 'I'll call you in when the test is ready.'

There is big smile on his face when she gets back into the room.

'Congratulations, Yana, you are pregnant,' he says.

Her body becomes numb and for a few seconds she is speechless. Eventually, she collects herself. She thanks him and he sends her off with advice on how to look after herself, what to eat and drink and gives her a prescription to help with the sickness.

Back home, she rings Katya.

Katya is silent when she tells her, as if she needs time for the news to sink in. After a while she asks her how she feels about it.

'I am still in shock,' Yana says.

'Are you going to tell Daniel?'

'I don't know.'

'Meaning?'

'Meaning,' Yana replies, irritated by the question, 'that I don't know. I don't know how I feel about it, and I don't know what I am going to do about it.'

Katya is quiet on the line and Yana wishes Mammy were here.

'Of course, I can't tell you what to do, Yana but you must think very carefully before you do anything you may regret later. Whatever you decide, I'll stand by you.'

Yana was truthful when she told Katya that she didn't know how she felt about being pregnant. A part of her feels that it is gift, carrying the child of the man she loves, a child made in love but another part, a larger part is angry with Daniel for abandoning her and she thinks that he doesn't deserve to know because of it. She is also scared, very scared. Would she be able to look after, bring up a child on her own? With Mammy gone, she will be completely on her own.

If she lets this baby grow, will it look like Daniel? she wonders. Dark eyes that look at her as if they have always known her, black hair that curls on the forehead? Or might the baby have her hair? She doesn't wish that on the poor mite. Not with all the teasing and name-calling that comes with it.

And if she didn't? She'd be free. She would do what she needs to do to get back to Wales and her studies. She will take her chances. Surely what they want from her isn't much; just listen to a few conversations and report back in exchange for being free to live her own life. And Daniel wouldn't need to know about it.

Chapter Twenty-Five

The call comes. This time, she is the only one waiting outside room 44 and after a few minutes she is ushered in. A small, wiry woman with short grey hair is sitting behind the desk in the corner. Yana is surprised, she had expected to see the man who'd interviewed her before. The woman is examining her passport and doesn't acknowledge her. Minutes pass then finally she looks up.

'Sit,' she says, pointing to the chair in front of the desk. 'We have your visa ready; we just need you to sign your agreement to help us protect our country from those who work against it. Then you must meet Comrade Stoichev. There are a few things he wants to talk to you about.'

The woman pushes the papers across the desk and points to the dotted line. 'Sign and date here,' she says. Her fingernails are painted red, the varnish chipped at the edges. The scent of cheap perfume is mixed with the smell of stale tobacco.

Lenin and Stalin look upon her from the wall.

Yana can hear the click of heels in the corridor and the faint mutter of voices. The clock on the wall ticks. Her heart is pounding.

She takes a breath. She holds the pen poised above the paper. The woman examines her nails and scrapes off a bit of varnish with her thumb nail. A door bangs shut nearby. Someone is running down the corridor.

Yana scrolls her signature on the line, next to her name printed in capital letters.

'Take her to Comrade Stoichev,' the woman orders the bespectacled man who she's summoned on the telephone.

He leads her up a large staircase, to the top of the building. She sits outside another room. This one has no number.

The person sitting outside the numberless, nameless door is not her but a character in a film or a play. She feels only curiosity as the door opens.

'Come in,' Comrade Stoichev says and offers his hand. She is taken aback; they don't usually make physical contact of any kind.

There is no ashtray on Comrade Stoichev's desk and the room smells fresh and clean. He is young, not much older than her and he wears an expensive-looking suit, obviously not bought in Sofia. On his feet are leather moccasins, the kind men wear in Italian films, and his linen shirt is crisp and white, with gold cufflinks.

'Sit down, comrade,' he smiles at her, pointing to the chair. She notices a pile of books on psychology and sociology on the shelves behind the desk.

He follows her eyes and says, 'I notice from your dossier that you have been studying psychology. I myself am a psychology graduate, studying for my doctorate now.'

She says nothing.

'I understand you want to return to your studies,' Stoichev continues. 'But I have been wondering whether that is the only reason you want to leave. We know that you have been seeing Daniel Greenberg. This is useful to us because, as you know, we want you to report on his friends, Elka and Vancho Danchevi, which you have agreed to do. So, the closer you are to Mr. Greenberg, the better for us and for you.'

'I am pregnant with his child,' Yana says and wonders where the words came from. She had not intended to tell him.

Stoichev's face is impassive, but his eyes have lost their friendliness. He pauses a while, then leans back in his chair.

'Motherhood must be such a special, unique experience,' he says. 'My wife and I have been trying for a baby for a while now, Mr. Greenberg and you must be delighted.'

Yana is silent, her body tense with fear.

'You've had a difficult life, comrade, haven't you?' Stoichev continues, concern clouding his eyes. 'Growing up without a father.' He looks pensive then adds as an afterthought, 'Tragic.'

Terror is making her body shiver. He looks at her kindly. 'Would you like some water? Or perhaps a little brandy?'

I will not let you intimidate me. Yana catches her breath and smiles a polite refusal.

'I'll come to the point, Yana,' Stoichev says, familiar with her now, as if they've known each other for a long time, but his eyes are hard. 'As you know, you have the honour of being selected to do some work for us in Britain. For the Party and the People. Your people. This baby is not part of the plan we have for you. It has come at the wrong time. We want you to be free to work for us.'

Then, after a pause, 'We can arrange everything, the best clinic, the best doctor, no pain.'

Her skin prickles as if cold fire is running over it.

'But of course, you must think about it,' Stoichev says, smiling benevolently but his voice is steel. 'It is your body after all, your decision. Think about it. A baby would make it difficult for you to do the work. And think of the consequences if you don't do what we are asking of you. Your life and that of your family will not be easy. But if you do decide to serve your country, then there will be rewards. Perhaps Katya can visit you in the UK. Perhaps she could even be sponsored to study there. And Vlado could be promoted. Who knows? Think about it but don't leave it too long. In the meantime, your visa stays with us.'

Outside the wind is howling and rain jabs her cheeks with sharp, cold fingers. People are hurrying along Boulevard Bulgaria, holding on to their umbrellas and hats and the yellow paving stones gleam, cleansed by the rain.

When Stoichev suggested an abortion, she knew with absolute certainty that she wants this baby. But now she is not sure. Keeping it would mean she would never go back to Wales. Stoichev's words ring in her ears *think of the consequences.*

She feels dizzy, black spots are dancing in front of her eyes. She grabs hold of a passer-by, an old woman who nearly loses her footing and they hold onto each other for a second or two. When they regain their balance, the woman looks shocked and angry then she sees Yana's face. 'I am feeling sick.' Yana says, 'I am pregnant, that's all.' The woman finds her a taxi and she is sick when she gets home. Afterwards, she lies on her bed, afraid to move in case the sickness comes back. She wants this baby, but she is terrified of what having it would mean for her, for Katya and for the baby too.

She must decide soon.

Part Two

Chapter One

February 1976

Yana comes round from her heavy, drug-induced sleep. It is dark in the room and the baby isn't there. She panics and calls for the night nurse. She lies alone for what seems like an eternity until the nurse brings her baby. 'We took her away,' she says, 'to let you sleep. You were exhausted.'

The baby opens her eyes. Blue eyes looking at her. She holds her close and feels the weight of her little body. 'Look at those eyes,' she says to the baby, 'how beautiful they are. Look at those little hands, how perfect they are.'

The baby hiccups, her body vibrating in Yana's arms. She gets up and goes to the window. A full moon is hanging in the sky. Its light floods the room and makes every little detail sharp and precise. The baby blinks at the moon and stops hiccupping. 'Look at the moon,' Yana whispers to her, 'look how wondrous it is. And the stars, how they shine for you. Your first night in this world. How welcome you are.'

The following morning, Daniel is standing on the pavement outside together with a few other new fathers who have come to see their babies. She takes Ellie onto the balcony and holds her up for him to see her.

'I didn't expect to meet my daughter this way,' he says, 'I didn't believe it when they said I couldn't visit you because of the rules.' 'Mother and baby must be kept

143

in sterile conditions' they said, 'no infection must be allowed to enter the ward.'

'Welcome to maternity Bulgarian style,' Yana says. 'I am so glad you came.'

'I would have come earlier,' he says, 'I didn't know until Mary told me. I got the first flight available. I would have liked to have been here at her birth.'

'You wouldn't have been allowed to; no fathers are ever allowed on the ward.'

'I've left some *banitza* and cake Katya made for you at reception. I hope you get it.'

'Feeding time,' the nurse comes into the room, her white coat sparkling clean and starched. Yana waves Daniel good-bye. She can't remember ever being so happy in her entire life.

Five days later, Yana comes out of the hospital carrying her daughter, swaddled in a white blanket. The baby is fast asleep. Katya and Daniel are waiting for them and a small band of *tsigani* is playing at the door. The men, dark-haired and moustached are wearing traditional costumes with wide trousers, tucked into knee high boots, red embroidered waist coats over loose, white puff - shouldered shirts. The wistful melody of the violins is accompanied by the reedy rhythms of the accordion and the soaring, lustrous sound of the clarinet. Yana smiles through tears.

Daniel pays the musicians and takes the baby from her.

'The taxi is waiting just round the corner.' He says. Yana and Katya follow him.

In the taxi, the baby smiles.

'It's wind,' Katya says.

'Maybe,' Daniel says, 'and maybe she is just pleased to see her Daddy.'

'I would like to call her after Mammy,' Yana says.

'You've never told me what Mammy's name was.'

'Elena,' Katya says before Yana has had the chance.

'I like it,' Daniel says, 'it is also a Latvian name, but it is pronounced slightly differently –*Yelena*. Shall we call her Ellie for short? Ellie is such a pretty name, don't you think?'

'Ellie it is, then,' Yana agrees.

They lie in bed with Ellie lying between them. 'I want to paint her,' Daniel says,' she is so beautiful.'

'I need to tell you something,' he says later, just as Yana is about to drift off.

Yana turns to him.

'I have wanted to tell you before, to warn you but it never seemed to be right moment.'

Her heart starts pounding.

'Sometimes I feel a rage that comes as if out of no-where. Ever since I found out about my grandparents. What happened to them in the Rumbala forest has crippled my heart.'

'Tell me what happened, please.'

'Twenty-five thousand Jews, among them my grand-parents, died there, lined up and shot in the backs by the Nazi. I hope they died quickly; I hope they didn't get smothered under the dead and half- dead bodies that filled the pit. I hope the bullet went right through their hearts and saved them from the stench of fear.'

Shivers creep down her spine. She moves closer and holds him. There are no words she could say that would make it easier for him.

'The rage,' he says, 'I don't know what to do with it. It stands between me and my work. And I am afraid it will stand between us too.'

'Hold me, Daniel, feel my heart beating. We are alive,' Yana says and holds him even tighter.

In the morning, he asks Yana to marry him. 'I went to the embassy a couple of days ago and checked out the formalities,' he tells her. 'The day we are married, you will become a British citizen and so you can travel back to Wales with me.'

Emptiness enters her heart where happiness should be.

If only he knew, Yana thinks, if only he knew what I have done, what I have signed my name under. But he may never know. They can't hold me to it once I become a British citizen, can they?

But the thought doesn't bring the re-assurance she needs.

She walks around, touching the furniture as if her hands could carry the imprints of her life here to her new home. For a long time, she sits in Mammy's winged arm-chair looking at the mountain and its silent presence makes her ache even more.

She tries to decide what to take with her. She finds Mammy's jewelry box, its red leather faded but still handsome, the white satin lining soft and smooth. Katya has told her she can take anything she wants so she puts it in her suitcase. She finds a photograph of the four of them, Mammy Tatti, Katya and her, taken not long before he left to be with Danna. She put that in her case too. Why did he leave? Sometimes I feel I can never forgive him, she thinks. Sometimes I still feel so angry with him for abandoning us. Am I doing the same now, abandoning Katya?

She pushes the thought away and snaps the lid of her suitcase shut. Tomorrow would be the start of her new life.

But in the morning, there is a plain brown envelope lying on the mat by the front door. *Don't forget your duty to the Motherland,* the note inside reads. *We will not forget you.*

Chapter Two

June 1979

The house they buy is near a town called Haverford-west. It is a large and rambling seventeenth century farm-house of grey stone, cheap, dilapidated and beautiful. There is a long, low outbuilding, which becomes Daniel's studio and half an acre of garden with an ancient cedar tree and a view of the Welsh hills in the distance.

Daniel puts down his brush and joins Yana and Ellie in the garden. It's only ten in the morning but the sun is already hot, and the bees are everywhere, filling up on the sweet scent of the garden. Yana is no gardener, and neither is he, but he is learning and spends most after-noons in the garden now, planning and planting.

Ellie is running around. She is full of wonder that her legs carry her any which way she chooses to go. She takes a few steps this way, then that way and laughs. Now she is standing by the delphiniums, investigating a butterfly sitting on a blue flower with the concentration of a scien-tist collecting data. Marcus strolls to her and rubs his fur against her and she goes for his tail. Yana scolds her gen-tly and takes her to the paddling pool under the pear tree.

The smell of lavender this morning is overpowering. It's mixed with the softer, sweeter smell of lilac, a plant Yana insisted on having in the garden because it re-minded her of summers in Sofia.

A small plane circles overhead, a witness to this peaceful homely scene and a reminder of the world out-side. For three weeks now, the phone has rung, at different times of the day. All she could hear when she picked up the receiver was music and loud breathing at the end of the line. Then a click and silence. The silence of threat. She knows this is meant to frighten her into action. She has kept her head in the sand for the last couple of years hoping that now she is out of the country, they wouldn't bother to pursue her. But deep down she knows they won't forget; they will keep her to her promise. She can't escape, there is no safety for her anywhere.

In the local parish playgroup Ellie always sits on Yana's lap and never ventures very far. When the teacher plays 'The Grand Old Duke of York' and the children march to the tune, Yana has to carry her because she won't be put down.

After playgroup, they walk by the Cleddau and Yana gives Ellie some bread to feed the ducks. Today, the ducks have been joined by two swans. They sail past them in regal repose while the ducks noisily circle the morsels.

The sun is beating down and Ellie's hat is missing, probably lost on the way. Yana pulls up the hood of the pram to give Ellie some shade and Ellie pushes it back and giggles, ready for another battle of wills. But Yana is not in the mood today. Today, she's had enough of Haverfordwest. She has been here now for nearly three years and the charm has worn off. She has walked the steep High Street hundreds of times and the Friday market, quaint and buzzing with people and goods, doesn't fascinate her anymore. When Daniel first brought her here and took her to the Castle and the ruined Abbey, then walked with her along the ancient sandstone bridges that cross the river to the Pendergast, she was captivated. It was like a fairy tale. But now she misses Sofia with an urgency that startles her. Every morning when she wakes, she imagines its streets and the mountain outside her window and when she thinks of Katya, her heart is tight with longing. Then caring for Ellie takes over and the days unfold in the monotony of routine, occasionally broken by visitors and her regular chats on the phone with Mary in Cardiff.

The ducks have finished the bread and Ellie is whimpering. An old couple strolling by stop and say something in Welsh to her and Yana smiles politely while Ellie, surprised by the strange sounds, stops crying. A little boy runs ahead of his mother who is pushing a baby in a pram. He looks at Ellie for a second or two then skips away and Ellie starts crying again.

Yana pushes the pram to the pedestrian crossing. As if from nowhere a car screech to a halt, an inch from the pram, then drives off leaving skid marks on the road. Startled, Ellie stops crying. A young man rushes over to them. 'Are you OK? You should report him, I've got his number.'

Yana's heart is banging against her chest. She knows that what just happened was not an accident. It's a follow-up to the phone calls. Wales used to feel safe, but she doesn't feel safe here anymore.

Chapter Tree

Katya

The Institute for Art and Design is in the middle of the city, not far from the old Turkish baths where Mammy used to take her and Yana when they were children. Katya still remembers the large steamy rooms with the marble floors and *teliachkite* who would scrub them vigorously until their bodies became pink and shiny and sweat poured down their rosy faces.

The tram that takes her there in the morning is crowded and she manages to squeeze in just as the doors are closing. She is late as usual. By the time she gets there the other students have started drawing the nude male model in the large room at the front. She slips in quietly and finds an easel at the back. The model is a short young man with stubby, hairy legs and a large torso. She gets her charcoals out and makes a mark on the paper.

The room is large, and sunlight is pouring through the high window, which today are open, letting in a gentle breeze and the smell of freshly cut grass. It's quiet, everybody is focused on their work, while the teacher walks around stopping here and there, whispering a comment or two before moving on to the next pupil.

A knock on the door breaks the silence.

The teacher walks up to the door and opens it a sliver. Katya can hear whispers in the corridor, then he comes back into the room and looks around. He catches her eye and walks up to her easel. 'The Director wants to see you in his office, comrade,' he whispers.

153

Comrade Antonov is a tall, lanky man with sand-coloured hair that flops over a pair of steel-rimmed glasses.

'Sit down,' he says, pointing to a chair by his desk. A framed poster of Maleevich's *Woodcutter* hangs on the wall behind his desk next to a hammer and sickle poster of the Russian Revolution.

A prickly uneasiness spreads in her body. She has never before been called to the Director's office.

'How are you enjoying the course, comrade?'

'Great course, I am loving it,' Katya says.

'I've been wondering how you are coping with your Mum not here anymore and your sister so far away.'

'I miss them both, of course I do but I am fine,' Katya replies. She wonders what this is all about, what is it leading to? It is highly unusual for a man in his position to take such personal interest in a student's wellbeing.

'It must be hard, though, with Yana so far away, married to an Englishman, unlikely to come back. Do you hear from her often? How is she doing over there?'

'She is busy, comrade, looking after her child, she tells me it takes up all her time,'

'Ah yes, that's understandable. And does she tell you much about life there? Does she like it?'

Katya shifts uneasily in her chair. She really is at a loss now. She has no idea what this conversation is about.

'I think she likes her life there, Comrade Antonov. But she does feel homesick too.' 'Understandably,' she adds.

'So she hasn't forgotten her roots, then. Still attached to her homeland.'

'I don't think it is possible to forget one's roots, comrade.'

'You'd be surprised, Katya, how many people forget about their birth land once they go the West. You'd be surprised. Anyway, I am glad she hasn't and that you are doing OK. Do let me know if you have any problems with your studies, I'd be only too happy to help.'

She gets back to the classroom, but her mind is not on the drawing anymore. The uneasiness she felt in the Director's office has turned into dread. Something isn't right, she can feel it in her bones, something to do with Yana isn't right. But what could it be? She left Bulgaria legally, she is a British citizen now, what would they want with her? She knows that here people are being watched almost constantly, what they say, where they go, what they do. There is a system of constant surveillance, a network of informants, everyone knows that. But Yana left all this behind so why are they trying to keep an eye on her too?

She walks through the Doctors' Park on her way home. There are people everywhere, sitting on benches, chatting, mothers and babies and old people making the most of summer. The flower beds are trim, with neat rows of roses, mixed with marigolds, their yellow heads standing out among the profusion of reds and pinks.

It is a lovely day, but her heart is heavy and tight.

The flat is empty when she gets back. She makes herself a cup of tea and sits on the small balcony overlooking the street. People are hurrying along, carrying bags full of shopping, some pushing prams, some leading small children by the hand.

Ordinary life, going on as usual. But in the pit of her stomach sits the knowledge that her life is about to change.

Chapter Four

December 1979

Dearest Yana,

What's up? Why are you feeling so low?? I must say your letter was a shock because I thought things were good in Haverfordwest, it sounds such a lovely place. Ring me, I am worried about you. And of course Ellie, she must know you are unhappy, remember how it was when Tatti left? Mammy was so good at trying to hide her grief, but we knew, didn't we?

Strange things are going on here. Do you remember Comrade Angelov who lives in one of the flats in the block across the street? The Party official responsible for our neighborhood? Well, he came to the flat the other day, he wanted to know how you were, as if you had been friends or something. Something isn't right, Sis, I can feel it in my bones. I felt very unsettled after he left. Then yesterday, the Director of the Graphics Department rang me to say we must set up a meeting to discuss my contract. The way he said it made me think I must be in trouble. It's probably nothing. You know what a worrier I am.

The big news here is that Mitko has defected! I bumped into a friend of his, Jerry, do you remember him? Apparently, Mitko married his boss's daughter, (he is a bigwig in the Party, Jerry said.) They went to Brazil for their honeymoon and Mitko disappeared. How about that? Obviously, he can never come back here now, they'll be after his blood. Jerry didn't know his whereabouts.

Otherwise, not much news here. Vlado seems happy with his teaching; I think he was born for it and I am glad he can practice on other people now. Joking apart, we are very happy, and I am beginning to think that getting married might not be such a bad idea after all. And having a kid.

I am sad that you are so far away, Sis, I miss you and I miss not seeing Ellie growing up. Give her a big kiss from her auntie and look after yourself.

Looking forward to speaking on the phone soon.

Much love,

Katya xxxxxx

Yana folds Katya's letter and puts it her pocket. The log fire is throwing out waves of heat, which enfold her body. The Christmas tree, laden with baubles and red ribbons, snowflakes and sparkly birds, twinkles in the corner and when she gets up to draw the curtains, she notices real snowflakes floating in the grey air outside. Her body is hot, but her stomach is a pit of ice. Cold runs down her spine. Soon she must collect Ellie from the nursery and carry on with the routine of tea and play, then supper and a bath. Daniel is in his studio; he hasn't been out of it all day and she knows he is thrashing at the canvas; she knows about the rage. When he is like this, she doesn't dare go near him but when it passes, he becomes gentle again and she tries to convince herself that this is who he is, not the raging man who cannot speak to her, who avoids her eyes. When the storm has passed, she will lie with him again, her head on his chest. The rages are like the weather, unpredictable hailstorms on a summer's day.

Katya's letter has distracted her from thoughts about Daniel. For nearly three years now the note from the Ministry has lain in the murky undercurrents of her mind, like sediment lying at the bottom of a pool. When the anonymous phone calls started earlier on this year, she pushed her fear away and didn't say anything to Daniel but the near-miss at the pedestrian crossing in the summer and now Katya's letter have stirred the muddy waters and she knows she cannot escape. Or if she does, Katya will suffer.

Don't forget your duty to the Motherland, we will not forget you. And Stoichev's words, 'Think of the consequences.'

They never forget, not even after you die, they never forget, and they make the ones that you left behind afraid too. They would have wanted her to get Katya's letter why else let it pass censorship? It is clearly a warning. She had thought that getting married to Daniel and leaving the country would have saved her from having to fulfill her contract, but she had been naïve. They have her signature, and they will not let her go.

Katya is in danger, and this is just the beginning.

She must do something to stop them from punishing Katya. She must not allow Katya to suffer because of the choices that she, Yana, has made.

Yesterday Daniel told her that the Arts Council are putting on an exhibition of Vancho and Elka's work after Christmas. The date hasn't been confirmed but it's likely to be late March. She has three months, and she must act quickly to stop them from punishing Katya and threatening the safety of her child. She will let them know that she is ready to fulfill her obligations.

Does she have it in her heart to do what she has always despised others for? To spy and inform on people? Her

159

mouth fills with the acrid taste of shame and the image of Katya's face, sweet and innocent floats in her mind. She knows she will be betraying Tatti and everything he stood for. Maybe that's why they were so keen to recruit her? To punish and humiliate him even in death?

She has to act, she can't delay. She can't allow her family to suffer because she, Yana, chose to get away.

I have to make a choice, she thinks. Tatti made a choice, he put his principles above the family, he spoke about his beliefs, and we all suffered because of it. And we are still suffering. Had he not died for what he thought was right, I might not be faced with this choice now. But I can't let my principles destroy Katya's future.

She picks up the phone and rings the Embassy.

On Christmas Day, Mary comes laden with gifts for Ellie. After lunch they sit by the fire and watch Ellie tear the wrapping paper, flush with excitement.

'I am so pleased that Vancho and Elka have had the go ahead for the show,' Mary says sipping her wine. 'Will you bring them to Cardiff?' she asks Daniel.

'Sure, I've invited them to stay with us here for a week, perhaps we could call by on our way back from London?' He seems happy right now.

Yana is dreading the show. The place will be full of people from the Embassy, and she knows that the eyes of the woman assigned to her would be on her the whole evening. But she would like to see London again and Daniel has promised to look after Ellie so that she could go shopping. They would show Vancho and Elka the sights before they drive them back to Wales. They would all stay the night in London with some Bulgarian friends of the Danchevi. Yana has never met them and is curious and for a second or two she forgets about the 'assignment.'

'You are quiet, Yana,' Daniel says. His voice startles her.

'Too much wine, I must get Ellie ready for bed.'

But Ellie is having none of it. She lies on the floor screaming and kicking, a valiant protest against routine when Mary is here and there are presents to play with.

'Let's go to the studio,' Daniel bribes her, 'you can use my brushes and we can paint a picture together, or you can open your new box of paints and try those.'

'Yours,' yells Ellie and climbs on his back.

Daniel always takes over as if he knows that Yana finds mothering hard. But she doesn't mind, he has a way with Ellie, they are a perfect fit for each other. Their love is easy, uncomplicated. With her, Ellie is often belligerent and sulky. It is as if she senses a vulnerability in Yana that threatens her.

After they've gone, Mary says: 'It must be difficult at Christmas with no family close by.'

Yana is silent, heavy with her secret. She has to pretend all is well. Life is ordinary, bringing up Ellie, a challenge. And yes, Haverfordwest is too small, she feels hemmed in and the hills that charmed her once now feel like the walls of a prison.

'Sometimes it's lonely here,' she says.

'I've often wondered why Daniel decided to buy the house here,' Mary says. 'He got good money for his parents' place, he could have bought property in London, near the gallery.'

Jane, Yana thinks, that's why. They must have walked the hills together and when he fell in love with her, he must have fallen in love with the place too. Jealousy stabs her.

'Tell me about Jane.'

'Not much to tell, I didn't know her that well. She was kind. They made a lovely couple.'

'Sometimes Daniel gets angry,' Yana says. 'There is a darkness in him.'

'I've had glimpses,' Mary replies. 'I know he has moods. Jane was loyal but she told me once'

She must have known about the Rumbala forest, Yana thinks. How did she cope with the brooding, the silences, the sense of total powerless to help. The rage that is like an impenetrable wall around Daniel when the mood takes him there. She is tempted to tell Mary, to explain but thinks the better of it. It is Daniel's story, it's not for her to tell it.

The fire needs stoking. Yana puts on a couple of logs and pokes the dying embers until a spark starts it going again, the flames tentative at first. The logs hiss and sprinkle fiery stars.

She loves the fire. The flat in Sofia had communal heating, *parno*, which was switched on centrally at the end of October and switched off in April, regardless of the weather. In the winter when the temperature dropped to fifteen degrees below zero, she was glad to come home to a furnace that quickly thawed her frozen hands and feet. But in March and April, spring mellowed the air and fresh breezes brought the smell of new life. It became stuffy in the flat then and there was no way of turning off the heat so Mammy would open all the windows to let spring in and leave them open, sometimes through the night. Yana would wake up at dawn to the sound of the first trams that stirred the city to life with the clank of their wheels on the tracks.

Spring in Sofia, the pigeons outside her window celebrating the sun. The mountain rising dark blue against a sky of a pale blue. The smell fresh and promising; hope rising. Each day a new beginning. It wasn't so bad then, was it?

What is it about her that pushes her away from those she loves? Did Mammy verse her in the art of leaving? When Mammy sent her away, did she release her from the bonds of love, did she teach her the bleak freedom of being apart, of not belonging. Even now, with Ellie, it is as if an invisible wall separates her.

Ellie and Daniel have come back from the studio and Ellie is tired.

'I'll bathe her,' Daniel says. 'You chat to Mary.'

'Mamma's tired,' Ellie says.

When they've gone, Mary asks: 'How's Katya? Is she still happy with Vlado?'

'Katya and Vlado are good together, they love each other very much but Katya is having problems at work, I am worried about her. I think they may be punishing her because of me.'

'Because you married an Englishman? What's wrong with that?'

'I should have thought about the consequences. It wouldn't have been hard to imagine that getting the visa the way I did would have angered them. It would have made them feel I slipped away from their clutches. They wouldn't have liked that. They like to know that we are all in their power. It makes them feel strong.'

'They must be very frightened,' Mary says, 'of losing their power.'

This is the oddest thing about it, Yana thinks. Fear rules us all, us and the ones that control us. They appear all-powerful but they too must be scared, fear breeds fear. And hatred. We are all in it together.

How strange this is when all her life she has thought of them as invulnerable. The thought doesn't take away her apprehension, it makes it worse.

She gets up to draw the curtains. 'You won't be going home tonight, Mary,' she says, 'your car's covered in snow. It's piled up inches deep.'

And she puts another log on the fire and pours them another glass of wine.

Mary stays for a week because of the snow and Yana is glad of it. It distracts her from the fear. But when she lies in bed with Daniel, her body is rigid, refusing to respond to his affection.

'What's the matter, Yana,' he asks her, concerned.

'Missing Mammy and Katya and Sofia' she tells him.

'Of course, I understand, it's Christmas. It must be hard to be away from people you love.' He holds her but the fear won't go away.

The light from the snow makes the morning air radiant. The drive and the cars are still covered with snow, which has settled and become hard over the last couple of days. Yana lets herself out into the garden and the snow crunches under her feet. The boughs of the trees hang heavy with it and the air sparkles. Magic has descended on this small corner on earth and for a moment her heart is quiet with the wonder of it.

Ellie comes rushing from the kitchen. 'Sleigh, please, Mammy, please, please.'

'Breakfast first.' She holds her hand and takes her back to the kitchen.

Mary's up. She's already made some coffee and Yana gets Ellie's breakfast. Daniel must be in his studio.

'Go and find Daddy,' she tells Ellie. 'Ask him to get the sleigh out.'

'I am concerned about you,' Mary says, after Ellie has gone. 'I don't want to pry but is everything OK?'

'Missing home badly, Mary.'

'Why don't you come and stay with me for a few days? The change would do you good. And you can meet up with Jenny.'

It might be a good idea to get away from Haverford West and Daniel and Ellie. The effort to keep things going as normal, to pretend all is OK is wearing her down. Being with Mary and spending time with Jenny would be a distraction.

'I'd love to, Mary,' she says.

Chapter Five

The snow has turned to slush on the streets of Cardiff and Yana decides to buy a pair of wellingtons to keep her feet dry. She goes with Mary to British Home Stores and chooses a pair printed all over with red tulips. 'You look like a walking garden,' Mary says, and it makes Yana laugh. Katya used to make her laugh like this.

She hasn't laughed for a while. In fact, she can't quite remember the last time. Being with Mary, no Ellie in tow is fun. It takes her back to the old days when she first came to Wales. She felt free then, those first months before Mammy was ill.

'Let's eat lunch somewhere nice,' Mary says, 'my treat.'

'The little Italian on the promenade?'

'It's changed hands since you were here last,' Mary says, 'I think the food is even better now.'

They find a parking space at the far end of the promenade. The sea is grey, speckled with a few seagulls skimming the surface, their screeching muffled by the sound of the waves crashing on the pebbly beach. A ship is anchored far in the distance, its hull like a cutout on the line of the horizon, motionless against the grey sky.

They walk fast, battling against the piercing wind. Yana's feet are freezing; the wellingtons were not made for warmth. Thankfully, a wave of heat greets them when they enter the Caprice and as she hands her coat to the waiter, she feels it seeping into her skin.

They choose a table by the window looking out to sea and order pasta and a carafe of red wine. Mary, her cheeks flushed with the heat, raises her glass.

'Here's to you, sweetheart, let's hope things with Katya settle down. Perhaps you can go back for a week or two to see her?'

For a second Yana wants to tell her the truth. That she is about to start informing on Daniel's friends. She is meeting with the Bulgarian handler in London in two weeks' time, the deal has been done now. She desperately needs to tell someone. The loneliness of the secret is a crushing weight. What would Mary say? She'd be shocked, no doubt, but what advice would she give?

'If I go back, they won't let me out again and if I stay, Katya will suffer,' she tells Mary after a while.

'It makes no sense to me,' Mary says, 'why would they want to punish Katya because you came to live here? You didn't escape, you didn't break any laws, you live here on a British passport, surely that isn't illegal in Bulgaria.'

'No, Mary, not illegal. But coming here the way I did meant that they couldn't control me anymore because I am now a British citizen under the protection of your Queen. I have escaped again, and it makes them furious. So, one way to get at me is to punish Katya, do you see?'

Mary doesn't look convinced. Having been brought up here, she has no experience of the fear. She could never understand a system that makes you choose between keeping you sister safe and betraying your husband.

'I have never felt safe since Tatti was murdered, Mary. I thought that coming here would free me from the fear but it's not so.'

'You are fearing for Katya, honey, I can see this.'

'And for myself. And the worst of it is that none of it is personal. They are furious because the system that keeps them in power has been challenged. It is an impersonal hatred, the more frightening because of it.'

'It sounds horrendous. It would be enough to make anyone feel paranoid.'

'It's not paranoia, Mary, it's real. I don't think I ever told you about the night when Mammy, Katya and I were woken by banging on the door. About the three-armed soldiers who burst into the room and bundled us into a lorry waiting in the street. I thought we would be murdered like Tatti.'

'What happened?'

'We were spared. We were interned to a village in the countryside as punishment for 'not promoting, with due fervor, the socialist ideology of the Bulgarian Communist Party and its glorious leaders.' We were lucky. The family we were accommodated with, Tanya and Vasko, were sympathetic, they had no time for the communists either, though they hid their views and pretended to be in line. Mammy got on well with them and we were all sad when the exile was over, and it was time to leave.'

Mary takes her hand and squeezes it gently.

'My dearest, I am so glad you survived. But what you have been through! No wonder you are still scared. Having your father murdered and thinking you will be too, that would be enough to make any one scared. I can see now how real your fear must be. You were lucky to escape his fate.'

The Danchevi may not be so lucky, Yana thinks.

Chapter Six

Katya

She knows she is being followed. It's a young woman, about her age, with dark hair in a ponytail. Ordinary looking. Fairly attractive. She was at the tram stop two days ago, dressed as if going to the office, carrying a brown briefcase. She sat at the table next to hers at the café when she met Julie yesterday. She bumped into her at the supermarket this morning. This time she was wearing jeans and a flowery top.

'She seems nice,' she tells Vlado when she gets home. 'If I weren't certain she works for them, I'd say hello to her.'

'What makes you so sure she works for State Security?'

'I know it in my gut, Vlado. It's too much of a coincidence. She is everywhere.'

'But what would they want you followed for? They know you've got nothing to hide.'

'I think they are trying to intimidate. That's why they kicked me out of the course with no valid reason whatsoever. Just being late for class a couple of times. No one gets kicked out for being late. Grant you, keeping time is not one of my strong points but even so.'

'If that is the case, if they are just trying to frighten you, there doesn't seem to be anything you could do about it. It's tough, I grant you that, but you just have to ignore them and carry on with your life. Open for business as usual.'

'Open for business as usual? What business exactly?' She folds her arms. 'You know I've been at a loose end, ever since I left the course. I've got nothing to do, nothing to think about.' Her voice is harsher that she intends it be.

'No need to take it out on me, Katya, I know you are frustrated, and it makes you irritable but none of this is my fault. And there is nothing I can do about it.'

Katya knows that the person she is really angry with is Yana. For leaving and letting this happen. She also knows that secretly, Vlado blames Yana too but he would never say so. The truth is that it isn't Yana's fault, all she did was follow her heart's desire. Got married and followed her husband. What could be wrong with that?

Deep down Katya knows what is happening is the fault of the system. She doesn't like to think about it because unlike Yana, she likes living here. She cherishes her home, Vlado, her friends. She loves how the mountain rises above the city, always there, a constant in her life. She would never want to leave. And yet they, the people who run the system are making it difficult for her to be happy and contended in her own country. She feels like yelling 'It's not fair, it's not fair, it's so not fair.' All she wants is stability, a simple life, work, the everyday. She doesn't want excitement or change. And least of all she wants fear.

The queue at the greengrocer's is long. 'They've got pink tomatoes,' the woman in front of her says. 'I've been hunting for them all over the place.'

Katya looks around to see if the girl is there, but she can't see her. When her turn comes, she buys a kilo of the pink tomatoes, a couple of cucumbers, a bunch of parsley and a bunch of dill. Next stop will be the grocer's for the cheese, then she'll have all the ingredients for the *shopska* tonight. She pays the bill and turns around finding herself face to face with the girl. This time her hair is down, and she is wearing a blue polka dot dress and a pair of sunglasses.

Katya walks away incanting *chupi se, chupi se; piss off, piss off* under her breath. Back home, she throws the vegetables on the draining board, washes them and using the sharpest knife in the drawer, starts slicing and chopping ferociously as if her life depends on it.

Chapter Seven

Yana

She tells Daniel she has arranged to go to London with Jenny for a day's shopping and did he mind looking after Ellie. Of course not, he said.

She takes an early train and meets Jenny at Paddington at ten. It is Saturday and the station is crowded. They push their way through to the underground and get on the Circle line to Kensington.

'Coffee first?' suggests Yana.

'I can murder one.'

'Barker's?'

'It's fine with me'

The café at Barker's is nearly empty and they find a table by the window. The waitress brings them the menu and half a dozen assorted cakes on a stand. She is a middle-aged woman, carefully made up and wearing a black button-through dress with a small frilly apron.

'Still quite formal here,' Jenny says, 'they don't seem to have moved on with the times much.'

'The cakes are good though,' Yana says, 'and there is quite a good Italian restaurant just round the corner. Daniel took me there when I first came here. We could go there for lunch if you like. Which reminds me, I'll have to leave you on your own after lunch for a couple of hours, I have to go to the Bulgarian Embassy to sort out some paperwork.' It's not far from here, across from the park. We can meet afterwards and do a bit more shopping before we head off back home.'

175

As instructed, she rings the bell at the entrance marked 'Staff Only.' The heavy black door has a solid brass knocker, polished to a high shine. Her heart is in her stomach, and she is breathless.

The door opens with a creak and a large man asks her name. He leads her down a dark corridor, past an office room where half a dozen women are typing at their desks then shows her into a room at the back of the building.

The woman behind the desk is small and plump with dark curly hair and a large hairy mole on her left cheek. Yana tries hard not stare.

'Sit down comrade,' the woman points to a chair a few feet away from the desk. 'So,' she continues,' the time has come for you to honour the contract you made with us. It took you longer than we had hoped for, but we understand that with a baby and toddler it would have been difficult for you to put your mind to it. But you are here now, that's the main thing.'

Yana is motionless but her heart is kicking against her chest.

'Here is the recorder,' the woman passes her a white box. 'As you can see, it is small enough to fit into your pocket. All you have to do is start it as soon as you hear the Danchevi speaking with people at the private view. The machine is practically soundless but is able to record every word clearly even in a crowded room. The latest invention of our brothers, the Soviets.'

This is for real, Yana thinks, it isn't a game. Although part of her feels as if it is. She feels as if she is a character in one of John Le Carre's novels, as if she is 'The Spy Who Came from The Cold.'

'Bring me back the recorder when the party is over, I'll be waiting for you here. And mind you don't mess up.

I'll be watching you, there will be consequences if you mess up. Serious ones. Think of Katya.'

Outside there is a fresh breeze but Yana's chest is so tight, each breath she takes hurts. How did all of this come into being, she wonders as she starts to walk towards the café where she is meeting Jenny again. One group of people establishing power over the rest? How did it happen that the men who took power in the name of freedom and equality became tyrants too? Is it that violence breads fear and fear thrives on violence? And that we are all drawn into it and become all the same, using whatever power we have over others to protect ourselves? Is that how the regime survives? If she carries out the assignment, if she uses the tape recorder as instructed, she becomes part of it too. She becomes like them.

Perhaps she should go back to Sofia and give up her life here. Would this help Katya? Unlikely. It's more likely it would make things worse; they would never forgive her for abandoning the assignment. And she might never see Daniel again. Taking Ellie away from him would break his heart. And what would Daniel say if she were to tell him the reason? Would he try to make her choose between her sister and his friends? She doesn't doubt that he knows how much Katya means to her. But how would he live with the knowledge that she had signed to betray his friends? He would leave her because she had considered informing on them, even if she hadn't done it.

He would hate her.

Either way, she can't win. There is no way out, she is trapped.

Chapter Eight

March

The tiny recorder vibrates in Yana's pocket. Her spine is tingling, and she is surprised that mixed with the fear there is some excitement. For a second it is as if she is five again and playing hide -and -seek with Katya. But what she is doing is not a game. Someone might end up dead like Tatti. It is not a game.

At the exhibition she walks around, attaching herself to this group or that, trying to piece together snippets of conversation while the recorder whirls noiselessly in her pocket. People talk mostly about the paintings. Vancho's new Art Naïve style pictures have proved a hit with the visitors. Comparisons are made with Chagall, peasants dressed in folk costumes flying over bell-domed roofs of churches and over sunflower fields.

The buzz of voices is deafening, and she feels herself burn with heat.

A waitress comes along with a tray of canapés, but she is too agitated to eat. At one point she notices her handler standing in the corner watching her and she feels her stomach clench. What had felt unreal, like a story from a spy thriller, is real now. She is making it happen.

The small Italian restaurant in South Molton street is packed and noisy and they have to speak loudly to hear each other. She puts her hand in her pocket and feels the recorder vibrating against her skin.

'Are you pleased with the turnout?' Daniel asks his friends.

'Pleased with it all, Daniel.' Vancho replies, his cheeks flushed with the wine. 'We couldn't have done it without you. But I still don't know how you managed to get the OK from the authorities at home to ship the pictures over here.'

'Well,' Daniel replies, 'I used my connections at the Arts Council. Connections are useful here too, you know.'

'Whatever you did, Daniel,' Elka says, 'we can't thank you enough. It's getting worse back home; they are tightening the screws. You have to go to private homes now to see anything interesting. Art in Bulgaria is being stifled completely, the only acceptable currency now is Social Realism.'

'Maybe next year we can get a residency for you, perhaps at one of the Art Schools in London or perhaps in Cornwall.'

'It would be such a relief to get out of Bulgaria,' Elka says, 'even just for a while.'

The tape recorder whirs on. Yana moves the pasta spirals round her plate with her fork.

Reporting Vancho and Elka's words is one thing, but can she do this to Daniel? But he'll be safe, they won't harm him, how can they? He is safe in his own country, isn't he? But a voice inside her says no one is safe, no one knows what they might do. She is a novice, an amateur, she doesn't know the rules. It is a game she'd never played before, and she is not sure what the risks are.

How much is on the tape, she doesn't know. It was noisy at the exhibition, and it is noisy at the restaurant too. In the report they asked for, she thinks she'd describe the exhibition and people's reactions to it in as general a

180

way as she can. She'd say that Vancho and Elka had been very pleased to have their work exhibited in London because they were finding it difficult to show their work in Sofia. She'd mention that the possibility of a residency sometime in the future had been discussed. She hopes no harm would come of it and it will buy her time to figure out what to do next. She has to help Katya. The thought of Katya suffering because of her is intolerable.

Later, when she listens to the tape, she hears Vancho, Elka and Daniel's voices clear above the din. She has fulfilled the assignment.

Chapter Nine

Ellie has taken a shine to Elka and follows here everywhere. 'Ellie Elka,' she intones repeatedly, 'same same.' Elka and Vancho have been in Haverfordwest for nearly a week now and they tell Daniel the place is like a paradise, away from the pressures at home, pure peace, they say.

Most days they go for walks by the river and the day before yesterday, Daniel took them hiking on the hill, Ellie strapped to his back. Yana said she needed to stay at home to prepare dinner.

The truth is she can't bear having Vancho and Elka there. The guilt is like poison in her body, she feels ill with it. It's like having the flu, one minute hot, next minute shivering, her throat is thick and not enough air seems to get into her lungs.

The worst is that they are so nice to her. They are in their fifties now and don't have any children of their own so treat her as if she were their daughter. They seek out her company, help her with the chores, hug her in the mornings and when saying good night. She can feel the warmth that emanates from them, and she feels awkward, askew with herself and the world, as if living a life outside of herself.

The evenings are the worst. After Ellie has gone to bed, they sit round the table eating, drinking and talking while the tape recorder works silently in her pocket. They talk about Art and about Elka and Vancho's struggles to exhibit their work in Sofia.

'We are required to paint in the state- approved style only, if we want our work to be accepted for exhibitions. It is unbelievably frustrating,' Elka says.'

'More than frustrating,' Vancho adds, 'it's like having a noose round your neck. The threat of being punished if you don't comply always there.'

'Social Realism has honourable roots in social and political protest in America in the twenties and thirties.' Daniel says. 'The Ashan school, people like John and Robert Henry are interesting, gritty artists. It was taken over by the Soviets after the Revolution and romanticised.'

'Yes, bland and idealising, the grit was taken out of it,' Elka adds.

'And yet, here you are, able to exhibit your works in the modernist, surrealist style of people like Chagall. Can't be that bad, can it?'

'Only because of you and your links with the British Council. They are keen to be seen as open to international co-operation.'

Yana shudders inside, these words are nails in Vancho and Elka's coffins. Stop exaggerating, she tells herself sternly. What's the worst that could happen to them? After all, they are not criticising the system as such, just the way it controls Art. But she knows what happened to Tatti when he spoke his mind. She fingers the recorder in her pocket. She can delete the recording, she can say it was by mistake, she can make that choice right now. But then she would never forgive herself if anything happened to Katya.

May

Two months after Vancho and Ella return to Sofia, Daniel walks into the kitchen holding a letter from the British Council. He looks puzzled.

'Vancho and Elka have been banned from showing their work,' he says, 'and they've been interned to the countryside to work on a farm. I don't understand. They had permission to travel and exhibit here. What's gone wrong? It doesn't make sense.'

Yana wants to run and never come back.

'I don't know,' she says as she turns away to pick up Ellie's toys. 'Sometimes there is no reason for these things.'

Daniel rings the British Council and goes to London to talk to his friend who organised the show. The friend says he doesn't know anything about it and there is nothing they can do. The British Council has no influence over political decisions made in Sofia.

Yana can't bear Daniel's anger and his sorrow when he returns. 'I feel so frustrated', he says, 'I don't know what to do'. Powerless and frustrated, he says, just as she's felt all her life. She wants to tell him what she's done, to relieve herself of the guilt but she knows that she can't. Her actions have drawn a line between them, which she can never cross. They now inhabit two different worlds and there is nothing that can bring them together again, close like they were when they first married and when all of this happening now was just an abstract idea.

She is caught in their web and can't get out. They will never let her go.

Three weeks later, she tells Daniel that she has enrolled on a part-time course on Teaching English as Foreign Language in London.

'Why London?' He asks. 'There are courses like that nearer home, in Cardiff and you can stay with Mary.'

'I want to do the best course 'she says, 'and this one in London has the best reputation. Besides, it would be good to stay with Jenny as I don't get to spend much time with her. You wouldn't mind looking after Ellie while I am there?'

'A big ask,' he says. 'But if this course gives you what you want, then so be it.' Then as an afterthought, 'I think you would make a good teacher, Yana.'

A part of her suspects that he doesn't mind her absence. He has been withdrawing from her and she puts it down to his depression after the critics slated his last show in London. But a part of her wonders if he doesn't also sense her withdrawing from him. At the British Council they told him someone must have informed on Vancho and Elka after the show in London. But he would never suspect her, would he? It is like a dance they are moving to, stepping around each other, mindful not to come too close and upset the silent fear that lies between them. Fear has followed her to Wales and will follow her wherever she goes. It has destroyed her marriage. It has made her love false. It has painted her heart black.

Chapter Ten

June 1980

Dear Sis,
I don't know what's going on here. I think I must be going mad! I feel as if I am followed every time I get out of the flat. The worst of it is that Vlado has now lost his job and it is so hard to make ends meet. Any hope of start-ing a family has flown out of the window.

I think of you lots and I hope things are OK your end, you have been quiet lately and I worry about you too. Please write or phone soon!
Love as ever,
Katya xxx

The phone call, when it comes is expected.

'The time has come for you to move to London,' the woman on the other end of the line says. 'Now that your daughter is at school, we want you nearer the action, nearer to where the traitors live and work against us. You are too far away in Wales. There will be repercussions if you don't follow the order.'

Yana tries to argue that it would be better if she weren't part of the Bulgarian community in London, that it would be safer to do her work from the outside, but the woman won't have any of it. She repeats: 'There will be repercussions if you don't.' Yana knows they mean it, she remembers the car, an inch away from Ellie's pram.

She is faced with a choice: stay in Wales with the peo-ple she loves or leave in order to protect them, Katya and

Vlado and herself. It is an impossible choice and yet she has to make it. The thought of losing Ellie and Daniel is as painful as the time when Tatti died although losing Tatti was something that happened to her, she'd had no choice. Leaving Daniel and Ellie would be her choice and she would have to live with the consequences.

The mothers outside the gates of Ellie's school are gathered in a group and as always, Yana finds it difficult to join in. It's not that they are unkind to her, quite the opposite, they are welcoming when she does join but she feels their politeness is of the kind extended to strangers. She feels an outsider, like she did all those years ago in the new school in Svishtov, the girl from Sofia with the funny accent.

A bunch of four-year-olds spills out of the gate, jostling each other, their socks wrinkled down to their ankles, their cheeks glowing. Ellie has a new friend; Katie and they are holding hands as they bounce up to Yana.

'We had nature study today, Mammy,' Ellie says, her eyes shining with excitement.

'We went to the woods,' Katie adds, 'it was dark there,'

Katie's mother joins them. 'Would Ellie like to come over for tea tomorrow after school? These two seem inseparable.'

'What do you think, darling? Tea with Katie tomorrow?'

'Nice,' Ellie says, 'good!'

'Aren't' they lovely at this age?' Katie's mother turns to Yana. 'Shame they grow up so quickly.'

Walking back home holding Ellie's hand, Yana's chest is hollow. Tomorrow, she will have to tell Daniel that she is leaving. The thought doesn't feel real.

The following afternoon, while Ellie is at Katie's, she finds Daniel in his studio. Sunlight is casting a shadow on his face. He is wearing a blue shirt, there are splashes of paint all over it and for a split second she forgets why she is here and thinks how nice it would be if they were to spread the old rug on the floor and make love like they used to.

He puts the brush down and looks at her. His eyes are blank.

'All right?' he asks.

'No,' she says. 'I've come to tell you that I will be leaving at the end of the week.'

'Oh?' He says sounding surprised. 'Leaving for where?'

'London. I've got a job at one of the English language schools there. We've been drifting apart for a long time now; Daniel and I am finding life in Haverfordwest claustrophobic. I feel constricted, as if I can't breathe freely.'

'And what about Ellie?' If he is shocked, his face doesn't show it.

'She is better off with you. You love her in a way I don't seem to be able to. I'll come back to see her at weekends. She'll understand.'

'You better tell her yourself.' His voice is angry now, his jaw rigid.

'Don't make this difficult for me, Daniel.'

'Why ever not? You've been mostly absent for over two years now, making Ellie my responsibility. You are not a child Yana, face up to it, you are just as responsible for Ellie as I am.'

After a while he asks, 'Is there anybody else?'

Yes, she thinks, a whole department, called State Security. A whole system calling itself 'Motherland.'

'No,' she says. 'I just need to be free.'

The irony of it.

'But why?' Katya is shouting down the line. 'Are you mad? What on earth has possessed you?'

'I am suffocating here,' Yana says,' I can't bear this place anymore. And Daniel and I are strangers now. I don't feel love here.'

'Love? How about Ellie? Don't you love her anymore?'

'She'll be better off without me, Katya. I am a bad mother. She'll be happier with Daniel.'

'What nonsense you are talking! You need your head examined! Or are you so selfish that there is no room in your heart for your own daughter?'

Yana puts the phone down on Katya. Her heart is beating wildly, and her throat is burning. The thing she would love most in the world right now is to be able to share her dilemma with Katya, the person who is the closest to her, but she can't because Katya is the dilemma. And in trying to save her, she is going to lose her.

That evening while she is putting her to bed, she tells Ellie she is going to live in London. Ellie doesn't say anything, nor does she cry but when Yana bends down to give her a good-night kiss, she clings onto her neck and won't let her go and Yana has to prize her fingers open. Daniel comes in with a new story book then. 'Leave now,' he says, 'and shut the door behind you.'

How could you? How could you leave your child who loves you? What mother does that? A rotten mother, rotten to the core. A mother who does not deserve to be loved. Ever.

She sits at the bottom of the stairs waiting for the sobs to come but her eyes are dry, and her stomach is so knotted, it makes breathing difficult.

She wishes for the ground underneath to open right now and swallow her, so she disappears forever.

Chapter Eleven

The streets of London are hot, and her days are long. She leaves her flat in Camden early every morning and takes the Northern line, then changes to the Central Line to Leytonstone. She walks for a few minutes, then turns down a narrow lane. There, a few yards from the corner is the British School of English. The school is housed up a flight of rickety stairs in an old building, which was once a leather goods workshop.

Today she is lucky and manages to find a seat on the tube. She skims through the first few pages of the *Evening Standard*, which she didn't have time to read the night before; the same news as always, high levels of unemployment, economic uncertainty after the recession, riots in Northern Ireland and picture of Prince Andrew and Sarah Ferguson after their wedding. Then she comes to 'What's on in London' and sees that Daniel has another show, this time at the Marlborough Fine Arts Gallery. She is glad he hasn't given up after the fiasco a few years ago. She misses him and Ellie terribly, her life is empty without them.

Some passengers in the carriage are sleeping, others are reading newspapers or books. The young man in the seat next to hers is pouring over a page of graphs in a thick book on Economics, oblivious to her surreptitious efforts to read over his shoulder. She catches herself; spying is becoming second nature to me, she thinks. A black woman in a colourful robe and a lime green turban sits opposite her. She flashes a shiny gold tooth in a friendly smile. 'Good morning,' the woman says and when Yana returns the greeting, the woman adds, 'It's nice to speak these words, nobody even looks at you here, let alone speak to you.' Yana enquires politely where she comes from. 'Ghana,' says the woman and moves to the seat next to Yana, which has just been vacated. 'Visiting my boy, he is studying medicine here,' she continues, and Yana can see the pride shining in her dark eyes. She thinks of Ellie, her bright eyes, her toothy smile, the dimple on her left cheek and feels she is the worst mother that ever walked this earth.

At the next stop, a dark-skinned man gets on, an accordion slung round his neck. He stands by the door and unbuttons the case then strikes the first mournful chords of a familiar tune. Yana is back in the summer camps of her childhood, and she sees herself sitting by the fire in the evenings, a young pioneer, red silk kerchief knotted round her neck, singing this very song about a mother's bitter tears as she sends her young son off to fight the Turks for the freedom of their country. The country she left in search for freedom.

The song is getting through to her, her eyes well up. The turbaned woman takes her hand. 'Don't upset yourself darling,' she says as the train shudders to a stop. She flashes her gold smile one more time and Yana can see the green peak of her turban bobbing along the platform above the heads of the crowd.

As always, Paul, the Director of Studies is there when she arrives, tidying the newspapers on the table in the common room and washing up the few cups left from the day before. *'Your Mother is Not Here to Wash up After You!'* reads a notice over the sink but some of the teachers regularly ignore it and call him 'Mother' behind his back. Yana feels sorry for him, he is a nice man and does his best to keep everyone happy, but this has only earned him the nickname 'Fusspot' alongside with 'Mother.' She likes him and would like to get to know him better, but she needs to keep a polite professional distance. Those are the instructions from the Embassy. Keep yourself to yourself, don't get close to anyone.

The Director of the school is Squadron Leader Rogers. When she was introduced to him, she thought his blind eye, covered by a black patch had been heroically acquired while defending British skies against the Germans but later it turned out that it was the result of a hunting accident.

Squadron Leader Rogers resides in a spacious office at the top of the building, as lofty as the skies he defended in the war. On the rare occasions when Yana visits his office, he is always to be found engrossed in the pages of the Telegraph.

Every Friday afternoon, Rogers descends from the heights of his office into the lower chambers, where his 'troops' reside, to dispense the little brown envelopes, which contain their weekly wages. He calls their names in alphabetical order and hands over the envelopes with a little fatherly advice about spending it wisely. He is loathed by his staff and recently there have been whispered discussions about joining the Teachers' Trade Union and getting rid of him.

She finds the atmosphere at work stifling, it is only made bearable by the students. Today Yana is sharing a class with Steve. Steve is gay and has short hair bleached blond and an impeccable sense of understated chic. He has a dry sense of humour and often makes Yana laugh and she likes him for it, so she tends to ignore his sometimes-bitchy jibes about the other teachers.

'How's that daughter of yours?' he asks at break time.

She doesn't like talking about Ellie and Steve is the only teacher she's confided in. She lies awake most nights thinking of Ellie, until sleep mercifully drugs her into oblivion for an hour or two. When light brings her to consciousness, her body feels sore as if a pack of dogs have mauled it. On Sunday she will be visiting Wales as she does most weekends. Her heart sinks at the thought.

'She is fine,' she tells Steve.

Chapter Twelve

December 1981

The woman shows her into the small room at the back where the interviews usually take place. In the six months she's been coming here, nothing in the room seems to have changed; the curtains are always half-closed, the ashtray always overflowing, the air stale with the smell of cigarettes.

The handler is a different woman today. She is tall and immaculately dressed in a black trouser suit, a crisp white blouse, a pair of patent black heels on her feet. The perfume she is wearing is subtle and expensive.

'Sit down, comrade,' she says with a friendly smile. 'I am new here, but I have been briefed about the good work you've been doing. The Danchevi's case was a real scoop, we had been trying to nail them down for years. They have been given the punishment they deserve now.'

The words float over her head like passing clouds. She knows what happened to Elka and Vancho but she cannot afford to think about it. Except at night, when they come into her dreams, always kind, always smiling and in the morning, she would wake up soaked to the bone, her pillow and her sheets drenched in sweat.

'We have a different, more unusual assignment for you this time,' the woman continues. 'There is a Polish student in your class. Take him under your wing. Soviet intelligence think he is planning an attack on the Russian Embassy, explosives they believe.'

'But as far as I know,' Yana says, 'I am working for you, not the Soviets. And I don't speak any Polish.'

'We are in this together, you should know this. And you don't need to speak Polish. You are his teacher; you take special interest in him because you are both Slavs. He is young and probably missing home and his mother. You could take care of him, look after him.'

Yana knows the boy the woman is talking about, Mikolaj, a sweet eighteen-year-old, as shy as a mouse. Not for a moment can she imagines him an incendiary.

The following day she asks Mikolaj to stay behind after the lesson. He looks surprised but stays after everybody else had left the room.

'How are you finding the course, Mikolaj?' she asks him.

'Good,' he says.

'How long are you here for?'

'Until the end of September. I have applied to study at London University but I need to bring my IELTS score to 7.5 in order to be admitted.'

He articulates his words carefully, the lilt of his Polish accent making them softer and more tuneful.

'You've got a way to go,' she tells him. 'From 6 to 7.5, a steep curve!'

He looks worried, disappointed, as if he'd expected better news.

'Don't worry,' she says, 'I am more than happy to help you, give you extra lessons after class. You don't need to pay me. I have a young lad back in Wales, he might need someone to help him too one day.'

How easy it is has become to lie.

At first, they work in the classroom, after all classes are finished. Mikolaj is studious and learns quickly. They practice conversation and he tells her about his family back home. His father is a doctor and his mother a teacher. He has a younger sister, Magdalena. She is still at school but would also like to come to London to study when she has graduated.

One afternoon, Mikolaj invites her back to the house he shares with three other students.

'You are helping so much,' he says diffidently, 'I like to give back to you. I like to cook Polish food; I think you like it.'

'Well, thank you Mikolaj, I really would like that,' she says stressing the *would.* 'Second conditional, do you remember? Used for the future, as opposed to the third conditional, which is used for the past. For example: *I would have liked to have come but I am busy.*'

Mikolaj blushes profusely and she laughs. 'Don't worry, Mikolaj, the conditional tenses are some of the most difficult grammatical structures in English. We will do more practice, don't worry!'

The house is in a leafy street in Holbourn. It is a large Victorian building on three floors, with shared facilities. Mikoaj's room is on the ground floor, overlooking a big garden, which has a couple of fruit trees, a weedy lawn and overgrown hedges. They eat in the kitchen, which is amazingly tidy and clean considering that it is being shared by four boys.

'First course,' Milkolaj says, '*Pierogi*, most common traditional Polish food. I make it with mince pork, but you can use any kind of meat. Or cheese,' he adds.

Yana bites into the flaky pastry and savours the moist, creamy filling.

'Delicious,' she says.

'Easy to make,' Mikolaj tells her, 'And you can make many and freeze them. I can teach you how to make them,' he adds.

Pierogi is followed by *bigos stew* with spicy Polish sausage and Mikoaj serves *ryz z jablukamy,* a kind of sweet rice for dessert. All delicious and very filling.

'Thank you, Mikolaj,' Yana says at the end of the meal, 'if everything else fails, you could certainly become a chef.'

'I make Polish tea now and we take it to my room because some of the others may want to use the kitchen,' he says.

The first thing Yana notices in his room is a large poster of Lech Walesa. She walks up to it and examines his face, strong features, a determined mouth under his signature handlebar moustache.

'He is my hero,' Mikolaj says, 'he fights for freedom for Poland. Freedom from the Russians. They want to occupy us. They are frightened of our freedom. They want to control us. But we will fight, we will never let them take over. Polish people love freedom. Polish people are strong. We will fight.'

The passion in his voice touches her heart while the tape recorder in her pocket vibrates gently. She likes Mikolaj, she would be proud to have a son like him, he reminds her of Tatti. And she might be sending him to the same fate, the small voice in her head says. It's not too late, she can destroy the tape. And what would happen to Katya then?

Her knees start to wobble, and she has to hold on the back of the chair to keep herself standing.

Two days later there is a knock on her classroom door. Paul opens it a fraction and beckons her out. 'Look at exercise eight on page 12,' she instructs the class and joins Paul in the corridor.

'There are two plain cloth policemen in my office,' he tells her. 'They have come to take Mickolaj away.'

'Really? Why?'

'Apparently they have information that he has been planning some sort of an attack on the Russian Embassy.'

'What rubbish,' Yana says, 'nonsense. I can't for as minute believe it!'

'Even so,' Paul looks worried. 'Ask him to come to my office when the class is over.'

Walking home that afternoon, Yana wonders about this new development. What would her handlers make of it? And if Mikolaj was really planning an attack, how did the British know about it? Counterintelligence, she thinks, they got to him before the Russians did.

At the end of the week, Paul tells her that Mikolaj has been deported. He was taken to the airport by the police and put on a direct flight to Warsaw. It is all she can do not to smile. He got away, she thinks, he got away. She feels joy, for the first time in years. And then she thinks of Daniel, Ellie and Katya and her heart sinks. She has failed the assignment and fears the consequences. Don't be paranoid, she says to herself, what happened was not your fault, it had nothing to do with you, you did what you were asked to do, outwitting British intelligence wasn't part of your brief. But reason seems incapable of conquering fear.

Chapter Thirteen

Late December 1981
Katya

The lights in the city have been switched on in preparation for the forthcoming New Year's celebrations. Sofia looks festive, some of its grey drabness hidden behind the glow of light. It's Saturday evening and the streets are teeming with shoppers, laden with bags and boxes, their coats tightly wrapped round their bodies against the cold. It hasn't snowed yet, but the air is bitter, and the wind is biting. A few lonely snowflakes swirl about half-heartedly chasing each other.

Katya has just finished her shift at the restaurant in *Gurko street* and she is slowly making her way home. Her legs are aching from having been on her feet all day, either serving customers or washing up in the kitchen at the back. The restaurant is part of a large chain but prides itself on being special for having procured an excellent chef and its reputation draws large crowds, particularly during the festive season.

Katya has been working there since she got expelled from her course at the Institute. Soon afterwards, Vlado lost his job at the school, and he is now driving a lorry for a cement factory. Between them, they manage to earn enough for their daily expenses but there is no spare cash and they promised each other not to buy presents this year but splash on a tree and some nice food for New Year's Eve.

On the way home she stops at the deli on *Oborishte* street to get some *lukanaka* for their New Year's spread. She queues for an hour and when her turn comes, she asks Bai Jelio to slice some *lukanka* for her.

'Four hundred grams, please,' she says.

'Sure,' Bai Jelio replies with a grin. 'Have you brought the *lukanaka*?'

'Ha ha, an old joke Bai Jelio, it's been going around for years!'

The lights on the tree greet her as she enters the apartment. Vlado is not back yet, and she feels the familiar stab of anxiety.

She hears the key turning in the lock and her restless heart settles. Vlado comes in, his cheeks and his nose are red with the cold, and she can feel her face glow with the pleasure of seeing him. She goes up to him and hugs him and he laughs.

'Let me take my coat off first, *dushko,*' he says, 'it's damp with the cold.'

He takes off his *galoshes* and paddles into the room in his socks. The large toe on his left foot is poking through the hole Katya has been meaning to darn for him for weeks. He wiggles his toe at her and says 'When?'

'You know I am not the domesticated type, Vlado,' she retorts, 'you've known this from the start. Maybe you should learn the art of darning yourself, I bet you would be better at it than I am.'

'Ok', he says, 'let's agree you are not so good at darning, but you are the best salad maker I know so how about it? I am starving.'

'I haven't heard from Yana since she left Wales, Valdo,' Katya says when they are the table. 'I am very worried.'

'You fell out last time you spoke, didn't you? From what I remember she put the phone down on you.'

'Yes, she was cross because I accused her of being selfish. Which I still think she is, leaving Daniel and Ellie because she found Haverford boring. I still can't believe she would do that. It's not the Yana I know. Something isn't right there, Vlado, I tell you.'

'She is probably still sulking, Katya. Let her be. She'll come around.'

But Vlado's words don't soothe her. She is worried about her sister. All she knows is that she is in London, but she has no address or telephone number for her. She wrote to Daniel asking for information and he wrote back almost immediately. Yana is OK, he said, she lives in London and visits Ellie most weekends. He didn't have an address or a telephone number for her, but he would tell her to get in touch with Katya. He would tell her Katya is worried about her.

Something must be very wrong. It's not like her sister to bear a grudge for such a long time. They have fallen out before many times, but they always made up quickly. This is different, it leaves a bad, heavy feeling in her stomach when she thinks about it.

Just as she and Vlado are about to get to bed, there is a power cut, the second this week. The flat is thrown into darkness and it takes Vlado a few minutes to locate the candles and the matches. He swears under his breath.

'We must make sure to keep them in the same place,' Katya says, 'we should be getting used to this by now.'

'It's a crap thing to get used to' Valdo says.

Chapter Fourteen

1987

'A new assignment for you,' says the woman in the small room at the back of the Embassy. She is another new hander, the third in as many years. She has greasy black hair, with a parting in the middle, showing a thick growth of white roots. She is wearing a pair of gold frame spectacles and is probably only a few years older that Yana.

'You have done good work in the last three years comrade,' the woman says. 'The Yankovi, the Georgievi and the Jeliabovi have all been punished for their heinous crimes.'

Yana wonders what happened to them all, but the thought is abstract, as if she's heard about these people but she has nothing to do with them.

'This is a very special case,' the woman continues. 'He's been in London for a long time, defected back in the sixties. Works for the BBC Foreign Service. She joined him a couple of years ago, jumped ship while on a state approved excursion. We need them followed and exposed, we believe they are working for the British.'

'How would I find them?'

'It won't be difficult. They live not far from you.'

She hands her a piece of paper with the address and a photo of the couple, Spas and Jivka Petrovi.

'They usually shop at Sainsbury's round the corner from you on Saturdays. Wait for them to come out and follow them. Engage them in conversation, get to know them. You know what to do now. We think you are getting very good at it.'

It's meant to be an encouraging complement, but it feels like a poisonous arrow piercing her heart. She is getting good at what she would have never believed to be in her nature; good at lying, pretending, manipulating, betraying, good at being heartless. It is becoming like second nature. But her heart knows better.

On Saturday, Yana hides behind a large tree outside the building by the canal where the Perovi live. They come out at eleven and head for the supermarket. She follows them there, gets a trolley and when the couple stop at the fruit counter, she stops too and stands close to them inspecting some apples as if trying to choose the most unblemished ones. The Petrovi are debating whether they should buy the red or the white grapes.

'The red ones look good to me,' Yana says in Bulgarian.

They turn to look at her, clearly startled. 'Are you Bulgarian?' Jivka asks.

'Yes, I live Just round the corner', Yana says, 'and what about you?

'Not far. Down by the canal.'

'What a coincidence!'

'Indeed,' Spas replies. 'Amazing! There aren't so many of us living in London.' He is smiling but his eyes are alert as he looks at her, taking her in.

'Yes, I know,' Yana says 'I rarely get to speak Bulgarian.' Then hesitantly, 'Are you free to meet for coffee after you finished shopping? It would be so nice to speak the language again.'

They meet at the café down the road. It is busy and noisy, but they manage to find a table in the corner.

'So how did you get here?' Spas asks her.

'I married an Englishman and went to live in Wales. It didn't work out, so I left and here I am trying to make a life for myself in London.'

'Must be hard,' Jivka says with genuine concern in her eyes. 'On your own in a foreign country. At least you speak the language well, which is more than can be said for me,' she adds with a sigh.

'I spoke the language before I came here. I teach at a school for international students now.'

'Impressive,' Jivka says. 'A Bulgarian teaching English in England. Well done!'

Spas isn't saying much. He seems to be more reserved than his pretty plump wife and Yana feels his eyes on her, probing and quizzical. It is more than reserve she thinks, this man is being cautious. It will take a while to gain his trust. Jivka will be her way in.

On parting, they exchange phone numbers, and it isn't long before Jivka calls her. They arrange to meet for coffee, then a few weeks later, for lunch at the British Museum.

'I am lonely,' Jivka tells her. 'I really miss my friends back home.'

'Have you made any friends here? What about the wives of Spas' colleagues at the BBC?'

'They are nice women, some of them tried to befriend me but to be honest, I find the English difficult to relate to. Too polite, I often wonder if it's genuine. Or standoffish, some of them are. It makes me feel inadequate and stupid. And not speaking the language well doesn't help either.'

'Why don't you join one of the classes at the school where I teach?' Yana suggests.

'What a good idea,' Jivka says, 'I'll talk to Spas about it.'

Later, Yana takes the information to the Embassy.

'Perfect!' The woman with the dyed hair says. 'It would give you more opportunities to get close to her. You are doing well, Yana,' she adds. 'We are proud of you.'

Another poisonous arrow through the heart.

Jivka is now in Steve's class and Yana often has coffee with her at break -time or after classes. One Saturday a month, when Spas is at the BBC, they also meet at the British Museum for lunch and look around the exhibits. Jivka is interested in history, and she says she values Yana's help with the language. They talk about their lives over lunch and coffee.

Jivka comes from Studena, a village not far from Sofia and her parents work on the local co-operative farm. She didn't go to University, choosing to train as a nurse in-stead. She met Spas, a journalist, through one of her friends on the course. It wasn't long before he became 'the love of her life' and she was devastated when he de-fected to Austria while working on an assignment in Czechoslovakia. Later, he settled in London and found work with the BBC and was eventually granted British citizenship.

Jivka saved money and joined a Mediterranean cruise with the help of a friend of a party member and after stop-ping off at a few ports in Italy, the ship docked in Nice, their final destination. They were taken sightseeing and were due to leave the port in the afternoon, so the passen-gers had to be back on board by midday. While having coffee with the others at a hotel on the quay, Jivka pre-tended she needed to go the Ladies and slipped out of through the deliveries entrance. She stayed in Nice with a cousin of Spas' who had left Bulgaria in the forties, until she was granted a tourist visa to Britain and eventually, she and Spas were re-united.

Spas came from a very different background. His family had been wealthy tobacco factory owners before 1944 and had everything taken away from them after the 'revolution' when private properly was appropriated by the new communist state. His father had served time at a forced labour camp, while his mother, a well-known children's writer whose books were banned in Bulgaria, was deported to work on a farm in the countryside.

'I am constantly worried about Spas' safety in London, particularly after the 'poisoned umbrella' case.' Jivka tells her Yana. You know Markov also worked for the BBC Foreign Service? The Bulgarian authorities consider it a source of anti-communist propaganda.'

Yana nods. 'Nothing stops them,' she says. 'I know all about it. My father was murdered when I was in my teens because he distributed pamphlets denouncing them. I know all about fear.'

She feels a wave of shame as she says this. Using Tatti who was above their lies, who fought for freedom from fear, using him to further her career as a spy, to gain the confidence of this innocent woman who is trusting her and whom she really likes is despicable, it is contemptible. She has never in her whole life felt more ashamed of herself. And yet, another part of her is almost proud of how clever, how inventive at this deadly game she has become.

She tells herself that only by doing what she has been told to do and doing it to the best of her abilities would she be able to protect Katya. But a part of her wonders whether being a spy is becoming an identity, something that cannot be done half-heartedly, something she is beginning to take pride in, despite the shame.

When she first started working for State Security, it had felt like a game. She remembered the first time she felt the tape recorder whirring in her pocket, the rush of excitement that came with it. She'd felt like a character in a spy novel. The guilt came later, when she was with Daniel and Ellie and the Danchevi or when she spoke with Katya.

Now that she is in London, she tells herself she can't afford to feel guilt. She is informing on her compatriots for the sake of the people she loves. But somewhere inside her, she doesn't entirely believe herself. She has become one of them. There is some fault in her that had allowed her to do it. Maybe believing as a child that she was betraying Mammy and Katya when she agreed to live with Tatti, maybe that set a pattern which made betraying others easy.

On Saturday, she takes the bus to the British Museum. Under grey skies, fine drizzle gives the streets an oily sheen. Rain settles on her coat like a damp blanket.

The café is crowded and noisy. Jivka has arrived before her and has found a table.

'Guess what, we are going away,' she tells Yana, her eyes sparkling with excitement.

'Really? Where?'

'The Maldives. Two weeks in the sun lying on a beach, can you imagine it?! Bliss!'

'Lucky you!'

'We have one problem though. The cat.'

'No problem,' Yana says, 'I'll look after her. I'll water your plants too if you would like me to.'

'Thank you, Yana, I'd do the same for you, you know that don't you?'

'Of course, that's what friends are for,' Yana says, hiding behind a smile. For this is what they have become, friends. Chatting most days at school, meeting for coffee most weeks, sharing confidences, talking about their worries. A couple of evenings ago, Yana invited Jivka to her flat and cooked a meal for her. Afterwards while they were having coffee, she showed her pictures of Ellie and she could feel herself welling as she looked at the face of her daughter, a happy smiling face, the child she had to leave behind because of the pledge she had made long before Ellie was born.

'Lovely little girl, she looks just like you, Yana,' Jivka said.

'Not so little anymore,' Yana replied, 'she'll be twelve on her next birthday. I don't know where time goes. It's nearly eight years since I came to live in London.'

'So, she was only four when you left?'

'Just over, and I know what you must be thinking, so say it. I know I am a bad mother. Not all women are cut out for motherhood you know.'

'I wish I could have had a child,' Jivka says sadly. 'But I have no idea what kind of a mother I would have made. You mustn't be hard on yourself, Yana, you did what you had to do.'

She has no idea how right she is, Yana thinks. I did do what I had to do and that has made me a bad mother. And a bad, evil friend too. She has cultivated a friendship with this lovely, innocent woman and in acting as if she is a friend, she has become one. A friend she is about to betray. She pushes the thought right down but her face burns with it.

You have a choice, the familiar voice in her head says, you could step back, pull out. But she knows this isn't the choice she is going to make.

The day after Spas and Jivka leave Yana lets herself in. She feeds the cat, a large tabby with long whiskers who greets her enthusiastically, rubbing herself on Yana's legs and purring loudly. The flat is spacious, much bigger than Yana's. It has large windows looking out on the canal and the floor is covered with colourful Persian rugs. On one of the walls is a big abstract canvas, which Yana recognizes as a copy of Kandinsky's *Composition IV,* a picture she'd come across in one of Daniel's art books and fallen in love with. In those early days of their marriage, she had wanted to learn about art so she could feel closer to him, and he had been a willing teacher, happy that she wanted to be taught.

The flat is quiet. The late afternoon light comes in through the windows and falls on the Persian rugs, making the colours even brighter and more vivid. The cat settles on her lap, still purring. A small clock on the mantelpiece measures the seconds and the minutes, its sound gentle, unobtrusive.

An hour passes and the doorbell rings. She lets the two men in paint-splashed overalls in. She watches them as they unscrew the light switches from the walls, fit some wires and screw them back on. She has seen something like that in a film. It's fascinating to be watching it happening in real life, in front of her eyes.

When Spas and Jivka return from their holiday she gives them back their keys, having made a copy for herself. She listens to their holiday stories, looks at the photographs and then gradually starts to withdraw. She has done what she had been instructed to do. Now there is nothing more to do.

About four weeks later, Jivka doesn't come to school and when she doesn't attend the following day or the day after, Yana rings their number. There is no reply. Yana tries again and a few days later, she goes to the flat. The curtains are drawn, and nobody comes to the door.

She lets herself in.

The flat is in shambles. The table and chairs in the middle of the dining room are overturned and the rugs on the polished floor are in a heap. In the bedroom, drawers' gape open spilling their insides, underwear and night-wear, scarves and tights. The bed sheets are twisted and torn in places. The light in the kitchen is on and there are two bowls on the breakfast counter coated with crusted cereal. There is no sign of the cat.

Yana lets herself out and goes straight to the Embassy. She asks to see her contact and is told the woman has left and is being replaced. They will be in touch when it is all finalized.

On her way back to her flat, a headline in the Evening Chronicle catches her eye. '**Bulgarian BBC correspondent, wife and cat missing.**' She buys the paper and reads that the police are investigating their disappearance. They believe it to be the work of the Bulgarian Secret Service. At her flat she sits on her bed for a long time, her mouth dry and her heart pounding. She fears the worst for Jivka and Spas and she knows nobody would tell her what has happened to them. She doesn't know who her next assignment will be. The embassy has given her no instructions. What will happen if they don't need her anymore? Will she be the next one? She has seen how ruthless they can be.

She should have stayed in Wales with Daniel and Ellie.

215

In coming to London to follow their orders, she has cut herself off from any possibility of help, or protection or redemption.

She is truly on her own now.

Chapter Fifteen

A year later
Summer

On her way back from work, the Northern line is packed tight, but Yana manages to push her way in before the doors close. She stands sandwiched between an old woman, her large bosom pressing against Yana's arm and a young man who is sweating profusely. The stale smell makes her queasy. It is infernally hot and stuffy in the carriage but mercifully a few people get off at the next stop and a seat by the door becomes vacant. She makes a beeline for it.

At the next stop a few more people get off and a tall fair man gets on. Yana glances at him absent-mindedly, then looks again. Mitko? It can't be. She leaves her seat and stands next to him. He is reading the underground map on the wall and hasn't noticed her. It *is* Mitko. He is the same, only his hair is shorter

She taps him on the shoulder, he turns, and his eyes widen. He takes a step back and looks at her incredulously then a tentative smile appears on his face, and he lets out a bark of laughter.

'Yana!'

Yana feels herself flushing with excitement. 'You, of all the people in London. What are you doing here?'

'Long story, how much time have you got?'

'All evening, as it happens. Where are you going?'

'Home. If you can call it that. A couch in someone's house.'

'Fancy a drink?'

'I thought you'd never ask!' They laugh at the clumsy joke and the years since they last met, and all the life that they contain disappear in a flash.

The pub on Camden High Street is full and people are spilling out on the pavement. There is a courtyard at the back, and they find two seats at a wooden table.

'I married my boss's daughter.' Mitko tells her what she already knows. 'He is high up in the ranks of the Party and I met her through a friend who knows him. A nice girl, I liked her, but I didn't love her. I had to get out, Yana, I couldn't bear it any longer.'

The things they make us do; Yana thinks. At least I married the man I loved.

'It got worse after you left,' Mitko continues. 'Remember Ahmed? We played together when you came to live with Tatti in Svishtov.'

'Wasn't he deaf?'

'That's right.'

'Muslim parents?'

'Yes. They lived in the South, growing tobacco and they'd sent him to the special school for the hard-of - hearing in Svishtov. He lived with the people next door to us, that's how I got to know him.'

Yana saw herself playing with them by the river one cold spring day, daring each other to dive in. Ahmed was first, his thin body plunging in then quickly coming up for air, his teeth chattering and his lips blue.

'Well, a couple of years ago the village where they lived was emptied. His parents and everybody else, Bulgarian Muslims who'd lived there for generations were told they had to change their names to prove they were Bulgarians or else go back to Turkey.'

'Yes, it was in the papers here too. What a crazy thing to do! But of course, we were taught to hate the Turks ever since primary school.'

'Five hundred years splattered with the blood of innocent Bulgarians, villages burnt to the ground, women raped to give birth to Muslim children. That's what was in the textbooks, wasn't it?' Mitko says and then continues:

'Many of the people in the village where Ahmed lived were of Turkish descent, but everybody was happy, and people had lived together in peace for a couple of centuries. Then that dickhead Jivkov decided that all Muslims had to take Bulgarian names to prove they were true Bulgarians. This is when the cleansing started.'

'I read that it affected the country badly,' Yana said. 'Apparently the wealthy Muslim tobacco growers took their money out of the banks and burnt it in the village squares before they went, leaving the banks empty.'

'Yes, I did hear about it,' Mitko says. 'Ahmed's parents weren't wealthy but they weren't prepared to change their names. Ahmed was told he would have to call himself Ivan and he wasn't having any of it. Neither did they want to live in Turkey where they didn't know anybody. So, they cleared their house and hid in the attic of some Bulgarian friends. But you know how it is at home Yana, particularly in small places, rumours spread, and someone tipped off the police. They went to the house and Ahmed jumped out of the attic window trying to run away. He died a few days later.'

Mitko pauses, his eyes are dark with angry tears. A picture of young Ahmed flashes in Yana's mind and a wave of grief hits her.

'They are all mad, Yana, none of it makes sense. Not that it ever did before, but we were born into it and for a long time we knew no better. I had to leave, or I too would have gone mad like them.' Mitko's voice is hard and bitter.

'That's why I too left, Mitko. When I was older, I knew there must be another way to live. I knew there was a world out there where people were free to speak, where things made sense. Where the shops had enough supplies so that people didn't need to stock up.'

'By all accounts it's getting worse.' Mitko says.

'Is everybody still carrying a string bag, in case 'they have let something out,' doesn't matter what?'

'Apparently, according to Jerry - do you remember him? We are still in touch – people buy stuff when they see it, it could be oranges one day or rubber boots another, it doesn't matter what, you buy it whether you need it or not, in case you never see it again.'

'And the queues?'

'As long as ever.'

'Do you remember how we used to queue for milk and bread? We used to take it in turns, Mammy was always on first command until Katya and I came back from school and then we would do our stints until finally we would reach the head of the queue by which time there was nothing left and then it was macaroni for supper with a little oil, if there was any in the cupboard and macaroni for breakfast too.'

'I know,' Mitko says, 'it was the same in Svishtov.'

'Do you know that when I first went to a supermarket in Cardiff I was so overwhelmed by the plenitude and variety that I cried! I stood by the biscuits counter and gazed at the rows and rows of different kinds of biscuits, and I wanted to buy them all. It took a while to remember that the shops were not going to run out of food or clothes or footwear and that I didn't have to stockpile.'

'Well, there are rumors they won't be able to hold on to power much longer,' Mitko says. 'Change is coming from the East, our brothers in the USSR are getting restless, so our own, homegrown tyrants are getting more vicious, madder than ever. I couldn't stand it anymore, I had to get out.'

'Yes, Katya told me. What happened?'

'I married Elena, and we went to Brazil for our honeymoon. Her father was loaded, as you can imagine. I walked off one morning while she was out shopping.'

Yana is shocked and then thinks, *who am I to judge*. 'But aren't you afraid they'll get you? Her father must have been enraged. He would never forgive you!'

'I moved from place to place for a couple of years. Then I came to London. I feel anonymous here.'

Yana knows better. Being with Mitko could be dangerous for him. She could lead them to him. She must warn him somehow.

'Don't underestimate them, Miko, they have tentacles everywhere. And long memories.'

They leave the pub after last orders and stroll down Camden High Street, holding hands. It feels good to be with him, walking hand–in–hand and she can sense her body longing to be touched again. The air is fresh and cool on her cheeks. The street is still full of people, some drinking on the pavement, others queuing to get into the clubs and the noise of chatter and laughter lifts Yana's mood.

I love living here, she thinks, despite everything. I love it that London is full of people from everywhere, visitors or exiles like me. I love the freedom of it. The wine, the fresh air, the bustle of Camden town and meeting Mito have made her feel light and for a moment or two, she forgets about her secret life, about the deceit and the anxiety. Then she thinks of Ellie and her belly tightens again. She is better off without me, she thinks, I am a bad mother, I carry too much mess. I don't want to pollute her too. And I must keep her and Daniel safe.

Back home, it feels strange to lie with a man who isn't Daniel. Her body seeks the familiar shape, the edges, the smell of linseed. Mitko's body is different, leaner and wiry and it smells of soap. He is an ardent lover, attentive and affectionate; making love with him has woken her to lust. She likes lying with him, she likes it a lot, but she is afraid for him. She knows she has been foolish to go to bed with him, it was loneliness that drove her to it.

Afterwards, Mitko lights a cigarette. 'I didn't think we'd make it like this, Yana, I didn't think you liked me enough.'

She strokes his shoulder. 'I do like you, Mitko. I always have.'

Mitko pulls on his cigarette and says nothing. Yana's mind is a whirlpool of anxiety. She knows that Mitko has had feelings for her ever since they were young, but she doesn't want him to think that there could be anything more than friendship. Now she has confused things between them. More than that is the worry that she might lead them to him. Meeting him by chance in London, a trusted friend from the past has been nothing short of the miraculous but now she is afraid for him and for herself. There is no way to tell him, no way to warn him that being with her could be dangerous, unless she tells him the truth and that may be even more dangerous for them both. It is best that he doesn't know. There are risks whatever she does and a part of her almost wishes she hadn't found him again.

The following day is Saturday and Yana thinks it might be safer if they got out of London, so she suggests a trip to the coast. They walk on the beach and the warm sea breeze soothes Yana's alcohol-addled, sleep-deprived head and clears her hangover.

They take a break at the beach café with cups of coffee and slices of moist fruitcake. Children are splashing in the water; sandcastles are being made and destroyed to the sound of shrieks and laughter. Life going on all around them, her life, a parallel universe.

'This is good,' Mitko says as he stretches in the sun, the luxurious stretch of a contented man. 'I am so glad we met again.'

'We must be careful, Mitko. I know a few Bulgarian people in London, and you know how it is, rumours fly. It is a small community; people know each other, and one could never be sure who is who and to whom people's allegiances are.'

Mitko is silent.

'I don't want them to catch up with you,' Yana says softly.' For all I know they may be watching me.'

'I can't go on hiding, Yana, and I think you are suffering from the old paranoia. This is a free country, remember? No one is watching anyone. At least no one is watching us. They have better things to do. We are part of the invisible masses here.'

But nobody is invisible to them, she thinks. And with a sinking feeling she wonders when her next assignment would be and who she would be instructed to spy on next.

'I need to find somewhere better to live,' Mitko says. 'At the moment I am sleeping on the sofa of one of the Poles I work with on the building site, but I can't go on much longer like this. It's hard work on the site and I am exhausted at night. I don't know what to do, I can't get references to rent a place of my own. I am illegal here.'

Yana is silent while her thoughts are racing. Should she ask him to stay with her? But no, that would be dangerous and irresponsible. What should she do?

'The lease on my flat is only for me. I have to be careful. You could come and stay with me for a day or two from time to time.'

'Thank you, Yana.' Mitko leans across the table and kisses her.

Chapter Sixteen

Autumn

Yana takes Monday off to be with Ellie on the first day of her new school. She gets to the house on Sunday evening in time for supper. Ellie and Daniel are in the kitchen, cooking together.

'Anything I can do?' Yana asks.

'Just sit yourself down, we won't be long,' Daniel said, with his back to her.

He is finding it difficult me being here, Yana thinks, he can't bear to be near me.

She goes up to Ellie and asks for a hug. Ellie half turns to her and allows herself to be hugged. Her long black hair is in a ponytail, and she is wearing a pair of jeans and a black and white striped top with the picture of a cat on it. She smells spicy and sweet.

'I'll have a walk round the garden while you two are busy. Don't want to be in your way. Call me when you are ready.'

Autumn colour has invaded the garden. The apple tree is laden with fruit and so is the pear tree near it. The asters line the border with light purple, side by side with the dark purple of the beauty berries. The Judas tree in the corner is swamped with yellow and crimson, its leaves shining in the early evening light. The virgin creeper covers the east side of the house in vibrant red. The air is cool and crisp. She catches the whiff of smoke coming from a bonfire somewhere nearby.

She was happy here. She believed that she had escaped. Now her life lies in ruins, with no future and no possibility of redemption. She has lost the people she loves and the only thing that is left for her is to make sure they are safe without her.

Guilt has built a wall between her and Ellie. She has let her down, she hasn't been the kind of mother she always thought she would be, the kind that gives all to her children, like Mammy did before Tatti died. She has failed. And when she is with Ellie, she feels so full of her own badness, it is as if there is no room for anything else in her heart.

She's failed Daniel too. In spying on his friends, she has betrayed their love. She has gone beyond love into a place where only fear rules. Fear has cancelled out love.

Daniel comes into the garden and joins her.

'I am worried about Ellie,' he says, 'she is not eating properly. I am encouraging her to cook with me, hoping that would make her more interested in food.'

Yana remembers that she stopped eating after Tatti died.

'Don't worry,' she says,' it's a phase, it'll pass.'

'She is losing weight,' he says, 'it does worry me.'

When they get back to the kitchen, she looks at Ellie more closely and yes, Daniel is right, she does look thinner.

Daniel serves the food, a mild vegetable curry and fluffy rice.

'Delicious,' she says after a forkful. 'Well done both of you.'

'It's a recipe Ellie found, didn't you sweetheart?'

'It's vegetarian,' Ellie says looking at Yana,' I am vegetarian now. I will never eat meat again. It's cruel to kill animals.'

'That's fine, *dusko*, as long as you eat enough to get all the nutrition you need.'

'I don't want to get fat either,' Ellie says. 'Melanie says it's good to skip breakfast and lunch, just eat once a day so that you can keep slim. I don't want to get fat. Fat girls get bullied at school.'

Daniel and Yana look at each other.

After supper, Ellie goes to her room to get her things ready for school and Daniel offers Yana a glass of red wine.

'I shouldn't have left,' she says after a while. 'I am too worried about Ellie. I remember that I stopped eating after Tatti died.'

'It's not as bad as all that, Yana. She missed you when you left, but then she got on with her life. It's not your fault, it's nobody's fault. It's teenage angst.'

'We didn't do much to help her deal with it, either. Both of us pre-occupied with our own angst. Both in our separate worlds, she was invisible to us.'

'Perhaps,' he says. 'I know I too have been away in my mind at times.'

There is so much more she wants to say but she can't. Her secret is a piece of sharp-edged rock, cutting her up.

'One day, perhaps we'll understand what happened to us. For now, it seems best that we live apart,' Daniel says, and she is startled by the hard certainty in his voice. She realises that a part of her had hoped he would ask her to come back even though she knew she couldn't. In her mind, she wills him to take her hand and for it all to be all right. But she knows it has never been all right and that it can never be all right. The seed of fear that grew into betrayal was planted in her from her very beginning. Love came to her, but she has lost it.

It is dark by the time the train arrives back in London. Rain is beating down on the roof of the station; she dives into the underground and when she gets off at Camden High Street, the crowds swallow her, steaming wet bodies, heads down trying to avoid the puddles that shine darkly on the pavement. A bus speeds past and raises a storm from the gutter and her shoes are filled with cold rain. She swears under her breath and squelches her way home, cold and wet and miserable.

By the time she gets to her flat, it is late, and the street is deserted. She unlocks the door and sorts through the pile of mail that has been left on the little table by the stairs, bills mostly then a handsome cream-coloured envelope with her name on it. It is a guilt-edged card, inviting her to an evening of '*Song and Dance*' at the Bulgarian Embassy. It looks innocent enough. Briefly, she considers her options, but she knows she doesn't have any. She puts the envelope in her bag and stops for a few seconds at her own front door to calm herself.

Mitko is in watching television and his face lights up when he sees her. 'I let myself in, I hope you don't mind. How did it go?' he asks.

She tells him about Ellie and how worried she is about her not eating. Mitko turns off the television and pours some wine.

'Come and sit here with me,' he says and when she does, he pulls her closer and holds her. Slowly, the warmth of him permeates her and the tension starts to drain, leaving her limp with exhaustion. She feels as if there are no bones in her body.

Later, in bed, her mind races and her thoughts are so loud she fears Mitko can hear them. *What it is they want from me this time?*

When Saturday comes, she tells Mitko that one of her students is having a party. It is a dull November day, and the smell of rotting leaves rises from the gutter. The streets are wet from the night's downpour and glisten under a metal sky heavy with more rain. She has the urge to turn back and go home but wills herself to walk on.

There is a Christmas tree outside the Embassy in Queen's Gate, decorated in the colours of the Bulgarian flag, stripes of white, green and red. She pushes the heavy door and hands her invitation to a dark-suited man.

Ornate crystal chandeliers hang from the high ceilings, giving out a bright, garish light that makes the faces of people standing with their drinks and canapés look pale, almost white. Another Christmas tree stands in the corner, hung with baubles and lights, with a pile of boxes wrapped in paper, the tri-colour of the flag under it.

Yana wanders around looking at the paintings, trying not to catch anyone's eye. She sees the dancers assembled in a smaller room, dressed in traditional folk costumes; the women's waists clipped tightly by wide silver-buckled belts, red aprons braided with green over dark pleated skirts, red roses in their hair; the men, brown *kulpatsi* on their heads matching their *poturi* and black *poiasi* wrapped round their waists, *tsurvuli* on their feet.

The music starts and the dancers file into the assembly hall. They make two lines facing each other, then join in the wild rhythm of the *rachenitsa,* their feet beating tiny steps, three to the right, then four to the left, then back again, hands whirling kerchiefs in the air in time to the music.

A tap on her shoulder and a woman, also dressed in a traditional costume, her hair gathered by a red scarf, ushers her into a room at the back of the reception hall. A brown leather sofa is piled in coats and hats and wet umbrellas are dripping in the corner. A picture of Todor Zhivkov on one wall. An ashtray overflowing on a small table. A mirror speckled with dust on the wall above the sofa. Curtains drawn. A musty smell of stale tobacco.

'Sit down,' the woman says, pointing to the chair while pushing coats to one side to make room for herself on the sofa. 'I want to tell you we are pleased with the work you are doing for the Motherland. Some of those who worked against us have been punished. But there are more, many more and some of them are here in London.'

She passes a piece of paper to Yana. 'Here are the names of a couple who have just come to London from Munich. Deserted the Motherland. They were sent as part of a trade delegation and didn't return with their group. We have their address here. We want you to follow them and find out where they go, who they meet, what they talk about. The usual, you know the form by now. Find a way to meet them. Make friends. They are new to London. They'll appreciate help and advice.'

Yana looks at the paper. She thinks about the Petrovi and wonders what happened to them. But she can't ask. She knows she has to do what she is told. This is what becoming a murderer must be like. Once you've committed the first murder you know you've sold your soul and there is no going back. There is no more to be lost.

'We also have another assignment for you,' she hears the woman say. 'Mitko Dimitrov, he is in London, and we know he is a friend of yours. We want you to report on him: where he goes, to whom he speaks. We have reason to believe that he is part of a network of traitors planning to damage the security of our state. This is of vital importance, and you are in the perfect position to do it.'

Her body freezes. This can't be happening. It isn't happening. It's a dream, a nightmare. But the woman is staring at her, her eyes are hard, and they don't leave Yana's face.

'I can't do that,' Yana says. 'We are lovers.'

The woman's eyes narrow. 'And who do you love the most? Doesn't the motherland come before all else?' Her words sound like a song Yana used to sing as a young pioneer.

'Think about it,' the woman says, 'and think about Katya and Vlado. And Ellie. Sort out your priorities but don't leave it too long.'

Back in the assembly room, some of the guests have joined with the dancers and a *horo* is winding its way out into the hall. Someone grabs her hand and pulls her in, and she joins the line trying to remember the steps.

Then she lets the music of her childhood flood her, every inch of her until there is nothing but the music and the rhythm of her body moving to it.

Chapter Seventeen

On the last day of school before the Christmas holiday, Rogers insists they should have a party for all the students. Paul is dispatched to the delicatessen for food while Yana is sent to buy paper plates, napkins, plastic forks and cups. Rogers supplies the drinks, squash and cheap warm white wine, which leaves a bitter metallic taste in her mouth. She can't wait to leave, she still has presents to get and she's arranged to have a night in with Mitko and a takeaway. He'd be at home, waiting, wondering where she is.

'Don't look so impatient to go,' Steve whispers in her ear, 'your face is a picture of frustration. It will leave a black mark in his book.'

'As if I care!' But she does, she needs the job, so she stays on until the end and makes sure Rogers sees her clearing up and tidying the room, ready for the new term.

It's dark when she leaves the school. She gets the tube to Oxford Street and battles her way through the crowds of last-minute shoppers. The bright Christmas displays in the shop windows are dazzling. She stops for a few minutes outside Selfridge's, mesmerized by the opulence of its window; a splendiferous snow scene in a magical forest, a fairy tale for adults dressed in designer clothes, snowflakes and silver stars raining on them.

There was no Christmas when she was growing up, only Father Frost. He came on New Year's Eve and gave children red-skinned apples if they promised to be good. Yana would eat hers straight away, but Katya kept hers in a drawer for months, until it shriveled. There was no money and no presents, but the red apple always made

233

her happy. Christmas is different for Ellie. When she was little, she had so many toys, one room was not enough to contain them all and Yana had to stop herself from feeling resentful and disapproving, even though she could hardly go past a toyshop without buying yet another toy for Ellie. It was Daniel who eventually said, 'That's enough.'

The Northern line is packed as usual. Yana manages to get a seat and tries to balance her purchases on her lap. One of the parcels slips and tumbles on the floor and somebody nearly steps on it, but she manages to retrieve it. She feels drained. The events of the last few months have crowded in on her and she is crushed by the weight of it all. She can't wait to get home and put her feet up.

The flat is dark. She expected Mitko to be waiting for her. He must have gone for a drink but it's not like him to forget to tell her. It must have been a spur of the moment decision. These things happen. Someone says, 'fancy a drink?' 'Just a quick one?'

She draws the blinds. The street is deserted save for a man standing at the bus stop outside her flat. There is something about him that makes her feel more anxious. His face is in shadow but as he moves slightly, it catches the streetlight, and she sees him clearly. High cheek bones, the skin dark, the nose prominent.

By midnight, there is still no Mitko. Now she is really worried about his safety. Would it have been better if she had agreed to spy on him? Would that have kept him safe? In her heart she knows the truth; no one is ever safe from their clutches.

She doesn't love Mitko, but they are refugees together, shipwrecked, far away from home, bound by fate of birth.

Had she betrayed him too, there would have been nothing left.

She loves her country, deeply and fervently. It is the ground on which she learnt to walk; her roots are in it. What kind of people ask you to choose between your country and the people you love? She remembers mad Magda's words all those years ago, after Tatti was murdered. *Don't mind them, they are crazy*. But Yana has been caught in their web of madness and there is no way out.

She paces the flat. The rain has stopped, and the pavements shine in the streetlights, washed clean of the day's dust and debris.

She manages to sleep but wakes in the night thinking she hears the front door opening. It's just the wind rattling the old window frames.

It's light outside when she hears the banging on the door. She must have fallen asleep again because it takes her a few seconds to know that she is not dreaming. A policeman and a policewoman are standing outside. The policewoman asks her when she saw Mitko last, then tells her that he is in hospital. He has been badly beaten. A man walking his dog found him early this morning. Yana's address was in his pocketbook.

They say there are a few questions they'd like to ask her, and she lets them in. When did Mitko come to the UK, does she know how long his visa is for? Does he have other Bulgarian friends in London? Did he ever feel he was being followed? How much does she know about his past life in Bulgaria? She answers their questions as best as she can, wondering all the time if The Security Services ordered the beating or whether it was Elena's father who tracked him down. She thinks the latter more likely; she thinks he got to him before they did.

After they've gone, the memory of room 44 and Comrade Stoichev's smooth, friendly voice comes to her. 'All we want you to do is take down the dates and times Daniel talks to Elka and Vancho, maybe make copies of letters. Nothing much, but you will be doing a great service to your country. We need to know who we can trust and who we can't.'

His words are like a pool of stagnant water at the bottom of a well, too dark to see but the smell is always there. She has done what they'd asked but it hasn't been enough. They want more. It will never be enough because it's not information they are after, it's her soul. And fear is the only way they know how to possess her. When she first went to Wales, she thought she'd escaped from them, but they still have her. They will always have me, she thinks. And if they want to murder Mitko, they may want to murder me too.

Chapter Eighteen

She finds it difficult to sleep and when she does drift off her dreams are full of images of battered bodies. Sometimes it's Mitko's, at other times it's Tatti and one night she saw herself in a ditch, blooded and bleeding.

The Embassy are quiet, and she knows that her career as a spy and an informant is over. She also knows that they will make her pay for refusing to spy on Mitko. They must be mad that they didn't get him, and she is an easy target for their rage. It is a matter of time before they get her and when they do, there will be no mercy.

She rings the school and tells them she is unwell and is taking a few days off. Then she writes to Daniel, a desperate little note telling him she is in trouble and could she go to Wales and stay with him and Ellie for a while. She says she will explain when she sees him.

She spends the next two days in bed with the blinds closed. She is sweating profusely, and her bedclothes are drenched. Every little sound in the building makes her flinch, she imagines footsteps where there are none. Her chest hurts with every breath she takes.

Daniel arrives in the evening of the second day and the look of shock on his face when he sees her, shocks her too. She sees herself in his eyes, her skin ashen, her hair matted, her unwashed face streaked with tears and sweat. A flash of anger catches her in the throat. She has asked to go and stay with him, not to come here, she knows the flat must be bugged.

'What on earth has happened to you, Yana,' he says. 'What's wrong?'

'Why have you come?' she asks angrily. 'I asked if I could come to you.'

'I couldn't get you on the phone, I didn't know what was happening, I was worried, I wanted to make sure you were safe.'

'We can't' talk here,' she says, 'We need to go as soon as we can. We'll talk in the car.'

She makes him a cup of tea, washes her face and throws a few clothes in a bag. It's ten o'clock by the time they leave and the roads out of London are clear. When they get to the motorway, Daniel sits back and looks at her briefly.

'Will you please tell me now what's going on?'

'A few days ago, a Bulgarian friend of mine was beaten up in the street and left for dead. I think it is likely that whoever did it was acting on orders from home. He angered someone important in the Party. I think they were teaching him a lesson or maybe they were disturbed by a passer-by so couldn't finish the job. Who knows?'

'My God! How is he now?' Daniel asks.

'Still in intensive care but they think he'll make it. He was lucky, the police said, whoever did it probably meant to kill him.'

'Why didn't you ring me straight away when it happened?'

'Because my line is probably bugged.' She is quiet for a while then speaks again.

'I never told you, but I may as well tell you now. Before I came to live with you in Wales, *Durjavna Sigurnost,* our equivalent of the *Stasi* in East Germany, recruited me to inform on Vancho and Elka. They asked me to keep a record of what they talked about with you and send them reports.'

Daniel is silent for what seems like eternity.

'And did you? Do what they asked?' He asks at last.

'Not at first. There were a couple of years after Ellie was born when I thought I had escaped. But then I started getting threatening phone calls, there was the incident with Ellie at the pedestrian crossing and Katya lost her job. So that year when Vancho and Elka came over for the exhibition, I did send a report.'

'About what?'

'About your conversations. About Vancho and Elka being pleased that you helped them bring their work out of Bulgaria. About the residency. But I don't think I told them anything they didn't already know.'

'So that explains why Vancho and Elka were banned from exhibiting in Bulgaria and sent to live miles away from their home.' Then after a pause: 'This is too much to take in, Yana. I need to think about it, we'll talk in the morning.'

They are back just as it is becoming light outside, and he lets her walk around while he unpacks the car.

'You can sleep in the spare bedroom,' he says. 'To-morrow I'll get in touch with the local police and see what they advise. And I'll tell Ellie that you are taking a holiday with us. She'll be pleased to have you back.'

'Are you still worried about her not eating?'

'She is better. Of course, they are all obsessed with being slim but Melanie has moved to another school, so her influence isn't there so much. I think she was a mixed-up kid.'

And how mixed-up Ellie must be, Yana wonders, with a mother like me. There one minute and gone the next.

She takes a cup of tea to the spare room and lies on the clean sheets, watching the dawn coming in from the window. Before she knows it, it is late morning, and the room is bathed in light.

Chapter Nineteen

She is a stranger in the house with Ellie and Daniel. They have a routine that she is not a part of, and she is not sure that Ellie welcomes her presence. Her twelve-year old daughter has become close to her Dad and independent of her. On the first morning after she got here, she offers to take her to school but Ellie laughs.

'I am not four anymore, Mum, have you not noticed? I think I can manage taking myself to school, don't you think?' she says, blue eyes flashing under the dark fringe that covers her forehead. Rubbing it in, Yana thinks, the years of growing up that she has missed.

'It's OK, Ellie,' Daniel says in her defense, 'your Mum is just trying to be helpful.'

'A bit late,' Ellie says as she picks up her school bag and shuts the door firmly behind her.

It hurts, of course it hurts. What did she expect coming back after eight years? To pick up the thread where she dropped it? To go back to the time when fear was buried underground, and love stood sentry.

But she has lived with fear for so long, it has become a part of her. It's like having two selves, she thought, one for love, one for fear. Twin souls always in conflict. And in a strange way, she feels more at home in the fear because she is used to it.

She read somewhere that fate is what you are born with, and destiny is what you make of it. Her fate was to be born in a country at odds with itself, never free from oppression for long, a country where sadness hangs like mist over the mountains, a country of beauty and sadness. She made it her destiny to search for a happier life elsewhere and in doing so, she has condemned herself to loneliness. She has become a stranger to herself.

After Ellie has left, she takes a cup of coffee to the garden. Winter has dulled the colours of autumn. The trees are bare, and their leaves lie on the damp ground, a thick moist carpet of orange and copper, deep dark reds and lighter scarlet. She sits on the bench under the apple tree, a few withered apples still hanging on its branches, the watery winter sun on her face. After a while, Daniel comes out of the studio.

'Did you manage to sleep?' he asks.

'I did. Thank you for bringing me back here.'

Daniel is silent for a while. Then he tells her that Mary is coming the day after tomorrow.

Yana is glad. She hasn't seen or spoken to Mary for a few weeks, so Mary doesn't know what happened to Mitko. It would be good to hear her calm, soothing voice. She always manages to put things into perspective.

But there is anxiety in Daniel's eyes, and she asks him how he is.

'Just tired,' he says, 'And still shocked and bewildered by what you told me last night. What made you an informer, Yana?'

She says nothing for a while.

'After Mammy died, I wanted to come back to Wales and the only way was to agree to become an informer. You had stopped writing and visiting, I thought you had given up on me. But I still wanted to live here. I didn't think through the consequences. I was angry with you but then Ellie came along, and everything changed. I thought they had forgotten me, but they hadn't. They threatened to harm Katya if I didn't do what they wanted me to do.'

'How did you keep it all to yourself? How did you manage it?' She could hear the anger in his voice.

'I learnt not to think about it.'

'You should have told me. It was wrong not to. On so many levels.'

'What could you have done? They would have always had Katya. And they would have hurt her, Daniel. I know that. I had no doubt then and I certainly have no doubt now. Would you have made me choose between her and your friends?'

'I don't know. I have no idea. The whole thing is absurd.'

'I am still on their books, Daniel. They made me move to London so I could have more opportunities to spy on Bulgarians there.'

'What makes you think you are in danger?'

'They asked me to inform on Mitko and I refused. They don't forgive or forget.'

'I need to think about all of this,' he says. 'We need to make sure that the police are aware of the situation so they can protect you here.'

It has been another mild day and the smell of fruit going soft and pulpy under the trees wafts through one of the windows of the conservatory they had left open.

Mary is wearing a black dress, which shows off her waist and her legs and Yana tells her she looks wonderful. She feels drab and unkempt in her old jeans and scruffy white tee- shirt. She regrets not having packed some nicer clothes.

'Here's to you coming back home, honey,' Mary raises her glass. 'Daniel mentioned trouble in London, he didn't go into detail. Tell me what happened.'

'A close friend got beaten up badly, the police think it was the Bulgarian Secret Service, he angered someone high up. I didn't feel safe in London.'

Mary's eyes widen with shock. 'But honey, you haven't done anything, have you? Why would they go for you?' She looks across at Daniel. He doesn't say anything.

'It's complicated, Mary, I think I've mentioned this before, they don't like the way I left. The way they didn't have the power to stop me.'

'I am finding it really difficult to understand your country, Yana. But tell me, is there anything I can do to help?'

Something in the way she says it doesn't quite feel right. There is something missing, it's as though there is something else on Mary's mind.

Yana looks at Daniel, but he is busy pouring them drinks and seems to avoid her eyes.

The air in the conservatory is still and apart from old Marcus purring under the table, there are no other sounds. The wine is going to Yana's head, she feels woozy. She savours the feeling of warmth that is spreading through her body and making her legs weak. She looks at Daniel and Mary, two of her best–loved people, and she feels happy. She wants this moment to last for a long time. She wants it to stretch and fill her world to the edge, banishing all dark thoughts and deeds from her memory.

She catches a look on Mary's face as she glances at Daniel and sees it reflected in his eyes. Yana knows that look. She's seen it in Daniel's eyes a thousand times before.

The last apple on the tree falls with a soft thud. Marcus purrs get louder. It is as if her ears have amplifiers, she can almost hear the plants in the conservatory breathe but it is her own breath she hears. She wonders if the others can hear it too.

Daniel and Mary go on talking. They haven't heard her heart hammering or the breaths that come out in long scratchy gasps. She sits very still.

When she was a child, she used to sit like this, hoping that if she was very still, whatever was bad would go away.

'You've gone very quiet, honey, are you OK?' Mary's voice is coming from far away.

'Headache. I think I'll lie down for a while.'

Daniel looks at her, concerned but she smiles and leaves them together.

She wakes up with a start when it's dark outside. No sounds in the house, no sounds outside. She has to leave again. She can't bear the deceit. Nowhere is safe any-more.

She had imagined safety here with Daniel, but he has betrayed her. She knows, of course she does, that she too has betrayed him, but this is different. She did it protect the people she loves. But she never expected that Daniel would betray her with Mary. Of course, she has slept with Mitko but he has never been a part of their lives the way Mary has. She's had a sense that Mary liking Daniel may be more than friendship, but she never thought Mary would act on it. But how is it different to you seeking solace in Mitko's arms, the voice in her head says. You left Daniel eight years ago, what was he supposed to do? Become a monk? You were not there, and he was lonely. Lonely people seeking comfort in each other.

Love can't be turned off like a tap, she thinks. Her love for Mary has been mixed with admiration and she knows she has been looking to her for guidance and comfort. Are her suspicions going to make that difficult, even impos-sible? She needs her friendship more than ever. Anger makes her blood hot. She tries to reason with herself. Mary and Daniel have known each other for a long time, she was there before me. She comforted him when Jane died. I am just an extra. Why do I think I should come first? It seems Mary has come to his rescue again.

She wants to scream but her throat is tight. She wants to hurt them both. Love is mixed with rage, and she doesn't know what to do with her rage or with her love. She doesn't know what to do with herself. Her body is vibrating, like a bomb waiting to explode. The silence in the room makes the noises in her head louder and louder.

She gets up, opens the window. It's still dark outside, but a line of silver in the east gives a faint suggestion of light. Morning won't be long, she thinks. She needs a plan.

She gets dressed and lets herself out of the house quietly. She walks along the river as far as the Castle and watches dawn flush the sky with pink and orange. She climbs Castle Hill until she can see the town spread at her feet, shimmering in the haze of the morning light. She stands at the top until the sun rises.

When she gets back, Daniel is in the kitchen making coffee and Ellie has already gone to school. Yana tells him that she has decided to go back to London.

'Why?' he sounds shocked and incredulous.

'You and Mary. I can't bear it.'

He doesn't deny it and he doesn't make excuses.

'Aren't you afraid to go back?' he asks. 'And what about Ellie, what shall I tell her?'

'Tell her I have been called back to work. She doesn't particularly want me here anywhere, does she? You are better with her, Daniel, she is close to you. I'll be back to see her.'

The sadness in his eyes has turns to anger.

246

'Sometimes I think you are the most selfish person I know,' he says, and she can't defend herself because she knows it to be true.

She packs her bag and leaves without saying good-bye. She knows she is risking her life going back to London, but she has already lost everything; the people she loves, her integrity, her soul. Dying doesn't seem such a bad idea after all.

Chapter Twenty

A year later

There is a crowd outside the Camden Arms, and she pushes her way through to the door. The room is packed, and everybody is clustered in front of the giant TV screen, cheering and clapping at pictures of people carrying banners and climbing up a wall. Then she sees the word FREEDOM painted in red. It takes a few seconds before she realizes what she is seeing. But her mind refuses to take it in. It's not possible, nobody ever thought it possible, it can't be.

On the screen, someone has taken a sledgehammer to the Berlin wall and a chunk of concrete flies through the air. The roars of the crowds on the screen mix with those in the room and outside. Suddenly, the man standing next to her hugs her. *It's coming down, it's coming down*! He is crying on her shoulder. She recognizes Vladek, her Polish neighbour and asks when it started. 'Have I missed much?' she asks. He is holding on to her as though he might collapse. A few others join them, they make a hugging circle and words she can't understand jostle with the screams of the crowds as another piece of the wall flies through the air.

I am dreaming, she thinks, this is a dream, and I am going to wake up any minute now. But the noise in her ears and the pounding of her heart are real. So are the arms of the people around her. It's happening. The Wall is coming down. The system that brought her up in fear, the system she loathed and tried to run away from, is crumbing in front of her eyes. She wells up, tears of disbelief and relief and joy that she has survived to witness this moment.

The months since she left Daniel again have been hard. It seemed that the Embassy had forgotten all about her, which made her feel uneasy, fearful as to what they might be planning for her. She lost her job at the school after returning from Wales and took up cleaning jobs in the neighbourhood to make ends meet. She saw Mitko a few times but things between them were tense, neither of them knowing what lay ahead. She felt as if suspended in time, unable to make plans. The only certain thing in her life were her visits to see Ellie on weekends.

Now that the Wall has come down, there may be a future for her.

She rushes back home to ring Katya, they haven't spoken since Katya's last call when she put the phone down on her, but the lines are down, and she can't get through until the following evening.

'Jivkov has been deposed.' Katya is yelling down the line. 'He is under house arrest. You should be here Yana to see it all happening. It's amazing! The streets are full, people are camping outside the Parliament. You should see it. The communists have gone, Yana. They are out. We've got the power. Nobody can stop you coming back now. They've gone. They've gone and we will never let them come back. Never! Come back, dearest!'

It is as if the eight years of silence between them have melted away in an instant.

As she puts the phone down, it rings again and it's Daniel. He's seen the pictures too. 'What are you going to do?' he asks. 'I must go back,' she says. She wants to be part of history making itself. The years of following orders are over. The people have taken the power in their own hands.

'Ellie's is here,' Daniel says.

'I am Ok, Mum. Will I see you before you go back to Sofia?'

Yana says yes, of course, I must see you before I go. And I'll be back, have no fear, I'll be back. Nobody can stop me now. The Wall has come down.

Her exile is over. But she still can't believe it. Joyful energy fills her body, and she jumps up and down with it, unable to contain it.

She phones Mitko and asks him over. They open the bottle of *rakia* she'd been saving and toast each other. They toast their survival. Two Bulgarian men have been arrested and charged with Mitko's attempted murder. He seems to be recovering but there is an angry scar across his right shoulder and across his forehead. He says he feels OK although Yana wonders. He cries in his sleep.

'When will you go?' he asks.

'As soon as I've seen Ellie. But don't wait for me, I am not sure yet how long I'll stay in Wales. It all depends on how Ellie is. And of course, how long Daniel will let me stay.'

She hasn't told anyone about Daniel and Mary. Events outside have overtaken her world. She feels part of history even though she isn't there yet. She is envious of people back home, they are in the front line, the breakers and the makers. By comparison, she is removed from it and yet in her heart she is joined with them. She needs to be there.

That night in bed, she and Mitko hold each other. The excitement of what they've seen has swallowed desire, so they talk. They talk of the future, of what it might hold for them, and they acknowledge that their friendship will probably never turn into romantic love but might be stronger because of it.

As Yana drifts into sleep, she pictures *Vitosha*, the mountain of her childhood, waiting for her, constant and immovable. Waiting to welcome her home.

Part Three

Chapter One

1990

At the airport, the official looks at her passport, then at her and smiles. 'Welcome back,' he says, 'and have a pleasant stay.'

Never before had a passport official smiled at her. She is unsettled by it.

She pushes the trolley past customs and through the green light. She walks slowly and steadily, resisting the urge to run. Her heart is beating so fast she has to take big breaths to calm it down.

She waits by the barrier but there is no sight of Katya and Vlado. Tearful embraces and welcoming cries of delight are all around her. She is back home but she feels a stranger. What to do? She has no *leva*. Can she change sterling at the airport to pay for a taxi? How long should she wait? Perhaps they have been delayed by traffic? But it's not like Katya. She would have been here at least an hour earlier than she needed to be. She is that kind of a person, that kind of a sister. Something must have happened, there can be no other explanation.

She sees Vlado's head in the crowd, and he waves her over.

'Where's Katya?' Yana asks after a quick embrace.

'Waiting in the car. She broke her leg a few days ago so they put her in plaster.'

'Oh, poor Katya.'

'She is OK, she's loving all the attention.'

Relief wells up and she wants to hug him again but remembers how reserved he is.

Vlado hasn't changed much. A few wrinkles here and there and a few white hairs but still the same, funny and kind. She is so happy to see him, she finds it hard to contain herself. Fourteen years of waiting and hoping, so much pent up missing, a volcano waiting to erupt.

In the car, the years and the hurts and grievances melt away. After the first embrace, Yana and Katya look at each other, quietly and intently, then yell so loudly that Vlado lets go of the wheel for a second and puts his hands on his ears, laughing. Yana and Katya are laughing and crying at the same time, and it is as if they are small again and had just come upon a hidden treasure.

Katya is a little plumper but still the same. Her black hair is streaked with silver, which makes her look even more beautiful.

'What happened?' Yana points to Katya's plastered leg.

'I fell running down the steps outside *Sudebna Palata*, it's been a mad few week, rushing everywhere, so much going on.'

'But what were you doing at *Sudebna Palata*?'

'I didn't want to say on the phone, I've been saving it until I saw you. Vlado and I are getting married, and I needed to pick up some documents to apply for the license.

'How wonderful, Sis, I am so happy for you! Will you have a wedding, a proper wedding?'

'A very small one, but yes, of course. There will be a celebration.'

'And so there should be! I am so looking forward to it. Hopefully Ellie would be able to come by then too, she'd love to be part of it.'

'We'll time it so she can, Sis, of course. It would be great to have her with us.'

The mountain, with its snow-capped peaks is sharp against a translucent sky. A tram is moving alongside the car, curving round the bend. Its sides are plastered with adverts for Coca-Cola, and the Marlborough man on his horse is looking at her from under the brim of his cowboy hat. Advertising used to be banned as a virulent capitalist ploy aimed at brainwashing the poor people of the West, making them want what they didn't have and didn't need. Buildings and trams used to be covered with slogans proclaiming eternal friendship with the USSR or Cuba or China or the might of the Communist Party or the Proletariat.

'Welcome to capitalism, Bulgarian style,' Katya says. A black shiny Mercedes, its windows darkened whizzes past them doing at least double the speed limit.

'It didn't take the party faithful long to change sides,' Katya says. 'They got the hang of capitalism very quickly. It's amazing how fast owning private property became a virtue, not a capitalist vice!'

'The *mutri* are becoming the new rulers,' Vlado adds and seeing Yana's puzzled face, Katya explains the term. For years the old communists had been stashing away funds in foreign banks and were now buying up the petrol stations, the factories and anything else they can lay their hands on that could make them profit.

'It's the mafia,' Katya continues, 'our home-grown version of it. Corruption is not hidden anymore. It's everywhere now. You can't get anything done unless you pay through the nose for it.'

'So, you never really got rid of them,' Yana says. The hope she felt at the airport is fading rapidly. 'You must be so disappointed, all of you people that marched in the streets and camped outside Parliament to get rid of them.'

'No, Yana, they are still here. They've just re-grouped. It was a palace coup, not a revolution.' There is bitterness and resignation in Katya's voice. Yana remembers the euphoria of the year before and it is hard to believe that it had all came to nothing. The hardship that Katya and Vlado and the whole country lived through in the last year: no money to pay the teachers and the doctors, no one wanting art when there was no bread in the shops. Vlado and Katya selling vegetables in the market to survive and Katya selling Mammy's piano to feed them.

Vlado decides to take the route past *Narodnoto Subranie* where a few of the tents remain. In the evenings, he says, people still gather there to sing and dance. As they drive past, Yana can see the make-shift stage, a couple of speakers standing on each side, the cables trailing on to the pavement.

What would Mammy have made of this, she wonders. She would have been out there on the streets, camping and protesting. After Tatti died, she hated the regime with a passion that grew with each passing year. And she would have been devastated now that the hope of liberation has vanished as if it had been nothing but a dream.

At the traffic lights, an old woman selling newspapers comes up to the car but by the time Katya finds some change, the lights have changed and Vlado drives on. Something about the woman's lined face and carefully pressed pleated skirt reminds Yana of Mammy and she wells up. At least Mammy never had to do this, selling newspapers to passing cars to make a living.

256

'Guess what, Sis,' Katya says in a voice high with excitement, 'the biggest news here is that the government have given people access to the classified files *Durjavna Sigurnost* kept on most of us.'

Yana's blood runs cold.

So now the tables have been turned. Katya is free but she, Yana will be forever bound by her past. She will have to account for her deeds. She will be judged and found guilty, and nobody will care why she did it. She will be found guilty of trading the lives of others to live in the West.

What a triumph it must have been for them to recruit me, the daughter of an enemy of the regime. As if taking Tatti's life hadn't been enough. Making his daughter work for them, the ultimate posthumous insult.

'I hope we can find the truth about Tatti,' Katya is saying. 'And you and me too, I know they had a file on me, my phone was bugged for sure.'

There is no way out of this now.

'You've gone terribly pale, Sis, are you OK?'

Yana nods. 'It's the shock of it,' she says. 'The shock of it all.'

The tenants in Mammy's flat had left and Katya has filled it with flowers. Long-stemmed chrysanthemums, their golden heads erect, earth colours clashing with the cherry red of the azaleas, cheap at *Jenskia Pazar* at this time of the year, Karty said.

After Katya and Vlado leave, Yana walks around, touching the familiar furniture and opening empty drawers. She feels as if she is suspended in space. Mammy smiles from the photograph on the wall above the dining table and Yana runs her finger along the smooth and shiny glass. But the touch fails to bring comfort. The magnitude of what she has done hits her again. She stands very still, waiting for the pain to subside.

In the kitchen, Katya has filled a large earthenware bowl with fresh walnuts, the shells still green from the discarded husks. Yana cracks one open and scoops out its milky kernel, then peels off the thin brown skin and puts the kernel in her mouth. It tastes sweet and bitter.

She sits in the large, winged armchair by the window, Mammy's seat, and closes her eyes. Nothing will bring her back. Like a river, life has flowed on, and left Mammy framed on the wall, smiling from behind the glass, a benign smile like a faint echo, an illusion of life. She has gone. Perhaps being away had delayed this moment of realisation.

Perhaps I only thought you were *dead and now I know you are*.

She knows now why she waited almost a year after the Wall came down to return. She has been delaying this moment when she would have to know that she will never see Mammy again. That she will never feel the warmth of her again or smell her scent. For fourteen years the reality of Mammy's death has been frozen in her mind and with it the reality of what she agreed to do after Mammy had died. Now, sitting in her chair, it comes to her with an inescapable clarity.

She feels hollow inside.

It grows dark outside. A bright moon has polished the roof of the building across the street with silver, and it gleams in the darkness, burnished with light. The mountain rises darkly in the moon shadow but tonight Yana finds no solace in it.

In the night, there is a storm, and the rattling windows wake her. She lies still for a while, trying to get back to sleep, then is woken up again by a crash somewhere close by. She pads barefoot to the kitchen and puts on the light. Everything is as she left it. She unlocks the door to the balcony and the wind drives spikes of rain in her eyes. It is difficult to see but she makes out Mammy's big clay planter which has been smashed, the soil laying scattered on the balcony, plants crushed by the weight of the pot.

She can't go back to sleep. Mammy's pot breaking feels like a sign; it is as if Mammy is angry with her because she has destroyed everything that was solid and beautiful in her life.

Chapter Two

Yana pushes the wheelchair and people make way for Katya's plastered leg. A large crowd has gathered in front of the Mausoleum, cheering and jostling with each other to get a better view. Yana stands on tiptoe, but they are too far back in the crowd to see what's going on.

'They brought it down in the middle of the night,' says the young man next to her, 'blew it up with explosives. Now they are clearing the rubble.'

Yana maneuvers the wheelchair and reluctantly people let them through until they are in full view of a couple of diggers piling blocks of cement and stone into lorries. Clouds of dust envelop them and its bitter dry taste fills Yana's mouth.

'We need masks,' Katya says. She takes a handkerchief out of her handbag and covers her mouth with it.

Yana spits out the dust then fumbles in her handbag and finds one for herself. A few people are by the lorries gathering bits of stone into shopping bags. 'You never know what they may fetch one day,' the man next to her says, 'I already have some from the Berlin wall. They may be worth lots of money in ten- or twenty-years' time.'

It seems strange to Yana that people should collect the relics of oppression as an investment.

'It's all about making money now,' Katya says. 'My neighbours did the same, went all the way to Berlin, just to pick up a few stones, never saw anything of the city.'

'What happened to the body? The Father of Our Glorious Revolution?' Yana asks.

'Buried somewhere in an unmarked grave, nobody knows where,' the man next to her says. 'They don't want the old guard making his grave a shrine for pilgrimage.'

Yana recalls seeing his body laid out in the dark chamber of the Mausoleum, the face like yellow wax and the dark moustache, enough to frighten anybody, let alone a small child. She is glad this edifice to absurdity has finally been demolished.

'It is going to be discothèque apparently', Katya says, 'How's that for a mad idea? Dancing on the grave of the dead.'

On their way home, they pass an old man rummaging in a rubbish bin. Years ago, the *tsigani* would look for discarded bottles and newspaper and metal for which they got paid a little money, a sort of a home-grown recycling system born out of necessity. This man is not a *tsiganin*. He wears a suit, which is old and worn-out but clean, with a spotless white shirt and a tie.

'Don't be shocked,' Katya says. 'This is a common sight these days. Some old people are sleeping in the streets. And these are good, decent people who have worked hard all their lives. It breaks my heart, it really does.' Yana can hear the tears in her voice.

'Shall we make *banitza?*' Yana says when they get back to the flat. 'The way Mammy used to make it, with spinach?'

'We'd be lucky to find spinach or feta, I haven't been able to get any for weeks,' Katya says. 'But yes, why don't we go on a shopping expedition? You can see for yourself what it's like.'

By the time they go out, it's four o'clock and it's getting dark. The grocery shop on *Oborishte* street is dimly lit and the shelves are empty, save for a packet of biscuits and a tin of dog food. But there is a queue outside the greengrocers', and they line up with the others.

'Leeks,' the old woman in front of them says. 'They've got leeks.'

'Do you know if they have any spinach?' Katya asks her.

'No idea, *dushko*, better wait and see.'

'Might as well,' Yana says, 'we could make *banitza* with leeks if we can't get spinach.'

'I suppose so, but it won't be the same, would it? But we have to get cheese and yogurt, *banitza* is not *banitza* without cheese.'

So, they decide to go further afield to the big new supermarket near the station. There is no queue there and when they get to the counter, it becomes clear why. They do have cheese but at triple the normal price.

'I don't think I can afford this price, Yana. This shop is not for people like us, it's obviously for the *mutri*.'

And so they go back home empty handed apart from half a dozen of leeks.

'No matter,' Yana says, 'I like leek soup, Mammy used to make a nice one, do you remember?'

It was never *that* bad during communism. She feels like a traveler who has come home to find her house ransacked.

They sit down with their bowls of steaming leek soup and chunks of crusty white bread. Finding the bread at the local baker's has been the highlight of their shopping expedition.

'I still don't get it, Sis, why you cut contact with me for the last eight years. I know that you got upset when I said you were being selfish, leaving Ellie and Daniel but to disappear the way you did, it still baffles me.'

Versed in lying, Yana replies,

'It was too hard to talk to you about my life then, Katya because I knew you were judging me. And I did feel ashamed of leaving Ellie, but I was so unhappy. Things between Daniel and me were very difficult at the time, he was depressed and withdrawn or raging in his studio and slashing his paintings. It was scary.'

'I would have understood if you had talked to me. I felt I had lost you forever and it hurt. It hurt terribly, I felt as if I had been orphaned all over again.'

What would you have said, Sis, if I had told you the truth?

She is glad that Katya didn't have to bear the burden of her dilemma. But would she be able to keep her from the truth now that the files have been opened? And would she understand, or would she hate her forever for betraying the values they grew up with?

'I am so very sorry, Katya, I hope you can forgive me.'

'You are here now, that's all that matters.'

'Yes, here I am again but I have no idea what to do. I have been out of my life here for so long, I have lost the thread.'

'English teachers are in great demand,' Katya assures her, 'you'll never be short of work and the pay is good. Business English, everybody is looking for Business English. Ellie can study at the Conservatoire when she finishes school, it would be wonderful to have you both living here.'

Yana wonders what Ellie would make of it all. A child who is growing up in a land of plenty, what would it be like for her to see her mother's country, stripped bare, wasted like an old beggar?

She wishes, for the thousandth time that Mammy were here. She feels woefully inadequate because she doesn't know how to be a mother.

And not just being a mother, she doesn't know how to be true anymore.

She would like Ellie to come and live here but doubts that Ellie would want that. Learning the language wouldn't be a problem. She can already speak some and although she is not fluent, she understands almost everything and with practice her writing will improve too. But would she want to leave her father and her friends in Wales? Perhaps Yana can give her the choice.

Mammy and Tatti had told her that she could choose, but they had already made the decision for her. She still resents them for it. She wonders if what they did has made her what she is now, forever split between two places, never certain where she belongs, never feeling at home in either.

She does not want this for her daughter. Perhaps she should go back to Wales for Ellie's sake; maybe the break with Daniel can be mended?

'More soup, Sis?' Katya asks.

'Yes, please and more of this delicious bread.'

They are friends again but for how long?

Chapter Three

Katya, December

Waiting at the airport for Ellie and Daniel, Katya can hardly contain her excitement. She hasn't seen her niece since Ellie was born and having her here with Yana, she feels her family is now complete.

Yana and Vlado are chatting while she keeps an eye on the passengers coming through Arrivals, pushing trolleys heaped with luggage, their eyes on the people behind the barrier, looking for a smile and a welcoming wave.

'There they are, Yana,' she shouts at her sister, 'coming through now.'

She hadn't expected Ellie to be so tall. She's taken after Mammy, she thinks, the same long legs, the same smile that is now beaming at her.

'Welcome to Sofia, my darling Ellie,' she says, 'welcome to the place of your birth.'

Ellie comes into her arms, and she hugs her closely, while Yana stands by, waiting her turn. Daniel is standing next to her, smiling.

'It's good to see you again, Yana,' he says.

'Thanks for bringing Ellie over, I am grateful to you.'

'No need, I wanted to come over anyway to see Elka and Vancho. They have an exhibition at the new Modern Arts Centre.'

Katya joins the conversation while Valdo is paying at the parking kiosk.

'It's a great show,' she says, 'I went to see it the other day. Bold and challenging. I wanted Yana to come with me but for some reason she decided not to.'

Yana and Daniel exchange a look and she wonders what's behind it. She wonders how much of their life she knows nothing about.

Traffic is heavy and it takes them a while to get to the flat. Yana has already laid the table before they left and is now busing herself, bringing in the food from the kitchen.

'Oh, *banitsza,*' Ellie exclaims, 'yum, yum.'

'Katya went to great length to find the ingredients just for you, Ellie. I told her how much you like it.'

'I love it too, Daniel says,' and the roast peppers. We've missed Bulgarian food, haven't we, Ellie?'

'Mmm,' Ellie says her mouth full of food, 'missed it lots.'

'A drop of our fire water, Daniel?' Vlado offers. 'The cure for all ailments.'

Daniel laughs. 'Sure, why not? There is a bottle somewhere in the house in Wales too, but it always tastes better here.'

'What was it like being with your sister after all these years Katya?' Vlado asks Katya back home.

'Strange at first, then it was as if we saw each other only yesterday.'

'She seems to be settling back here, what do you think?'

'Yes, I think she is trying to, but it must be hard after so many years. And so much has changed here since she left. But she shouldn't be without work. If she decides to teach English, there is plenty of demand as you know.'

Although Katya knows Vlado is glad that she has got her sister back, there is an edge to his voice when he talks about her. She knows that secretly he resents Yana for leaving and for the trouble that caused them. Katya was truthful when she told him that seeing Yana again, it was as if they had never parted but it is also true that her sister has changed. She is moodier that she remembers her and seems to be constantly on edge. And seeing her with Ellie, she has become aware of the tension between them, a nervousness in the air when they are together. It's not surprising, Katya thinks, considering they have lived apart for so long. It must be difficult to get used to being with each other again. She is also aware of something unspoken between Yana and Daniel. She remembers how much in love they had seemed when they were first married; to see them so distant from each other now makes her sad.

I too must get used to having Yana around, she thinks. It will take time before things between us feel as they used to.

Chapter Four

Katya and Vlado marry the week before Christmas. It is a small affair, just a few close friends and afterwards they go for a meal to the Russian Club. Katya, wearing Mammy's wedding dress looks radiant and Vlado can't take his eyes off her. Yana loves seeing her sister so happy and having her daughter here too: all of them a family.

It brings memories of her own wedding. Ellie had been a few weeks old and had slept through most of it. Yana had never felt such happiness before. Now it feels as if the day belonged to someone else.

Today she must stay present to her sister's happiness.

The Club is busy and there is a party of ten people at the table next to theirs. Their chatter subsides when Katya, Vlado and the rest of them walk in. All eyes are on them. 'Bulgarians love weddings,' Yana whispers to Ellie as they take their seats. The orchestra at the far end of the room takes up a familiar melody, the theme tune of the Godfather. A couple get up from their seats and make their way to the dance floor.

The wedding table, covered in starched white cloth has been decorated with blood-red berries and a small Christmas tree takes centre stage. The waiters bring the *rakia* and the *shopska salads* and Jordan, Vlado's best man makes the first toast.

'To Katya and Vlado, may you live long and happy lives and may your troubles stay behind you.' He presents them with his and his wife's Zhenia's wedding gift: a large silver bowl, the edge decorated with tiny angels.

271

'To keep you safe and happy,' he says, pointing to the figures, 'till the end of your days.'

Yana wells up and Ellie, who is seated next to her takes her hand.

The waiter brings a large loaf of bread and hands it to Jordan who holds the loaf over his head and invites Vlado and Katya to take each end and pull. 'Whoever breaks the biggest piece will be the boss,' Yana whispers in Ellie's ear. After much tugging, Katya ends up with the larger piece. 'Of course,' Vlado says, putting on a sad look, 'the story of our lives.'

And then the feast starts. Roast pork on silver platters, soured cabbage, roast peppers, pickled vegetables, *pitka* with *liutinitsa,* wine and honeyed cakes, the food keeps coming. Yana wonders where it all came from then remembers that the club had recently been bought by the former minister for agriculture who had been demoted after1989.

After the meal, they return to Katya and Vlado's apartment and drink champagne, a gift from Daniel. Vlado is tipsy and unusually talkative. He decides there should be more speeches, stands on a chair and proclaims his love for Katya. 'We had hard times, but we got through them together,' he says, 'and it has made us stronger. We are stronger than ever.'

'Sister-in-law,' he says and there is a hardness in his voice, which Yana has never heard before. 'I am so glad you and my niece are here with us to share in our happiness. Yana, you left us for a better life, but you are here now and what could be better? Welcome back to your family.'

Yana looks at Katya, but Katya looks away.

Vlado steps down from the chair and pours himself another drink. Yana goes to the kitchen to make coffee and he follows her.

'What were you thinking?' He spits at her. 'That you would escape and there would be no repercussions? Well, there were. Katya lost her job. They watched every step we took. They threatened to send us to the labour camps.'

Yana says nothing.

There is no excuse for what she did.

And Vlado doesn't know the worst yet.

He stares at her, a glass of whisky in his hand and for a second, she thinks he is going to throw it in her face, but he gives her one last look of disgust and walks away.

Chapter Five

She wakes up to a snowstorm. The wind howls and rattles the windows and the air is thick and white with it. She goes into the kitchen to make herself a cup of coffee and Ellie comes in, rubbing the sleep off her eyes.

'Whoa, Mum, have you seen the snow?'

'Yes, *dushko*, are you excited? You don't get to wake up to snow like this in Wales, do you?'

'No, just ones, do you remember when auntie Mary came to stay and couldn't get back home because of the snow.'

Yana remembers, of course she does. That was when her career as a spy and an informer started. That abhorrent, loathsome part of her life. A part of her life that is far from over. Yesterday Katya told her that they have been allocated the date to read their dossiers and those of their parents. The date, December 29 is imprinted on her mind; the inescapable advancing and closing in, leaving her with an icy stomach.

The phone rings and Ellie rushes to answer it. It's Katya with an offer to take them both to the mountain tomorrow.

'She says the snowstorm is going to subside later on today and tomorrow is forecast to be calm and sunny.' Ellie can hardly contain her excitement and it takes Yana back to those happy days in Wales when Ellie was little, and Yana had somehow managed to push her pledge to *Durjavna Sigurnost* to the back of her mind.

It's lovely that Ellie is here now but as always Yana feels that she can't give her all of herself. Her secret life stands between them like an impenetrable wall, invisible but always there. She looks at her pretty daughter, tall and gracious like Mammy was and she tries to imagine what it would have been like if she could rewind the tape to that moment when she chose to sign her name on the dotted line of betrayal. Ellie would have been born here; would she have been able to mother her the way she was mothered by Mammy? Perhaps. And perhaps she is kidding herself, perhaps the part of her that made her sign the contract would have always been there, making her restless, dissatisfied and always searching for something else. Maybe she is not cut out to be a good mother.

On Sunday morning, the sky is spotless, and the air is transparent with light. It's early and the city is asleep. A church bell sounds faintly in the distance, but the familiar sound of trams is muffled by the white softness that has descended upon the city.

Home.

It is good to be here in the city of her childhood. And for a moment it feels as if she has never left. She stands by the window as still as a tree on a windless day. There is nothing but this snow-filled city.

Until she remembers. It won't be long now before she and Katya will be sitting side by side, reading their dossiers. Should she tell her before they go? If so, when?

But she knows she won't do it. A tiny hope lays hidden in her heart; perhaps she can avoid letting Katya see her file somehow. But how? She would need Divine intervention and she does not believe in the Divine. No one would be there to help her when she sees the horror on Katya's face.

At ten o'clock Katya comes to pick them up for the hike. 'Hurry up you two, Vlado is waiting in the car.'

They pile into the car, bundled up in coats and scarves, fur hats pulled over their ears. They drive through the frozen streets, the winter tires ploughing through the drifts.

'I've never seen so much snow,' Ellie says, 'except in films.'

'This is nothing,' Vlado tells her, 'Some years we can't open our front doors and have to dig a tunnel to get out. One-week last year, the drifts were ten meters high.'

'I wish I had been here then,' Ellie says, 'it sounds so romantic.'

Vlado laughs. 'How are your muscles? Digging a tunnel in the snow is hard work.'

Yana puts an arm around Ellie's shoulders. 'When Katya and I were children, we used to pray for the snow to come in the night so we wouldn't have to go to school. But the caretaker would be up at dawn and by the time we woke up, the snow outside the front door would have been cleared and we would have to walk to school through the drifts, spare socks in our pockets. Our feet would get soaked and our coats would be soggy with the snow.'

'And the classroom would be steaming with all the coats drying on the radiators.' Katy adds, 'and we would be running around in our socks, and it always felt like a holiday. Somehow lessons didn't feel so serious when we had no shoes on.'

'Speak for yourself,' Yana says 'I don't remember lessons ever being too serious for you.' And Katya returns the dig, laughing. 'Well, you were the family swot, big Sis.'

'I wish I could have had a sister,' Ellie sighs.

'It wasn't always fun. Your Mum could be a real bossy-boots at times.'

'Now, now girls,' Vlado says, smiling. 'Stop it. You are not at school anymore.'

The cable car lurches a couple of times, then rapidly gains height and in a few minutes, they are high up over the mountainside. It is snowing heavily, and the air is thick with it. Like lace, it covers the trees and crevices below and makes them look unreal, magical in their stillness. Higher and higher they climb, until there is nothing to see but air dense with snow.

They are quiet in the cabin. Katya has her arm through Vlado's and Ellie moves closer to Yana. 'This is wonderful, Mum,' she says.

The car judders to a stop. The weather station is nestled close by against the steep slope of the mountain. Yana can just about make out the shapes of a few brave climbers heading for the peak.

'What does *Cherni Vruh* mean?' Ellie asks.

'It's called Black Peak in English,' Vlado tells her. 'Some people think it is because of the dark colour of the rocks but it could also be that a long time ago there were pine forests here and people burnt them down to make pastures.'

'I thought there might have been a more mysterious reason than that.' Ellie says.

'You've been reading too many Gothic novels, *dushko,*' Yana says, and Ellie gives her a black look. 'Speak for yourself,' she says and turns her back on her mother. She takes everything I say as a rejection, Yana thinks sadly.

The restaurant at the station is more of a canteen, with trays of steaming food on the counter. There is a huge pot bubbling on a hot plate, giving out a spicy smell.

'Pork belly soup,' Yana tells Ellie. 'Good food for a hangover. When I was a student, we used to have it at the cafeteria round the corner from the University on our way to lectures, after a night of poker and wine.'

'You played poker?' Ellie looks incredulous.

'Your Mum was a whizz kid with the cards,' Katya says. 'Her winnings paid for a quite a few meals out and she even bought me a pair of new boots once after a big win.'

There is a small queue for food and when her turn comes, Ellie asks for a bowl of the belly soup.

'Sprinkle some dried chillies on the top and add a splash of vinegar, that's the only way to eat pork belly soup.' Yana tells her. Ellie helps herself to the coarse white bread and takes her bowl to one of the tables. Yana, Katya and Vlado join her.

'What do you think?' Vlado asks Ellie.

'Delicious, like nothing I have ever tasted before,' she replies. 'Can we make it at home?'

'Sure, anything you like. I am so happy to have you here,' Katya says.

And then it's Christmas time and the day for the reading of the files approaches fast. On Christmas Eve day Yana wakes up early and lies in bed still like a mummy, trying to contain the fear that has invaded every fibre of her body. If it isn't for Ellie, she would stay in bed all day, hiding, but Ellie is up, singing quietly to herself as she puts the last of the decoration on the Christmas tree.

At ten o'clock Katya comes in with the turkey she has insisted on getting for Ellie to make her feel at home. The sight of the large limp bird makes Yana feel sick.

'Why such a big turkey?' she asks, 'it's only the four of us tomorrow. Have you forgotten that Daniel will be spending the day with the Danchevi?'

'I thought I'd ask them all to come here' Katya says.

'No, please don't, I think I might have a tummy bug or something, I don't know how I would feel tomorrow.'

Katya looks at her carefully.

'You do look peaky, are you really unwell?'

'I am sure it's nothing serious, Sis, just a bit of an upset stomach.'

The thought of having Elka and Vancho here threatens to make her vomit. She has not seen them since that time in Wales when the tape recorder whirred in her pocket. She knows that they too would have access to their files and if they haven't done so already, they will soon find out who betrayed them

If she could dig a hole in the ground and bury herself there, she would do it.

But she gets on with the preparations and when Daniel arrives, the table is laden with food, and they are ready to open the champagne that he gave them a couple of days ago to keep chilled in the fridge.

Daniel looks good. His face is rested and a strand of his hair, which is mostly white now, still curls on his forehead. He used to be the love of her life and he still is. There has never been anyone to replace him.

He greets her with a kiss on the cheek and for a moment desire takes over the fear. But he keeps his eyes away from hers. He is the only one here who knows the truth and it is clear that he finds it difficult to face her. He is here because of Ellie.

She has lost him, and she is about to lose Katya too.

Chapter Six

On the way to the archives office, they pass room 44 and Yana wonders what happened to the people she saw there and to Comrade Stoichev, the psychology graduate. What happened to all these people, communist stooges who had spied on their every move, opened their letters, installed 'ears' in walls? She could have never imagined that she would become one of them. She should say to Katya that she is not feeling very well, ask to postpone the visit for another day, but she knows that she will have to go there eventually and that she can't prevent Katya from seeing her file.

'They own the new shopping malls now,' Katya says, 'all these people who worked here. They own the restaurants and cafes on Vitosha Street. And the banks and the concert halls. The new hotels on the coast, and the ski lifts in Pamporovo and Bansko. What used to be the property of the Peoples' State is now the property of those who used to rule the State.'

The archives office is in a cavernous hall, its windows shuttered against the sunlight outside. Yana feels the dust particles of old paper creeping into her skin and her hair. A stout woman, her face heavily made up, red lipstick smudged in the corners of her mouth, hands them the files and invites them to sit at a trestle table. There are four people already there, an old man at one end, his walking stick propped against his chair, a man and a woman sitting close to each other, and a haggard-looking woman at the other end.

'*Citizen 7545, parents of bourgeois origin.*' Yana reads. '*Maternal uncle married to an ex-Gestapo medical officer now residing in Munich. Father, dissident writer and agitator of anti-communist propaganda (refer to operation code name Zvunets, 1958). Family relocated to the countryside. Grandfather- anti- communist views. Continue to monitor the family.*

Sofia University, English Philology. Information on beliefs and activities, Citizen 1243. Anti-communist views. Left for the West 1974. Married Daniel Greenberg, 1976, suspected British secret agent. Resides in Wales. One child, a daughter. Subject recruited to pass on information about Greenberg and underground painter friends V. and E. Danchevi. Information provided insufficient and infrequent. Action: pursue subject, extract more information, assign further cases, operation code name Jelio.'

The lines burn her.

Katya has finished reading her file, which she tells Yana, contains nothing she didn't think they'd have. Summaries of Yana's letters, bits of transcribed conversations and some information about Vlado's background. Tatti and the reference to 'operation codename Zvunets' is also there.

I can give my file back to the woman with the red lipstick, Yana thinks, and Katya would never know about the spying. She hesitates, the file still in her hands. She can feel a vein in her neck pulsating, marking time. Seconds trickle away.

'There is more in mine,' she says as she passes the file to Katya and watches her read it. She watches her sister's face drain of colour.

Katya looks up. Paper rustles as people turn the pages of their dossiers. Somebody coughs. Pale light sneaks in through a slat in the shutters and makes a line of dusty yellow on the floor. A door somewhere bangs shut. A woman's high heels click rhythmically as she walks across the wooden floor.

Katya walks out and Yana follows her.

'Why, when you managed to get out anyway?' Katya whispers.

'I did it for you.'

'For me? Why?'

'I agreed to become an informer so they would let me leave. But then Daniel proposed, and Ellie was born, I thought I had escaped. But when you lost your job, I knew they would do worse.'

'I would have rather suffered the consequences than have you do what you did. Do not make me part of it now.'

There are no words that Yana can say. The shock has silenced Katya too.

The sun goes behind a cloud.

After a while Katya says sadly, 'That's why the Danchevi disappeared from Sofia, and nobody knew where they were. No wonder you couldn't stay with Daniel.' Her eyes narrow. 'I can't believe it. I feel I don't know you at all. How could you do it? Become one of them? After they murdered Tatti? You defamed our parents, what they stood for. With the dossiers open now, everybody will know what you did.'

Yana looks away. 'I think that's why they chose me, the ultimate insult to Tatti's memory.'

'Don't expect sympathy from me. Or the Danchevi for that matter.'

'There were others too, after they made me move to London.'

'Made you?'

'They threatened there would be consequences if I didn't. I didn't know what they might do.'

It is Katya's turn to look away.

'It's the truth and I have to live with it.' Yana says.

'And I have to live with it too. I hate you for it.' Katya's face is as tight as a fist ready to punch.

'I am going back to find Tatti's file. You don't have the right to see it now.'

But Tatti's file is missing.

'Happens all the time,' the red lipsticked woman says. 'People come looking for information, but the files have either been destroyed or pages have gone.

Operation code name *Zvunets 1958*. The reference had been in Yana's file. 1958 was the year Tatti was murdered. The man convicted of his murder had pleaded guilty on the grounds of crime *passionel*, stating that he'd believed his wife and Tatti were having a sexual relationship. He served eleven years for the murder. Katya heard from a friend whose father worked in the courts that his family had acquired a new house and a car while he was in prison. Later when he was released, he and his family disappeared.

The past hovers like a ghost among the files. Memories flood in. Mad Magda on the stairs, telling her about Tatti's murder. The death certificate confirming Magda's account. Cause of death, brain hemorrhage due to a ruptured cranium. Yana hates these memories. She wants to be rid of them. Another life, not hers.

A void opens up inside her. She is not here; she does not exist. She is a missing person who has been impersonating herself all these years, pretending to be Yana.

'Let's get out of here,' she says. 'I need fresh air.'

Katya's face softens. She takes the files back to the woman and leads Yana outside as if she is blind.

'You look dreadful. Let's walk to the park and sit in the sun for a while.'

Sitting on the bench with Katya and watching people strolling around and children playing, Yana feels a little better.

'Do you sometimes feel as if you don't know who you really are?' she asks Katya.

'No, I don't think so,' Katya replies after a while, 'but you have always been the philosopher in the family. You are shocked and overtired,' she continues. 'Are you going to tell me more about the spying?'

'I will but not now,' Yana says 'It's too painful. But I will, I promise.'

After a while she tells Katya about Mitko.

'I am not surprised,' Katya says. 'He was nuts to do what he did. Leaving Romanov's daughter in Brazil. Did he think he'd be safe in London?'

Yana tells her about Mary too. 'I was deceived by the two people who were the closest to me,' she says.

'Look who's talking about deceit! I think you are feeling sorry for yourself, Yana. Daniel and you were deceiving each other.'

'I think he's forgiven me, but I don't know if I can forgive him. Or Mary.'

'You left him,' Katya says. 'After everything you've done, it is not your place to forgive anyone!'

They sit for a while in the pale wintery sunshine, wrapped in their own thoughts.

'You are my sister,' Katya says after a while, 'I'll have to come to terms with what you have done.'

But will I ever come to terms with what I have done, Yana thinks. How can I ever come to terms with the fact that I have ruined my life and the life of others?

285

Chapter Seven

Katya, Early January

A new model is posing in the studio today, a young, small- breasted girl with the hips of a boy. Katya has made a few marks on the paper in front of her, but her mind is not on the drawing. Her sister's revelations have shaken her to the core.

Yana, her big sister, her mentor and protector, the person she has most looked up to after Mammy, has crashed; the image she had of her smashed to smithereens and she feels heavy with the grief of it.

The worst of it is she hasn't told Vlado because she is afraid of what he would say. And yet, she knows she must tell him. He is her husband now; they are not meant to keep secrets from each other. She wonders what it must have been like for Yana to keep her terrible secret all those years, year in year out living a double life, the world around her never knowing who she really is.

She feels sad for Ellie and Daniel too, she knows how much in love he was with Yana, what must it have been like for him to find out that she had been spying on his friends. And yet he seems to have forgiven her, can she, Katya forgive her sister? And how can she expect Vlado to forgive her if she herself is still angry with her?

On her way home, she buys two large slices of *garash torte,* Vlado's favourite dessert. In preparation for the conversation, she must have with him later on tonight.

'Are you celebrating a special occasion?' the girl behind the counter asks.

'Sort of,' Katya tells her, 'It's for my husband, he has been a bit angry with me lately.'

'Well, I am sure the *torte* will help. You know the saying, don't you? The way to a man's heart is through his stomach. I don't think any man can resist a slice of our *garash torte.*'

It will take more than a slice of *torte* to sweeten Vlado after the bitter truth she is about to share with him.

He is not home when she gets in and she starts to make the salad. She lays the table and warms up the stew they cooked last night.

Soon after he comes in, his cheeks glowing with the cold.

'It's lovely and warm here,' he says as he unwraps himself from the layers of winter. 'So good to be home. What's for dinner?'

'Sit down, my love, let's have our drink first. I have something to tell you.'

'You look serious, Katya, what is it?'

'It is very difficult, what I have to tell you.'

'Well, get on with it then, don't keep me in suspense.' She can hear the alarm in his voice.

'It's about Yana,'

'Yes? What about her?'

We went to *Durjavana Sigurnost* the other day to look at our files.'

'And?'

'And I looked at mine and there was nothing much there, except about Yana and how she had let her county down to live abroad.'

'It figures, she did leave, and it makes sense that that's what they would think. Nothing new here so what's the problem?'

'I also read Yana's file.'

288

'So?'

'I really don't know what the best way to tell you this is, Vlado.'

'Tell me whichever way you like, I just need to know what you are going on about.' He is tapping his fingers on the tabletop now.

'It turns out that she has been spying for *Durjavana Sigurnost* for the last eight years or so. Spying on Bulgarians living in London and informing on them. Also spying on the Danchevi when they were in Britain.'

There it is, she told him.

She can see his body stiffen. He turns away from her.

'Aren't you going to say something?'

After a while, he turns to her.

'What do you want me to say? What is there to say?'

'You are shocked, just as I was when I found out.'

'Stating the obvious, aren't you?'

'No need to be angry with me.'

He looks down and examines a small cut on his thumb.

'I wish they made better pliers these days so one doesn't have to cut one's fingers every time one tries to pull a nail out.'

'We need to talk about this, Valdo, no point changing the subject.'

'Talk away.'

'She is my sister. She has done bad things, but she is still my sister. The only family I have left, apart from you.'

He doesn't say anything for a while, continues to fiddle with his thumb.

'I knew telling you was going to be hard.'

'It's you I feel for, Katya. She is your sister; it must be hard for you to swallow this. What with your Tatti and everything.'

'It's hard, but I have to forgive her. She says she did it for us. She says they threatened to harm us if she didn't do as they asked.'

'I can believe that. You being kicked from the course and me losing my job, this must have been meant as a warning for her.'

'She said that, yes.'

'Why else would she do it?'

'I know.'

Neither of them feels like eating the stew now. She tells him about the *torte* and he laughs.

'I am not angry with you, dusko. In fact, I am not angry with Yana either. Just shocked. The bastards. And no punishment for them either. Still lording it over us with their big cars and their women dripping with gold. I hate them. I hate them in my guts, and in every cell in my body.'

There doesn't seem anything more to say so she takes the *torte* out of the fridge.

Chapter Eight

They meet in the park by the pond with the water lilies. A thin layer of ice shimmers on the surface of the water, reflecting the light of the winter's day.

Daniel is wearing a sheepskin coat, which he tells her he bought in Sofia a few days ago.

'You won't have much wear of it in Wales,' Yana says.

'I am leaving it here, with Elka and Vancho. They will keep it for me for when I come back another winter.'

And then he takes her hand. Tentative at first, as if unsure whether that's what she wants. But she holds his hand firmly and they walk along the frozen paths just like they did all those years ago when he first came to Sofia. Then it was spring, and primroses and daffodils lined the paths, and the woods were carpeted in bluebells. Breathing in the warm spring air, she knew love for the first time. Time has streaked his hair with white and she loves him more than ever.

She wants to tell him this, but she can't. So much has happened since love was easy between them. And yet they are still strolling and holding hands just like they used to. Is it possible that the chasm between them could be bridged? Could they be stronger for having lived through the wreckage of their younger selves?

As if he knows what she is thinking, he says: 'It's nice being with you like this again, Yana.'

'When we are together like this, I wonder if things between us can mend. I still love you.' She says.

'And I still have feelings for you, too, Yana.'

She can hear the 'but' in his voice.

'Do you think what happened, the way I wounded you, do you think that can ever be repaired?'

'I don't know. And I had a part to play too. I don't think I ever made it easy for you to tell me the truth. Too wrapped up in my own stuff. Too self-centered as Ellie sometimes tells me.

'So that makes two of us then,' Yana says. 'Poor Ellie.'

'Yes, and she is such a lovely kid. So kind.'

'Do you think she can ever forgive us?'

He says nothing and for a while they walk in silence. The park is nearly empty, it's too cold and the wind is starting to pick up. Suddenly a gust of it drives a big black cloud over the sun and it makes the day as dark as if night is about to descend on them.

'I guess we need to forgive ourselves first,' he says as they turn and start to trace their steps back to the city.

'And what about Mary?' she asks as they start crossing the street. He puts his arm out in front of her to stop her from moving as a car approaches fast.

'She is and always will be a close friend of mine,' he says as they reach the other side of the street.

'I had a letter from her,' Yana says, asking if she could come and visit.

'And what did you say?'

'Of course she can, she is a close friend of mine too, remember? I just wanted to know if you are still lovers.'

'I am tempted to say that it's none of your business, Yana. That you left me and cut contact with her for nearly eight years. So, you hardly have the right to ask. But I do understand that you need to know before you see her. All I can say is that nothing has changed between us, we are still the same close friends we have always been.'

How's that for an ambiguous answer, Yana thinks, leaving me none the wiser.

At the airport Ellie gives her a big hug before going through Departures.

'I've had a lovely time, Mum,' Ellie says, 'I can't wait to come back. It' been wonderful.'

Yana hugs her trying to hold back the tears.

'It was wonderful to have you here, *dusko* and yes, please come back soon. Easter time can be wonderful in Sofia.'

'We'll come during the Easter Holidays,' Daniel says, 'We'll be here.' And they both turn back and wave at her as they walk towards the departure sign.

She takes a taxi to Katya's.

'I've been expecting you,' Katya says as she opens the door. 'Come in and drink *rakia* to drown your sorrows. Vlado has gone to a football match.'

Yana examines the pale liquid in the glass that Katya has just handed her.

'I am still crazy about him, Katya.'

'Did you tell him?'

'I told him I still loved him. I asked him about Mary, but he didn't give me a straight answer.'

'Will you talk to Mary when she gets here?'

'I am dreading it. To be honest, I don't really want to see her. I am still angry with her. I know I shouldn't, but I still feel hurt.'

'But Yana, it wasn't just her. If you want to be angry with anyone, perhaps it should be with Daniel. And with yourself.'

'I am angry with them both. But Mary, I did trust her. I feel I understand Daniel better, why he did it. But I had never doubted my friendship with Mary. What she did was so hurtful.'

'And the Danchevi? Have you thought of them? How hurt they must feel too? Are you going to make amends, are you going to apologise?'

'I know I have to, Katya, but I don't know how.'

'And how about Ellie, are you going to tell her the truth?' Katya fires at her again.

'I am so scared of losing her. I don't know if she would understand.'

'She loves you, Yana, you are her mother. And I love you too. I don't excuse what you did, but I've forgiven you. You are my sister and I love you. I want you to know that.'

'Perhaps I need more time.' Yana says, 'to gather courage.'

Back home, she moves about the flat aimlessly, picking up objects and putting them down again. Katya's words are just, but they feel like stones in her chest. She knows she has to open herself up to Ellie. She knows that she might lose her if she doesn't and yet, she can't. Her mind has been trained so efficiently; the secrecy embedded in her so completely, perhaps she can never be honest now.

Would she ever be able to say what she really thinks, how she really feels?

How can anybody understand her when she can't understand herself?

Chapter Nine

Waiting at the airport, Yana realises she is looking forward to seeing Mary. Last time they'd met was in Wales when she found out that Mary had taken her place. Ellie had needed a mother and Mary had filled that need. Sweet, loving Mary, she had done the same for Yana when she first lived in Wales, still a child, all those years ago.

That's what is so difficult to reconcile in her mind; Mary's love for her and what she feels is her betrayal. The child in her is filled with the old longing to hug Mary and be hugged by her, secure in the knowledge that she is loved. The woman in her wants to draw blood, a rival invading her territory, keep off my man, stay off my patch. But when Mary appears at the barrier, looking older but the same Mary she's always known, a fine-boned, beautiful woman, her hair tied back to show off the heavy silver earrings Yana had given her many years ago, pleasure melts the bitterness in Yana's heart.

'Good to see you, honey,' Mary says, 'I've been looking forward to this for weeks.'

'I am so glad you are here,' Yana replies, and they hold each other for a long time. Neither of them says much on the way to the flat and once there, Mary unpacks while Yana prepares supper. She's cooked butter beans with herbs, Mary's favourite dish, but when they sit down at the table, neither of them feels like eating. They toast each other with *rakia*, then pick at their food while Mary talks about Wales, what has been going on there and about the opening of the new arts centre. 'It's exciting,' she says, 'after all the planning and the hurdles, it's actually happening. And Daniel has agreed to offer a drawing session at the opening, his name is sure to draw crowds.'

Daniel. She knows more about him that she, still his wife does. Her heart tightens again, and she clenches her jaw, but Mary seems unaware of the tension. Or if she is, she doesn't show it.

After a few more glasses of *rakia* and more small talk, they fall silent, the old clock on the wall marking time, awkward minute after awkward minute.

'It feels difficult between us right now, Yana,' Mary says after a long while. 'I don't know where to start.'

'Why did you do it?' The question comes out sharp, like a dagger. 'I know you were lonely, but I trusted you. I still can't believe you did it. It still feels like something I might have dreamt of.'

'You left, Yana. You didn't return my calls. I didn't know how you felt about Daniel. I am sorry you are upset but you just disappeared. I don't feel I have anything to explain or apologise for. Daniel wanted me. We wanted each other. It wasn't about loneliness.'

That is not the response Yana expected and it shocks her into silence. She thought Mary would be apologetic, that she would try to explain, to justify herself. She wasn't prepared for this, and she has no ammunition left. She says nothing.

The last rays of the evening sun come through and lay a wavering line of light from one end of the room to the other. Then in a second, it is extinguished as the sun sinks behind the roofs of the houses opposite.

'I picked up the mess when you left, Yana. I was there for Daniel and Ellie when you weren't. I love Daniel too. It may be a different kind of love, but it is love nevertheless and it is enduring.'

296

'You can't leave people behind and expect them to wait and pine for you forever,' she continues. 'You can't blame people if they leave too.'

'I am sorry I left the way I did. There were things I couldn't tell you at the time. It wasn't safe to. Daniel knew but I guess he never told you. It was too big, for him and for me.'

'You are talking in riddles now.'

'This is difficult, Mary. You'll be shocked.'

'Perhaps you should tell me anyway.'

Yana's heart starts banging against her chest.

'I was recruited to spy and inform on Bulgarians in Britain. *Durjavna Sigurnost* threatened to harm Katya if I didn't agree to do it. And I informed on Daniel's friends, Elka and Vancho too when they visited.'

The shock on Mary's face makes Yana cringe. They sit facing each other for a while and Yana tops up their glasses.

'It is difficult for me to understand or judge,' Mary finally says. 'I wasn't brought up in a society so devoid of scruples and humanity, so I find it hard to understand how people can do such terrible things to each other. I am at a loss what to say.'

'There is nothing anybody can say. I made a choice, and I ruined Vancho and Elka's lives. They paid the price for my desire to be free, to live abroad. But it was a waste of their suffering. I never felt free.'

'I am sorry, Yana that you had to make such an awful choice. There is nothing else I can say.'

'And us? What about us? Where do we go from here?'

'Where do you want to go?'

'I still love him, Mary and I can't bear the thought of sharing him with anyone, not even you.'

'Daniel and I are old friends and I have loyalties to him just as I do to you. Don't expect me to drop our friendship. That wouldn't be right.'

'I want him back, Mary.'

'That's for Daniel to decide.'

'And us?'

'That's for you to decide. My feelings for you haven't changed.'

The last light of the day has gone now, and the windows darken with the approaching night. Yana gets up and closes the curtains. 'I love having you here, Mary.' She says.

Chapter Ten

'Let's go to Denko's, the new restaurant on Oborishte Street,' Mitko suggested. 'They are offering tasting menus and apparently the food is unbelievable!'

They are given a table by the window, looking out onto the Doctors' Park. As a child Yana used to run up and down the paths, playing 'hide-and-seek', hiding behind the stone Obelisk, bearing the names of the doctors who died in the First World War.

Denko's is a smart restaurant and looking at the prices, it caters for the new rich of Sofia. Pot-bellied businessmen flashing heavy gold cufflinks, designer-dressed women, carefully made-up and coiffured to perfection. Yana feels out of place in her jeans and Marks and Spencer's woollen top. Having lived in Britain for so long, she'd forgotten what it is to dress up. Nobody does there, not even for the opera, unless they are old-fashioned. It took her a long time to adjust to the more casual style of her adopted country and for a long time she felt over-dressed whenever she wore anything more glamorous than a pair of jeans. Now she feels it would take a lot to make her wear anything but a pair of jeans.

Mitko wears jeans too but they are immaculately cut, pressed and not at all faded.

'Calvin Klein', he said, 'don't you know?' and it makes her laugh and the memories of their London days come flooding back and fill her with tenderness. He seems to have recovered from the beating in London and looks well and happy.

'When did you get back?' she asks.

'About four months ago.'

'Why didn't you get in touch earlier?'

'I've been busy. You know the coffee shop on Stamboliiski street? The one we used to go to when we were students? A friend of mine, Jerry and I put some money together and bought the lease. We did it up and it looks very different now. All modern, shiny chrome, Italian leather, really chic.'

'Like your jeans', Yana laughed.

'Nothing wrong with looking smart, you should try it yourself!'

'Touché!'

The waiter brings the menu. They have a choice of either five or seven tasting courses, each with a wine to go with it.

'I am feeling overwhelmed,' Yana says, 'help me choose.'

'Shall we blow caution to the wind and have the seven-course menu? We haven't seen each other for over a year. And being a tasting menu, the portions would be small.'

'OK, but you might have to carry me home.'

'Always at your service, Madam,' Mitko affects a bow. It feels good between them, like in the old days, bantering and teasing, secure in their affection for each other.

'I am in love,' Mitko says after a while.

That explains it, Yana thought with a pang, why you didn't ring me before.

'Who, when, how?' she asked cheerfully, trying to hide her reaction. Did she think that Mitko would always be there for her, that they could have a future together? She may have to give up on Daniel and make a life for herself here, in Sofia. It would not be with Mitko now.

'Jery's sister, Rada. I want you to meet her.'

300

Yana nods. 'I am so glad for you dearest Mitko, you deserve to be happy.'

'Don't we all?' Then after a pause, 'And you? Are you happy, Yana?'

'Having Ellie here for over a month made me happy'

Then after a pause, 'There are things about myself I haven't told you, Mitko.' Her body tenses. Why is she telling him? Because it's better that he found out from her than hear it from others.

'Did you ever wonder how they found you in London? This is difficult but here we go. Years ago, before I married Daniel, I got recruited to inform for *Durjavna Sigurnost* in exchange for an exit visa. Then Daniel proposed, we got married and I got the visa anyway. I went to live in Wales with Daniel and Ellie, and I thought, foolishly that they would forget about me. But they didn't. They took Katya's job away and threatened worse unless I agreed to work for them. I couldn't have lived with myself if they harmed her, so I agreed to spy on Daniel and his friends, the Danchevi.'

Mitko is silent, his face blank.

'It wasn't just the Danchevi, there were others too.'

Her cheeks burnt. The silence between them shut out the noisy chatter around.

'It wasn't safe to tell anyone about it,' she says.

Mitko puts down his knife and fork and finishes his wine.

'There's more. At the end, they asked me to inform on you too.'

All colour drains from his face.

'And did you?'

'No. I couldn't do it. I couldn't bear the thought of going to bed with you and kissing you, knowing what I was doing. But I think they found you in London because of me. They knew we were seeing each other. So, I feel responsible for what happened to you.'

He looks away. 'But how could you do it? Join the enemy camp?'

'I did it to protect Katya,' she says, and it sounds to her like a stuck record playing the same tune again and again. 'I am not sure what I would do if I were faced with the same choice again. But I've wrecked my marriage and my relationship with Ellie and the lives of other people. Do you understand?'

'I am not sure, Yana,' Mitko says 'it's too much to take in. I feel as if I don't know you.' He looks dazed.

'I am so sorry for deceiving you.'

'Look at what I did,' Mitko says after a while. 'I married Elena to get out, then dumped her. She was in love with me, and I broke her heart. Extreme times, extreme measures.'

The waiter brings another dish, three tiny fish filets in red current sauce, garnished with sprigs of rosemary, arranged in the shape of a fan. He gives a complicated explanation about the ingredients of the sauce and the provenance of the fish. Suddenly, anger takes the place of shame and the heat of it flushes through her. She stifles a yawn. She didn't want to be rude, but the pretentiousness of the place is getting through. She tries to hide her irritation, but Mitko knows her too well.

'What's the matter?' He asks.

'I hate this place. I was so looking forward to seeing you and I wanted it to be like it used to be. Remember the Lock Tavern in Camden? Beer and fish and chips and nobody pretending to be anything they are not. I don't like what is happening to Sofia. I don't like the flashy cars, the designer shops, the glitz and the money. Dirty money laundered in expensive restaurants like this one. I don't like it, Mitko. I know you wanted to give me a lovely evening and I am sorry, I really am.'

She can see she has hurt him.

They sit in silence, the candle on their table flickering in the draft from the door opening to let new guests in. She watches the flame shudder, fragile light trying to hold on. The restaurant is getting noisier, the wine seems to be loosening any inhibitions the clientele may have had. Shrieks of laughter pierce the air and booming voices pound her ears.

'I am scared, Yana,' Mitko says quietly, and it is as if the words push the noise back, compress it against the walls. Silence hangs in the air, empty and new.

'I felt like this in London,' he continues, 'I think I am being followed again.'

'You are being a bit paranoid, Mitko, these days are over. Thankfully.'

The waiter is at their table again, sweeping crumbs from the starched linen tablecloth. It is a welcome distraction.

'Shall we pay and go?' she suggests. 'Perhaps I can come back to yours for coffee? I'll get a cab later.'

Outside it is snowing again and the crisp air makes her face tingle. She puts up her hood and holds Mitko's arm to stop herself from sliding on the wet snow. They cross the road to the park and walk down the main path past the snow-capped Doctors' Monument, past the fountain with the marble cherub pouring water from an urn and past benches heaped with snow which sparkles in the dark. The park is empty save for a man, sitting on one of the benches, his hands in his pockets, his face hidden under the shadow of a hat. The sight of him makes Yana feel uneasy and she squeezes Mitko's arm, seeking to reassure herself.

'Probably pissed, trying to sober up before he gets home to his wife,' Mitko says.

'I hope he doesn't freeze to death here; they are forecasting a cold night. Should we wake him up?'

But before they could do anything, the man gets up. He sways for a moment, then walks past them, huddled against the cold, hands in his pockets, his face still hidden beneath his hat.

A silver moon, almost full comes out from behind the bare branches of an oak tree and for a few moments the park is flooded with light. Then a cloud sails past and darkness falls, broken only by the eerie light of the snow. They make their way home through snow- filled streets, their footsteps falling softly on the padded pavements and the dark sky hangs upon them, silent and brooding.

Chapter Eleven

Springtime in Sofia. It's unseasonably warm and people have thrown off their winter layers. It's early evening and the streets are full of couples strolling. The scent of lime blossom fills the air, heady with the promise of summer.

The windows of Mitko's café are thrown wide open, and he has put smart wrought iron tables and chairs outside on the pavement. It's the second time Yana's been here, and she is still impressed with the way Mitko has transformed the old student café. Gone are the oak bookcases and the old scruffy counter, everything has been replaced by shiny chrome and gleaming white Italian leather straight out of the pages of a design magazine.

Mitko seems inordinately pleased with it and proud of himself for having been able to set it up so well in the short time he's been back from London. Yana is pleased for him, but she misses the old worn- out bohemian comfort of the place where she and Katya and their friends used to soothe each others' love wounds and put the world to rights. It feels too new, too smart; like many of the cafes and wine bars that have mushroomed on Vitosha Boulevard, it's trying too hard to be 'modern', to be 'western', to move away from the grey drabness of socialism into a hopeful gleaming future of money and progress.

'Have you heard from Daniel?' Katya asks, watching the stream of people passing by their table.

Yana doesn't answer and the question floats away on the warm evening air. She is remembering her conversation with Mitko a few weeks ago.

'I am worried about Mitko's state of mind,' she says. 'He thinks he is being followed.'

'Why would he be followed?'

'I don't think he is, Katya, I guess it's a bit of the old paranoia. After all, you can't really blame him considering that he got nearly killed in London.'

'I think we have all been so conditioned to worry about everything,' Katya says. 'It's difficult to believe that life can be normal, with normal worries like a broken heart. Have you heard from Daniel?' she repeats the question.

'Not since Mary went back.'

'So, are you going to spend the rest of your life pining for him?'

'Things could never be the same between us. I think what happened, what I did is like a wall between us.'

'And Mitko? How do you feel about him?' Katya continues to interrogate her. It's annoying but she knows that Katya cares for her and wants to be helpful.

'He is an old friend, you know that. Sometimes when I lose all hope about Daniel, I wonder if I might make a life for myself with Mitko. But it's just a silly dream. He's in love with Rada, Jerry's sister.'

'Let's see how long that lasts. She is not known for sticking with the same boyfriend for any respectable length of time.'

Katya brings two more glasses of sauvignon blanc to the table and Yana savours its icy crispness, smooth and sparkling. She wonders about Mitko's relationship with Rada. She is surprised that she minds. She doesn't say this to Katya. They sit in silence, together but separate. A tall man, wearing a wide brimmed fedora hat passes by their table. A faint memory stirs up, she knows she's seen him before, but she can't for the life of her remember when or where.

They meet in Mitko's and Jerry's café again the following Sunday. It is *Tsvenitsa,* the Day of Flowers, the last Sunday before Easter. Buckets of daffodils, tulips, anemones, cornflowers and roses stand on every pavement and people carry sprigs of catkins on their way back home from the many churches that have thrown their doors open to receive the light of the coming Resurrection.

How things have changed. When Yana was growing up, people lost their jobs and students were expelled from University if seen entering a church. And yet, on the night of the Resurrection, many defied the sanctions and went to the Nevski Cathedral to light a candle at midnight. Those who couldn't find a space inside, thronged outside, holding candles, and listened to the chanting and the singing that poured into the square. The night was studded with lights that flickered in the darkness. She recalls walking home from church with Mammy and Katya, trying to keep her candle burning. Katya and Mammy did too because it meant you were a good person. Yana still remembers the disappointment when her candle was extinguished by a sudden gust of wind.

How easy it was then to think of goodness so simply. To think that good people did good things while all the bad in the world came from bad people. She knows now that a person who tries to be good can do terrible things. Living with that is her challenge: how to mend the damage she has done, the anguish she has caused. How to repair the fragile threads of love.

Mitko appears with some food and joins them at the table.

'You two look deadly serious.'

Yana looks at Katya then half-smiles. 'Sister stuff, you know. It can be 'deadly' serious! Anyway,' Yana continues, 'How's it going with Rada? How's love on this beautiful spring Day of Flowers?'

'To tell you the truth, I don't know. Or care.' He looks at his hands.

'What's got into you?'

'It's more a question of what's got into her,' Mitko says.

'Oh, I see, so what has got into her?'

'You better ask her. I haven't got a clue. All of a sudden, she's unavailable, can't meet today, busy tomorrow, away for Easter. I don't know what's going on, but I am pissed off and I tell you what, I am not hanging around waiting for her.'

Katya gives Yana a knowing look.

'Plenty of fish in the sea,' she says gently to Mitko.

'I am too old,' he replies, looking forlorn.

Yana puts her arms around him. 'You are not too old,' she says 'and there's plenty of life out there and broken hearts do mend. There'll be others.'

Chapter Twelve

Two bullets in the head. It was in the papers three days later. Photographs of Mitko's body on the pavement outside his apartment, lying in a pool of blood.

The papers say the Mafia was behind it. He owed someone money for the café and had fallen out with the people who were supposed to 'protect' his business.

The days that follow pass in a daze. Yana is unable to eat or speak. Sleep, when it comes, is a deep dark pit of oblivion. Her lungs ache with every breath and her skin feels clammy.

Katya holds her and rocks her like a baby. She moves in temporarily to look after her. She can't believe that Mitko is dead. The shock and terror of Tatti's murder all those years ago has poured itself into her grief for Mitko. She grieves for them both and for the coldness that had crept into her heart when Tatti died. She sees how, starved of love's vitality, her heart had shrunk, then closed itself round the fear.

She can't believe that he is dead. She thinks of his shy, lopsided smile and her heart aches.

When she can breathe again, she wants to move, do things. She tells Katya she wants to clean the flat before Ellie and Daniel arrive.

Katya offers to help but Yana says she wants to do it on her own. She wants to clear her head before going to the airport to meet them. She goes through the flat, sweeping, scrubbing, polishing, and when she's finished, she rests in Mammy's chair and watches the sun pouring through the newly cleaned windows, making a pool of golden light that shimmers on the polished wooden floor. She feels empty.

Thursday before Good Friday

'I've always thought there was something I didn't know about you,' Ellie says facing Yana across the dining room table. They sat down to have breakfast more than two hours ago, but the coffee has gone cold and so has the toast.

'I need to see Dad. I need to speak to him.'

'It's shock for you, Ellie. Dad is good at times like this.'

Ellie nods and her eyes fill up. 'I was happy when I was little,' she says after a while, 'but then you changed; you sort of went into yourself. And then you left. I don't trust you, Mum. I don't feel I know you.'

Hard words to hear. There is nothing Yana could say.

So, they clear the dishes, pour away the cold coffee and throw away the toast. Then Ellie takes the bus to Vancho and Elka's flat, where Daniel is staying. Yana sits for a long time, until the sun goes down and a crisp breeze comes through the open window and makes her shiver.

She thinks about her own death. Nothing is safe here, she thinks. When the wall came down, we thought everything would change, but it hasn't. Murder and corruption have just become open for all to see. Maybe I should go back to Wales, she thinks. Be near Ellie and Daniel and Mary, try to repair the past somehow.

But she knows she can't go back. It isn't only that she will miss Katya and Vlado; there is a new energy here, a buzz in the streets and in the markets and in the parks. Despite the corruption, the poverty, the want, people look different. The layer of grey hopelessness has been stripped away to reveal tiny, fragile buds of hope.

She dreams of Tatti. He's been away for a long time and now he is back. They are in the kitchen; he is wearing a colourful shirt. A Panama hat is on his head, and he is suntanned. He's been on holiday, he says. Then Mammy comes in, carrying a bowl of fruit. 'Look who's here, Mammy,' Yana says and after a brief moment of surprise, Mammy opens her arms and embraces him.

Waking up, Yana feels gladness. On the night of the Resurrection, she will go to the cathedral and light candles for them both. She is not sure if she still believes there is a God, but she, Katya and Mammy used to light candles. She will ask Ellie to come with her and she will ask for forgiveness. She will ask Daniel to forgive her, too.

She is just about to make herself some coffee when she hears the bell. Daniel is at the door, a bunch of pink tulips in his hand. Her belly flips.

'I thought I'd look in on you,' he says as he comes in. 'Have you got something to put these in?'

Yana takes the flowers from him and goes in search of a vase. She finds the old yellow pot that Mammy loved and puts the tulips in it.

'They are lovely, Daniel, thank you. I am just about to make some coffee; would you like some?'

'That would be great.'

He walks about the flat while she makes the coffee and comes back to kitchen with the picture of the three of them that Katya took when Ellie was born.

'Little did we know then, did we,' he says as he sits at the table. 'I heard about Mitko from the Danchevi and came to see if you are alright, if there is anything I can do to help. The shock of it, I can only imagine.'

'I thought we would be safe after the wall came down. I was wrong.'

'Are you worried about yourself, Yana?'

'Not really. There is no reason for them to be interested in me now. I am sure that Mitko's murder was in revenge. I am pretty sure it was Romanov, his ex-wife's father. I don't think he ever forgave him for dumping his daughter so unceremoniously. I am sure it was his men that tried to kill him in London.'

'It makes sense,' Daniel says, 'as much as anything here makes sense. But I wanted you to know that now I truly understand why you did what you did. I think that for the first time I understand the fear.'

'I hope that you have it in your heart to forgive me.'

'I already have, Yana. Now I need to forgive myself for letting you down.'

Good Friday

A crowd has gathered for Mitko's funeral on the square outside the church of St Sofia and Yana elbows her way through the door, only to find that the entrance is blocked by reporters and photographers.

Someone thrusts a microphone in front of her face and a woman shouts:

'Were you Mitko Dimitrov's girlfriend? Did you know they were going to kill him? What do you know?'

A wave of chanting rises from the crowd, it gathers momentum and rolls through the square with an almighty roar.

'Stop to corruption! Stop to killing! Red parasites out! Out, Out, Out!'

As the crowd surges forward, a tall, long- haired man pushes his way to the steps of the church and snatches a microphone from one of the reporters.

'Bulgarians, children of this land of heroes, it's time to rise against oppression again, it's time to claim our freedom. Go to the barricades, friends, bring down the fat-bellied bastards that suck us dry to fill their pockets and their Swiss bank accounts and build their villas and sail their yachts! Bring them down and bring them to justice! '

'Justice, justice, justice!' The crowd chants in response as it surges forward, a forest of fists and placards swaying in the spring air.

Excitement and anxiety grip her: anxiety about missing the funeral service that is shortly to begin inside the church, and a wild desire to join with the crowd and shout, shout out the years of oppression, and free her senses from fear. Then a small nasty voice whispers in her head: *You traitor, you coward, you weakling. You have no right to protest, to shout against corruption when your own heart is corrupted. You are as bad as any of the 'fat-bellied bastards.' You, who have brought punishment upon so many innocent people.*

She shrinks inside.

Vlado has managed to push his way through. He grabs her by the shoulders and propels her forward and through the church door, using himself as a shield against the surging and swaying mass behind them.

Inside, it is cool and dark, and the scent of incense fills her lungs.

She sways for a second or two, unsteady on her feet and Valdo takes her by the elbow and walks her to the far end where the open coffin is laid out on a large marble dais.

She joins the mourners a few feet away from the coffin and stands next to Mitko's mother who takes her hand silently, her wizened body bent with age, her face mapped with deep creases like a furrowed field.

The priest, dressed in black, his stovepipe hat like a shiny black chimney, intones the first notes of the *Trisagion*, then the choir comes in softly chanting *Gospodi Pomilui, Gospodi Pomilui*, their voices rising then falling to a whisper, then rising again in a sweet melody, a hymn to divine forgiveness and everlasting life.

The music ebbs and flows, the voice of the priest rising above the choir, a deep sonorous baritone, smooth and rich like wild honey, then falling to a whisper as the voices of the choir soar above his, *Gospodi Pomilui, Gospodi Pomilui*, God Have Mercy.

She is still. The music envelopes her like a soft cloud and she is peaceful. The prayers end and the priest invites the mourners to file past the coffin to say their last good-byes to Miko.

His mother, led by the priest is first. Her sobs *chedo, chedo* pierce the still air and echo off the walls, *my child, my child.* Then a silence descends as the priest leads her away and waits with her by the door.

It's Yana's turn. She steps forward, hesitates, then gathers herself and goes to him. His face is peaceful; his once blond hair is now grey and swept away from his brow, his blue eyes are closed. She has the crazy urge to shake him awake. She bends over and kisses his forehead, which is cold like marble.

Goodbye Mitko. She sees him walking by the Danube on a distant summer's day, throwing sticks into the brown water and watching them float away. Which one goes faster, yours or mine? *Goodbye my dear friend.*

Chapter Thirteen

After they bury Mitko in the old cemetery, a few of his old friends join them at the flat. Yana is in a daze and Katya and Vlado make sure everyone has enough food and drink. They toast Mitko's life and shared memories and their voices, subdued at first, get louder and louder, their faces flushed with the drink and the tears.

Yana tries to talk to people but the words hang in the air and crowd the space around her until she feels she can't breathe. Time seems motionless. The four days since Mitko was murdered seem like an eternity. She had loved him since they were children, since they held hands at the banks of the Danube, but it was not the love she felt for Daniel. Perhaps it was more like love for the brother she didn't have. She knew him almost as well as she knows herself and there had been comfort in that, and perhaps the possibility of a future together when things with Daniel fell apart. She knows Mitko felt more than brotherly love for her and she felt guilty for not reciprocating and for wanting him to comfort her. She also felt glad in the knowledge that she had refused to betray him. Was this an act of redemption? For him it made no difference; they killed him anyway, they would have done it whatever she did or didn't do. It mattered because she had, for once, stood up to fear.

After the guests leave, she watches the evening slowly descend upon the mountain, painting it pink, then violet. In the emptiness inside her there are tears she can't cry, but the mountain rises to the sky, big and tangible, and she doesn't feel alone.

After a while, Mammy and Tatti come into her mind and with that the tears flood. They burst through the wall of numbness and reach the sadness that has been there for as long as she could remember. She cries for Tatti and she cries for leaving Mammy and Katya behind and for leaving Ellie and Daniel too. She cries for Mitko, the tears she couldn't cry at his funeral. She sobs hard like a child for the mistakes, the suffering, the waste. The hot, salty tears blind and choke her and when the floods subside, she feels calm. She says her final good-byes to all the people she had lost.

Then the people that are part of her life now come to her, Daniel and Ellie and Katya and Mary and she thinks of the future and hopes that Ellie will always be part of it. She sees Daniel's face, strong and kind and looks into his dark eyes as if there she can find him again. She holds him and feels him solid and firm against her skin and the smell of him comes back to her. She keeps him in her mind like this for a long time, inhaling his smell and sensing the smooth firmness of his skin and she knows that she could never lose him because the feel of him is imprinted on her body. The knowledge makes her ache with desire, and she wants him now, here. She wants to call him but then remembers where he is and the thought of Vancho and Elka cuts through the desire and fills her with anguish again. She wants to go to them and fall on her knees, but she knows that nothing she does now can repair the damage she has caused.

She will have to live with consequences of what she has done. There would be no way to erase the guilt. But she must not let it stand between her and Ellie because Ellie is the future, and the future carries the possibility of redemption. She must not let fear keep her closed. Fear and sadness have been a part of her life for so long, they have become like old friends, familiar and safe. She must break free and claim the possibility of joy and gladness that might still be waiting for her in the future. She must open herself to life, whatever it holds, whatever the risks are. She owes it to Mammy and Tatti and to Mitko and most of all, she owes it to Ellie.

She will write to Mary. She will thank her. She will let gratitude flush out resentment and jealousy. She must clear the decks and prepare her ship for the journey ahead.

Easter Saturday

On Saturday morning Katya brings the eggs she has boiled and painted the night before and lays them out in Mammy's silver bowl with the fluted edges. She opens the window in the living room and the coloured eggs, red and blue, yellow and mauve catch the sunlight and sparkle with a kaleidoscope of lights.

'Did you manage to sleep?' Katya asks.

'I slept a bit and thought a lot.'

'About what?'

'About my life. About the mistakes I've made. And I thought of the future too.'

Katya doesn't say anything for a while.

'Shall we go to Easter Mass tonight?' she asks after a few minutes. 'Remember how we used to go with Mammy, painted eggs in our pockets, ready to break them at midnight? Yours were always the last to break and it always made me feel envious and grumpy. And the candles, remember how we carried them home walking ever so slowly to keep them burning until we got there?'

'I never managed to keep mine alight, but you did, most years you took yours home still burning.'

'Shall we take Ellie with us? Perhaps Daniel will come too, shall I ring them?'

'I doubt Daniel would come but you could try.'

'Do you want him to?'

'I don't know. Too much has happened, too much water under the bridge and I don't know if the bridge is still standing. But I would like Ellie to come, perhaps we could all come back here when the mass is over?'

'Let's see how it goes, shall we? I'll ring Ellie and see how she feels about it. I know it's difficult for you to ring her while she is staying at the Danchevi's.'

As they approach *Alexander Nevski,* the cathedral stands seeped in light, its golden domes shining in the clear night. They go through the heavy doors into the nave, which is filled with thousands of candles flickering from ornate gilded chandeliers. The candles throw light on the richly coloured icons of saints with long, sad faces and more candles flicker from the gold-plated candle-holders that surround the sand-filled trays where people place candles for the dead.

The cathedral is already packed with people holding lit candles and the choir is singing. Katya buys candles for the four of them, herself, Yana and Ellie and Vlado. Yana lights hers from the candle of a man standing next to her and offers her light to Ellie. The two of them make their way through the crowd to the centre of the cathedral where the alter is covered with a gold cloth, embossed with the pictures of saints. Katya and Vlado follow behind.

The music from the organ rises and the choir takes up the melody. Then the voices of the soloists fill the air, the bass and the baritones deep and rich, the sopranos clear and sweet.

Someone taps Yana's shoulder. She turns around and finds herself face to face with Ivanov.

'What are you doing here?' she whispers. 'I'd have never thought you were a church goer.'

'I am these days,' he whispers back, 'nothing to lose.'

'Meet me after the service for a drink?' he whispers again.

His eyebrows are white and so is his hair, or what is left of it. But his eyes are as dark as ever.

'This is Ellie, my daughter,' she says quickly, 'visiting from Wales.'

He offers his hand, large and coarse like a bear's paw. 'How do you do,' he says, bowing slightly. Ellie smiles a polite 'fine thanks' and moves closer to Yana.

'I knew nothing about the murder,' he whispers. 'Rumour has it was Romanov, but you might have already guessed that.'

'Shhh, not here.'

'Your daughter. Well, well. She is beautiful, but not as beautiful as you. I'll wait for you at the Russian Club later on. Don't worry if you can't get away tonight, I'll ring you tomorrow.'

And with that he turns and disappears into the crowd.

'Who was that?' Ellie asks.

'An old friend.'

She puts her arm round Ellie and draws her close. The light of the candles makes Ellie's skin look luminous and her eyes are shining. Yana kisses her forehead, which is slightly damp with the heat and smells of incense.

Katya and Valdo stand behind them. Katya whispers, 'Daniel and the Danchevi are here.'

The cathedral bells chime midnight. Solemn and majestic, they fill the air as the Patriarch intones *Hristos Voskrese,* Christ Has Risen, and the crowd echoes *Voistina Voskrese,* Indeed He Has Risen.

Katya offers around the painted eggs and Ellie chooses a bright blue one speckled with silver. 'Hold it like this', Katya says to Ellie 'and I'll try to break one end with mine, then you turn yours over and try to do the same with mine.'

But Ellie's egg is stronger and neither end breaks, so Yana offered hers. Ellie manages to break both ends of Yana's egg too while her own egg stays intact.

'You've got a winner there,' Katya says. Ellie smiles and puts the egg in her pocket.

People are starting to drift towards the exit and the four of them follow, carrying their lit candles, careful not to let the draft from the open doors extinguish them.

Daniel is standing on the steps outside.

'Elka and Vancho have gone home,' he says. 'I'll walk you back.'

They say good night to Katya and Vlado and start on their way home, Yana and Ellie shielding their candles against the gentle breeze from the mountain.

And all around them the darkness is filled with lights flickering in the warm night air.

THE END

Index